You Killed Me

Ian Walker

SPEAK EUNIQUE

Editing/publishing by Speak Eunique
eunicewalker@mac.com

Original cover art: Ock Draws
X formerly Twitter @OckDraws – Instagram @ock_draws
Facebook Ock Draws

ISBN 9798280849471

Disclaimer

This is a work of fiction. Except in the case of historical fact, any similarity to **persons, living or dead, or actual events**, is purely coincidental.

13th of August 1981

We met in the bar of the Portland Hotel. We always met in the Portland as it was in the centre of town and there was plenty of parking. It wasn't just my friends who gathered there. Most of my classmates would be in the bar that night before they moved on in groups to other pubs. Some would do a tour around town, whereas others, such as my friends and I, would venture out to pubs in the Peak District.

The reason why we went to country pubs was because we could. Some of us had passed our driving tests and had access to a car, either our own or those belonging to our parents. Driving was a new and exciting experience for us. It opened up a whole new world.

And it wasn't just new pubs we were discovering. There were new fish and chip shops and discos to visit. Mind you, most of the discos in the Peak District weren't anything to write home about. The majority were held in village halls and were hardly up to the standard of somewhere like Stringfellows. In fact, they were not even up to the standard of the Adam and Eve nightclub in Chesterfield and that was pretty dire. However, what they did give us was a whole host of new girls to chat up, girls who weren't used to sophisticated townies like us, not that we ever succeeded in getting off with any of them. The truth was that we considered ourselves lucky if we managed to persuade any of them to stop dancing around their handbags and dance with us instead. But that was as far as we ever got. We couldn't even persuade them to give us a snog, let alone go for a quick grope down a dark alley.

I was one of the lucky ones who had a car. Mine was a 1973 Hillman Avenger GL in Baltic Blue, and it was my pride and joy. I'd saved up all the money from my Saturday job as a petrol pump attendant at Walton Motors to be able to buy it. I really loved that car despite it having 85,000 miles on the clock and a top speed of only eighty miles per hour. According to my mother, it was a good job that it wouldn't go any faster than that. If it had been down to her, I think she'd have fitted a limiter to the engine, which would have restricted my speed to thirty.

It was always inevitable that I would buy a Hillman as that's my surname. My dad claimed we were distantly related to William Hillman who founded the company in 1907 but I've never seen any evidence to back up this claim. Even if our family connection to the company isn't real, the fact is that my dad has owned a Hillman all his life and currently owns a Hillman Hunter. It's the top of the range GLS version in metallic gold with a vinyl roof, which he maintains in immaculate condition. You never have to move old crisp packets and empty coke cans out of the way before taking a seat in his car like you do in mine. Mind you, it's five years old now and he's going to have to replace it soon, which poses a problem. You see, you can't buy a new Hillman anymore after the company's takeover by Chrysler. If he wants to maintain the family tradition of having the same surname as the car he drives, my dad will have to change his name by deed poll. If he does, I might suggest that he changes it to Porsche or Lamborghini.

"If only I was called Dino Ferrari or Merak Maserati, my future choice of vehicle would be far more promising," I used to think to myself.

But I was plain old Nigel Hillman and that was why I had to put up with an old banger patched up with Plastic Padding and a heater that wouldn't work. It was a car that would only go at its maximum speed when heading downhill with the wind behind it. Still, it could have been worse. My surname could have been Lada or Yugo, in which case I really would have had something to moan about. When it came down to it, I was very fond of my car. It may have been an old banger but it was my old banger, my first car, and it was going to stay in my heart long after I'd forgotten about all the others.

"What colour is Bostik Blue?" my sister asked when I was considering buying it.

I'd told her I was going to look at it after seeing it advertised for sale in the *Derbyshire Times*.

"Baltic Blue," I corrected her in disgust.

My sister's lack of knowledge about the seas off northern Europe and her complete ignorance of shades of blue never ceased to amaze me.

"It's a dark blue named after the Baltic Sea," I retorted.

"I've never heard of the Bostik Sea," she replied. "Where is it?"

"It's the sea between Sweden and Finland," I snapped back. "And for the last time, it's Baltic, not Bostik. Bostik is glue."

If you could see the bits that kept falling off my dashboard, it probably would have been better if it had been Bostik rather than Baltic. At least I'd be able to stick them back on again.

"Well, I think it's stupid," she continued. "Everybody knows there are only two shades of blue, light and dark. Who do they think they are trying to impress by naming it after a sea nobody has ever heard of?"

Geography was never my sister's strong point. She was not academically minded. It's no wonder she failed to get into one of the town's grammar schools and had to go to a secondary modern instead. Mind you, Phil Brown, one of my classmates, wasn't much better. When his dad bought a Triumph Dolomite, he had to look in the atlas to find out where the Dolomites were. Phil is hoping to study geography at Keele University next year. Consequently, his ignorance about the mountain ranges of northern Italy is extremely worrying.

We wouldn't normally go to the pub on a Thursday but there was a very good reason. Our A level results had just been published and we were going out to celebrate or possibly commiserate depending on how everybody had got on.

I'd been to school earlier that day to get my results and was pleased to discover that I'd got the grades I required for my first-choice university. The only thing I had to do now was to find out if my friends had done likewise.

There were six of us in total: Alex Singleton, Steve Bowler, Martin Howarth, Bruce Young, Dan Podgorski and me. Dan's real name was Dianielek, which is Polish just like his surname. But none of us could get our heads around that when he first told us. So he was just plain old Dan from that day on.

We became friends in our first year at Chesterfield School and had remained good mates ever since. Some of the friendships had become a little strained at times, which had led to a few arguments. When I was younger, we used to have arguments about important things, like who had the best conker and who was the best at Subbuteo. But as soon as our balls dropped, there was only one thing we ever fell out about and that was girls, especially the girls who went to St Helena's High School. It wasn't as if we had much experience of girls in those early days as their school was on the other side of town.

However, when we reached the age of sixteen, we started going to a local youth club where the problems started. In fact, the worst moment came earlier this year when Steve's girlfriend Jessica finished with him and started going out with Bruce instead. At one stage I thought Steve and Bruce were going to come to blows over her. But peace eventually returned after Steve took up with Jessica's best friend, Martha. Nowadays, all four of them usually hang out together. They still come out with the rest of us but now they've formed a little subgroup within my circle of friends.

Everyone says Martha is better looking than Jessica, which made Steve think he'd ended up with the better deal. But that just goes to show how shallow he is. Jessica definitely has the best personality.

Shortly after Bruce started going out with Jessica, he told Steve that she'd given him a blow job in the back of his mum's Ford Escort. That wiped the smile from Steve's face. He suddenly felt shortchanged as she'd never practiced fellatio on him when he was going out with her. Not that the rest of us believed Bruce's story, especially since he still hadn't passed his driving test. I very much doubt that his mum was sitting in the front seat of the car while Jessica was doing the dirty deed. That said, I guess there's one way we could find out if it's true or not. But since nobody had the courage to ask Jessica to confirm whether or not she'd done it, we had to leave the matter there.

The rest of us haven't got any girlfriends at the moment. Dan had been going out with Maggie for two years but he finished with her last month. He's expecting to go to

Loughborough University next month to study international relations, whatever that may be, and he wanted to clear the decks before then. If he was hoping to get a new girlfriend at university, I've got bad news for him. I looked up Loughborough University in the *Sunday Times* university guide and it seems that its student population is 94.5% male, which is one of the worst male to female ratios in the country. So it looks as though the only relationship he's going to have for the next three years is with his right hand. In fact, I wouldn't be surprised if he ends up visually impaired and having hairs growing on his palms. That also might be the fate that awaits Alex and Martin, as neither of them have girlfriends yet.

That said, Alex told us he got off with a girl whilst he was in Ibiza on holiday with his parents last year. He said she was five years older than him and was on the pill. I didn't believe him. He told me her name was Vicky and then told Steve her name was Julia, which didn't exactly lend credence to his story.

As for myself, I went out with Claire for six months. She was great to start off with. She'd even let me take her bra off in the back of my Avenger after I'd pulled into a layby on a dark country lane late at night. However, she wouldn't let me go any further than that and I finished with her just before I sat my A levels.

And I say Steve is shallow. I guess it just proves that where shallowness is concerned, I'm just as bad as him.

You see, the reason why I finished with her is the same reason why Dan finished with Maggie, except that I expect to have far more success than him during the next three years. In six weeks' time, I'm off to Heriot Watt University in Edinburgh to study brewing and the male to female ratio is far better than at Loughborough. There are also four other universities and colleges in Edinburgh all bursting with crumpet. So I'm bound to be able to get a new girlfriend. It would be statistically impossible not to. They'll all be desperate for a shag having been recently released from the restriction of living with their parents. Personally, I can't wait to get started.

Heriot Watt is the only university in the UK where you can study for a degree in brewing, and I'm very lucky to have a place there. They get lots of applicants each year and many fail to get in. However, I did well in the interview and have some knowledge of the subject after receiving a home brew kit for my sixteenth birthday. It sparked my interest in brewing and now I've decided to take it up as a career.

The six of us plus the two girls will be going out tonight. I'm taking my car and will have Alex, Martin and Dan with me. Steve will be the other driver as his dad allows him to use his Ford Granada. It's a company car and I don't know if London Refractory Services, the company his dad works for, knows that he lets his teenage son drive it. Even if they do, I doubt they would approve of the way he drives, which is usually flat out.

Since Steve will have Bruce, Jessica and Martha with him, they won't be heading back with us later for last orders at the Highfields Hotel in Newbold. Instead, they'll be parked up somewhere just off the Matlock Road for some heavy snogging, which usually ends with stains on the Granada's fabric upholstery. It might be quite a spacious car but the Avenger is far better for removing evidence of teenage sexual activity. The seats are upholstered in leatherette, which may be hell to sit on in the summer but at least they are easy to clean with a sponge and some soapy water.

I arrived that evening in the bar of the Portland at seven o'clock to discover Martin and Dan were already there.

"Go on then, what did you get?" asked Martin.

"Four Bs," I replied. "So I'm off to Heriot Watt. I only need three Cs."

If I was honest, I'd been hoping for an A in Chemistry but who was I to complain. I was going to have three years of drinking, shagging and a little bit of studying. I was the first in my family to go to university. My mum and dad were extremely proud, not about the drinking and shagging bit, of course.

"You're not including General Studies, are you?" said Dan. "Everybody knows it's not a proper A level."

"Too bloody right I am," I replied. "Go on then, what did you two get?"

"I got an A in Physics, a B in Maths and Chemistry and an E in General Studies," he replied.

"It's no wonder you didn't want to include General Studies then," I laughed.

"It's immaterial though," Dan continued. "Loughborough only asked for a B and two Cs."

"How about you, Martin?" I asked.

"I got an A, two Bs and a C," he replied. "I've got the grades I need to go to York."

Martin had accepted an offer to study Politics at York University. When we asked him why he'd chosen Politics, he said he thought it would be interesting. Personally, I thought it sounded extremely dull. It might not be so bad if it led to a job in the Cabinet, less so if it led to a job on Chesterfield Borough Council.

Dan and Martin had nearly finished their first drinks, so I went to the bar and ordered two pints of Stones bitter and a half for me. I was drinking halves because I was driving and would switch to Coke later. There was no way I was going to lose my license, especially since I was intending to take my car to university. Having a motor was bound to make me stand head and shoulders above the other students, with their cycle clips and student rail cards. My Baltic Blue pulling machine was undoubtedly going to help me find a new girlfriend.

Shortly after we'd got our beers, Bruce, Steve, Jessica and Martha arrived and I asked them how they'd all got on.

"I got a C, two Ds and an F in General Studies," replied Bruce.

"How the hell did you fail General Studies?" I asked him. "You must have spelt your name wrong on the exam paper."

"Ha, ha, very funny," he replied. "Anyway, it makes no difference as it's still enough to get me into Trent Poly."

Bruce was the only one in our group who'd applied to go to a polytechnic where he intended studying mechanical engineering. He thought he would be in a better position than the rest of us to find a job after he'd graduated, which was very mature of him. Personally, I hadn't thought further ahead than the freshers' fair.

Steve had the best result. He got two As and two Bs.

"What did you get Bs in?" I asked him.

"History and General Studies," he replied.

That was good news as I knew he needed an A in English to get into his first choice of Durham to study Law.

Jessica and Martha went to St Helena's and they had both passed their A levels with good grades. Jessica was off to study Chemistry at Newcastle and Martha was going to Exeter to study History. It was good news all around and the whole group was in a party mood. Alex still had to arrive, of course, but he only needed a C and two Es to get into the University of Kent at Canterbury where he was going to study English.

There were many of our other classmates in the bar that night and the general impression was that most of them got the grades they wanted. But then Alex arrived looking dejected.

"Christ almighty, Alex," I said. "What's the matter?"

"I got a C and to Es," he replied.

"Well, that's alright," said Dan. "That was what you needed, wasn't it?"

"Except that one of my grade Es was in General Studies, which doesn't count. Even though I got a C in English, which they were asking for, I won't be going to university, and it's all because I failed Economics. It's so unfair. It's all Cec Thompson's fault."

Cec Thompson was the Economics master at our school. He was quite a good teacher and I surmised that Alex's failure had more to do with his lack of revision than anything Cec had done.

We had a solution for Alex's problem and that was to get him pissed. We thought it would cheer him up if he tried to go for a personal best that night. Alex's previous best had been seven and a half pints three weeks earlier. Tonight he was going for the full gallon.

"You'll still be able to go to university though," said Bruce once he'd bought Alex his first pint. "And you'll probably be able to study English as you got a grade C. You'll just have to go through clearing and if you don't get into university, you can go to a polytechnic with grades like that. Perhaps you'll even end up at Trent Poly like me, which would be great. The two of us will be able to go out on the pull together."

That remark cheered Alex up a bit more but it didn't go down too well with Jessica. However, her mood soon improved when she spotted another of her friends on the other side of the bar. She was a pretty girl called Sue Pearce who was there with Giles Harrington, her boyfriend.

Giles was the head boy at our school and a right prat. He was a year older than the rest of us and had returned to school for an extra year to do his Oxbridge entrance exam after getting four As in his A levels the previous year. He was also the captain of the first fifteen. Well, that's what he was until he broke his collarbone when his shoulder hit the post whilst scoring a try against Lady Manners School in Bakewell. This was quite a common injury in the days before post protectors.

I'd always thought that post protectors was an odd name. It makes it sound as if it's the posts that need protecting from the players, rather than the other way around. Anyway, it served Giles right for playing rugby rather than football.

His injury kept him out of the team for the rest of the season. But he was fully fit again for the start of the cricket season when he scored a century off fifteen overs in his first match against Mount St Mary's College in Sheffield.

We should really have been in awe of him as he was good at almost everything. But we weren't. Instead, my mates and I considered him to be a right arsehole. He'd never been in trouble for having his hair too long and he liked pop music rather than punk rock and heavy metal. He'd also never smoked a cigarette behind the bike sheds. In many ways, he reminded me of Peter Perfect from the cartoon series, *Wacky Races*. That said, he did like a drink as I discovered when he won a yard of ale drinking competition in the Terminus Hotel one Saturday evening. It took him just eight and a half seconds and he didn't spill a drop. It was quite an incredible feat when you consider that, at nineteen, he was by far the youngest in the competition and all the others were hardened drinkers.

He had another skill, which Claire told me about. This had been revealed during a discussion in the sixth form common room at St Helena's. On that particular day, the girls were discussing their boyfriends' sexual prowess and Sue had told them that Giles was quite a stud. It seemed he could do wonderful things with his tongue. Sue had described it as prehensile, a bit like the ones giraffes have, and she said she'd experienced three orgasms the last time he'd gone down on her.

To sum him up then, Giles was intelligent, could hold his drink, and was good at sport. He was also getting his leg over regularly. It was no wonder we all hated him.

"What did you tell them about me?" I asked Claire when she mentioned the girls' discussion.

"I said you were like a banger on bonfire night," she replied.

"Really?" I said with a smile. "What, exploding with passion, you mean? Banging away all night?"

Not that Claire had ever allowed me to bang her. Still, it was good of her to keep up the illusion that we were regularly having it off. In fact, I felt quite impressed by her description of me. But I was soon brought back down to earth again.

"Not really," she continued. "I said that if I wasn't careful, you'd go off in my hand."

Claire and I split up shortly after that particular discussion. I thought at the time that she'd be upset that our relationship was over. But she wasn't. By the following week she'd already found a new boyfriend called Dave Willis, and she was later to describe him as being like a Saturn rocket. Naturally, I hated his guts.

After they had spotted our group, Sue and Giles came over to speak to us. Giles congratulated us all on passing our A levels. Mind you, he managed to do it in a supercilious way, which was his way of saying, "You've all done really well, but not as well as I did last year."

"Did you pass your Oxbridge entrance exam, Giles?" asked Bruce.

"I got the result a couple of weeks ago," he replied. "I'll be studying astrophysics at Trinity College Cambridge next term."

"Of course you will," I thought to myself. "How could you be studying anything else? You complete toss pot."

"My dad bought me a new sports car as a reward for getting in," he continued.

"How wonderful," I said, before pretending to sneeze into my hand and at the same time shouting "wanker".

Jessica chose this moment to drop a bombshell.

"I hope you guys don't mind," she said. "But I said Sue and Giles can come out with us tonight."

"Good God, no," I thought to myself.

"Yes, I thought I'd give my new motor a run out," added Giles. "And we are celebrating Sue's three As and a B."

He spat out the B with disdain. It was just as if he was describing a dog turd someone had stepped in.

"Of course you can," said Bruce. "The more the merrier."

He didn't mean it. He'd only said it to get back in Jessica's good books after his comment about going on the pull with Alex. He knew full well that his fun would be severely limited later on if he didn't.

We all knew that was why he'd said it and we all gave him black looks behind Giles's back. This was supposed to be a fun night out to celebrate our exam results, not a night out with the school twat. The thought of Giles accompanying us was almost as bad as if Mr Price, the headmaster, had agreed to come out on the piss with us.

"Drink up then," said Steve. "We've got pubs to visit and beers to drink."

"Where are we going first?" asked Giles as we were walking to the car park.

"We're going for a game of pool in the Peacock in Barlow," replied Dan.

Giles wandered over to his new car with his arm around Sue. Of course, by 'new' Giles had meant it was new to him rather than something bought from a showroom. Giles's parents may have been rich but they weren't stupid enough to buy a brand-new car for their teenage son, especially one who'd only recently passed his test at the fifth attempt. It seemed that Giles wasn't as good at driving as he was at astrophysics, sport and cunnilingus. Still, I suppose nobody can be good at everything. I'm absolutely rubbish at knitting.

Giles's parents had decided that it wouldn't be quite as bad if he came back from a drive out with one of the corners missing from a car that had only cost them £500, rather than from one costing £3,000. That said, the eight-year-old Triumph GT6 in Italian racing red was an impressive sight. All the lads gathered around to get a better look.

"It's got a two litre straight six engine with twin carburettors, delivering 104 break horsepower," said Giles. "And it's got a four-speed gearbox with overdrives on both third and fourth. It's got a top speed of 107 miles per hour and does nought to sixty in under ten seconds."

He was showing off.

"You see that power bulge on the bonnet," he continued. "They had to do that in order to shoehorn the larger engine into a Triumph Spitfire body. I'd never have let my parents buy me a Triumph Spitfire. They've only got a 1300 engine, a real hairdresser's car, if ever there was one. The GT6, however, is similar to an E-type Jag. It's a real man's car."

What he didn't tell us was that his parents had wanted to buy him a three-year-old Ford Fiesta but Giles had pleaded with them to get him something sporty. In the end, he had worn them down and they had capitulated.

For a few seconds, all eight of us stood looking at the red two-seater in amazement. It had a curvaceous body culminating in the bulge on its bonnet. It may have been the poor man's E-type but the contrast with my Hillman Avenger, which was next to it, could not have been greater. Giles's car cost more to insure than mine had cost to buy. As a result, my loathing for him had reached a new level.

After we all got into our motors and fastened our seat belts, we set off. Steve led the way with me close behind him and Giles followed at the rear. Fifteen minutes later, we arrived at the Peacock where we parked in the car park behind the pub.

As I got out from the driver's seat, I noticed there was an immaculate powder blue MGA with wire wheels parked near the pub's entrance. It may have been twenty years old but it was in showroom condition. Next to it was a brand new Lotus Elite. It had white paintwork just like the one Roger Moore drove in *The Spy Who Loved Me*. I went over and peered through the window. Giles had also spotted it and had wandered over for a closer look.

"I bet you didn't know that the casino in Monte Carlo has only three parking spaces in front of it," he said whilst admiring the car's pop-up headlights.

I had to admit that I didn't know this before wondering where this particular conversation was going.

"They insist that the punters with the three best cars fill the spaces," he continued. "When you arrive you have to give your keys to the concierge. If you drive a top-of-the-range Merc and you arrive fairly early, they'll probably let you park at the front with another couple of expensive motors. But if someone arrives after you in an Aston Martin, they'll remove your Merc and put it in the underground car park so the Aston can take its place. I've always thought they ought to adopt that policy everywhere. If they did that here, there'd be no prizes for guessing which three cars they'd choose, would there?"

As he was saying this, he gave my Hillman Avenger a disparaging look, before disappearing into the pub with Sue.

"What an arsehole," I thought to myself again before following them down the steps into the tap room.

Giles won the first round robin at pool and, to make matters worse, he put *Chant Number One* by Spandau Ballet on the jukebox. The bloke obviously had no taste in music. Martin put on *Ace of Spades* by Motörhead next, so we didn't have to listen to crappy new romantic rubbish all night. Martin was a big fan of Motörhead and had been ever since he discovered that the band's drummer, Phil 'Philthy Animal' Taylor, had been born in Hasland just like him.

Once the first game of pool was over, Giles, Steve and Bruce went and sat at one of the tables with their girlfriends whilst the rest of us had another game.

"Thank God we don't have to spend all night talking to that knobhead," I said to Martin as I broke the pack at the start of our second game.

"A knobhead drinking pints," added Martin. "The bloke only passed his test three months ago and is driving a powerful sports car. It's a sure recipe for disaster."

Someone placed a fifty pence coin on the pool table, signalling that they wanted to play next. It was time to move on anyway. When the game was over, we downed our drinks and got ready to leave.

"Where to now?" asked Giles as we walked up to the table where the others were sitting.

"I thought we'd go to the Devonshire Arms in Beeley," I replied. "If you do a left out of the car park, you'll eventually hit the A621. I'll lead the way."

"Right, let's go then," added Giles, before downing the rest of his pint and getting out of his chair.

The Devonshire Arms was one of my favourite pubs. It was located close to the Chatsworth Estate and, although it was predominantly a food pub, it also had a small snug to the right of the bar. That was where we always went as there was a dartboard.

Steve turned out of the car park with me following him and Giles behind me. It was a narrow country lane and I was not best pleased to have Giles right up my arse. Since it was nearly half past eight on an overcast day, we all put our headlights on. But Giles's headlights were on full beam.

"Jesus Christ, doesn't that bellend know where his dip switch is?" I cried out whilst adjusting my rearview mirror so that I wasn't completely dazzled by his headlights.

We reached the A621 and after we'd turned left towards Baslow, Giles shot passed me.

"Bloody hell," said Bruce. "That GT6 sure has some acceleration."

I immediately turned the main beam on to give him some of his own medicine. However, he was rapidly pulling away from me and catching up with Steve in his dad's Ford Granada.

It wouldn't be as easy for Giles to overtake the Granada as it was to overtake my Hillman Avenger, despite it being a heavier car with four people in it. After all, it was a Granada GL with a two litre V6 engine, which had almost the same acceleration as the GT6. Thinking about it, it was a pity it wasn't the Ghia version as that would have had leather seats. That would have made it a hell of a lot easier to wash the spunk stains off.

The fact that the car Steve was driving was almost as powerful as his GT6 didn't stop Giles. At the roundabout just outside Baslow, he saw his opportunity. This particular roundabout is pretty large and has only three roads leading to it. One of these is the A621 from Sheffield, which was the road we were on, one is the A619 from Chesterfield and the third, the one we were going to take, was the A623 to Manchester. What this meant was that we had to go all the way around the roundabout before taking the last exit. Except that Giles didn't. Instead of turning left and going around the roundabout the normal way, he turned right, taking the shorter route and getting ahead of Steve at the same time.

It was incredibly dangerous, of course, a bit like deciding to head south on the northbound carriageway of the M1. If anybody had been coming in the opposite direction, he probably would have hit them head-on. But, fortunately for him, there wasn't and he disappeared off into the distance towards Beeley.

When we arrived at the Devonshire Arms, Giles was already in the bar with Sue. They were cuddled up together looking for all the world as if they were joined at the hip. Giles was drinking a pint of Theakston's and looking smug, whilst Sue had a glass of Chardonnay. The expression on her face made her look as if she couldn't wait for the evening to end so she could reacquaint herself with Giles's prehensile tongue.

"That was bloody dangerous, you idiot," said Steve. "Are you trying to kill yourself?"

"You're just annoyed because I got past you," replied Giles. "Anyway, it wasn't dangerous. I could see that nobody was coming in the opposite direction. It's getting dark, so you can see the headlights coming from miles away."

"It wasn't pitch black though," added Steve. "Someone might not have put their lights on yet."

"Well, more fool them if they didn't," added Giles.

Fortunately for us, Giles decided that he didn't want to play darts. We left him in the bar with the three girls whilst the six of us went into the snug.

"Why did you say he could come with us tonight?" I asked Bruce as he was pulling his darts out of the board. "He's a complete fuckwit and he's ruining our celebrations."

"Sorry about that," replied Bruce. "I didn't realise he was such a dickhead. The thing is, Sue is one of Jessica's friends. I could hardly say no, could I?"

"I see he's drinking another pint," added Dan. "That makes three he's had to my knowledge, and we don't know how many he had before we met him in the Portland Hotel. He'll lose his license if the police stop him."

"Talking of pints, how many have you had, Alex?" asked Martin.

"This is my fourth," he replied, "halfway towards my gallon."

A few minutes later, Alex went to the toilet. Martin took his dad's hip flask out of his jacket pocket and tipped some of the contents into Alex's pint.

"Vodka," he announced. "I did the same thing the last time Alex tried to drink a gallon and that was why he only managed seven and a half pints. He never realised that he'd drunk half a bottle of vodka as well. He threw up all over his bed that night and his mum was furious. Don't tell him, will you?"

We all agreed not to mention it to him.

"I've been doing some thinking in the gents," said Alex when he got back.

"Each to his own," replied Martin. "Personally, I go there to have a piss."

"Well, I was thinking whilst I was pissing. I reckon we ought to leave Giles behind in the next pub."

"We'll never get the girls to agree to that," said Steve.

"Why don't you have a word with them in the car and see if you can persuade them?" suggested Dan.

"I'll mention it to them," Steve replied. "But I wouldn't hold out too much hope if I were you."

With that agreed, we continued our game of 'around the clock', which I won. Next we had a game of 501, which Martin won. Alex could barely hit the board by this stage. He was starting to get really drunk.

"Have you guys finished yet?" asked Giles, who'd wandered over from his seat in the bar just as we were finishing.

"We have," Steve replied. "We were thinking of going to the Horseshoe in Matlock if you're up for it."

"And no racing this time," I added.

"I bet you wouldn't be saying that if you were in a GT6 rather than that load of crap you're driving," replied Giles.

By then I wanted to smash his face in. But I remembered the words of wisdom espoused by that master lyricist, Jilted John in his classic track, also called *Jilted John*. Towards the end when describing Gordon, the moron, he says, "I ought to smash his face in. Yeah, but he's bigger than me, in't he?" So taking a leaf out of Jilted John's book, I just said, "yeah, yeah" in a disdainful way instead. Perhaps, like in the song, I could get my mate Barry to hit him. Except, I didn't have any friends called Barry.

Fortunately, the journey between Beeley and Matlock is mainly along the A6, an extremely busy single carriageway road. As a result, Giles didn't have the opportunity to do any racing or overtaking before we reached the Horseshoe.

The Horseshoe is one of those old-fashioned pubs with an outside gents' toilet. Giles went to pay a visit as soon as we arrived. Sue went to the ladies at the same time.

"Well, did you broach the subject?" I asked Bruce once they were out of earshot.

"I did," he replied, "Tell them, Jessica."

"Martha and I think leaving them behind is an excellent idea," she said.

"But I thought Sue was a friend of yours?" I added.

"Not really," she continued. "She likes to tag along with us, which was just about bearable before she started going out with Giles. Now all I want to do is to strangle her. I'm not surprised Giles is going out with her. Believe me, they deserve each other. She's such a terrible snob. She keeps going on and on about how, just like him, she's decided to stay on for another year to take her Oxbridge entrance exam."

"Oh, I wouldn't be seen dead at a red brick university," added Martha doing an impersonation of her.

"She's planning on having a gap year," Jessica continued. "Daddy's going to pay for her to go to South America with one of these charities that rich kids go with. I mean, you're supposed to raise the money yourself in order to go on the trip. It's part of the challenge. You're not supposed to get your parents to pay for it."

"So we are all agreed then," I added. "We leave them in the pub."

"Why don't we just go now?" asked Martin. "We could sneak away whilst the two of them are in the bogs."

"I thought we were going for chips next," said Alex who had started to slur his words. Bruce had slipped some more vodka into his pint whilst he wasn't looking.

It was a tradition whenever we went to the Horseshoe that we always went to the chip shop across the road from the pub afterwards. In my opinion, it was one of the best fish and chip shops in Derbyshire. Furthermore, it was the only one we knew that sold haggis. We had planned to visit it as we usually did. But we wouldn't be able to if we were going to run off leaving Giles and Sue behind. It was a dilemma but one that was soon resolved when Giles reappeared from the toilet. It meant we were going to the chip shop after all.

Giles sat down next to us with his pint of Bass, his fourth of the night. A couple of minutes later Sue returned as well.

"God that wine is awful," she said after taking a mouthful of her drink and pulling a face like she'd just sucked a lemon. "This pub is really awful. Can you believe that they serve their wine from a fake hand pump? All they have on offer is a cheap red and a white wine that tastes of petrol. This place isn't a patch on the Devonshire Arms. At least they sell proper Chardonnay direct from the bottle there."

"You want to drink draught Bass," said Dan. "It's excellent."

Sue gave him a look as if he'd just suggested she should try drinking meths.

We all finished our drinks and piled into the chip shop. Most of us had haggis and chips, although Giles had chicken and chips and Sue had a saveloy.

"I bet she chose saveloy because she wants some practice for what she's going to be doing later tonight," commented Dan once we were back in the car eating our food. He put his finger in his mouth and pretended to give it a blow job.

"Thanks, Dan," I replied. "You've just put me off my haggis."

"I'll eat it," said Martin.

"I was only joking," I said.

We'd already told Giles that we were going to the Kelstedge Inn before heading back to the Highfields Hotel. We quite often finished up at the Highfields as a few of our other classmates also would be in the bar. The pub was popular with the girls from St Helena's, so we usually ended up there in the hope of pulling one of them. It was the ultimate triumph of optimism over experience, as none of us had ever been able to get off with any of the girls who went there. In that respect, it was no different to the discos in the Peak District.

Steve and Bruce wouldn't be going to the Highfields, of course. They already had girlfriends and didn't need to go on the pull. Instead, they'd be visiting one of their favourite remote spots and have a competition to see who could stain the upholstery in Steve's dad's car the most. Besides which, Bruce had been banned by the landlord the previous December when he'd caught him nicking baubles from the Christmas tree after getting as pissed as a fart on Stella.

Anyway, that was the itinerary where Giles was concerned. However, between Matlock and Chesterfield was Slack Hill where the road was three lanes wide, and we knew that Giles wouldn't be able to resist putting his foot down and overtaking both of us. The plan was to let him get ahead and, when he pulled into the car park of the Kelstedge Inn, we would carry on to the Red Lion at Stanage instead. Well, that was the plan, except we hadn't realised there were roadworks on Slack Hill. The road was down to one lane with traffic lights at both ends.

"Shit," I said as I joined the queue waiting for the lights to change. "What are we going to do now?"

"We switch to plan B," said Bruce.

"We don't have a plan B," I added.

"I do," Bruce continued. "We go into the pub and when Giles goes to the toilet again, we leg it."

"What? And leave our beers behind?" queried Alex, who'd been asleep in the back until that point.

"It would be for the greater good," replied Martin.

That was what we agreed to do and as soon as we pulled into the car park Bruce went to Steve's car to tell the others.

However, it turned out that we didn't need to waste any of our beers. Giles went straight to the toilet as soon as he entered the pub. It seemed that the extra fifteen minutes we'd spent at the chip shop in Matlock had stretched the capacity of his bladder to its limit.

"Come on everybody," I shouted as soon as Giles had disappeared into the gents. "Let's leg it."

We all dashed out again leaving a bemused looking Sue wondering what the hell was going on.

We were all laughing as we emerged into the car park. But none of us could imagine what was about to happen next and how it would come back to haunt us many years later.

Chapter 1

"May I have everyone's attention?" announced Bert Pieters. "I'd like to say a few words before you have too much of the falling down liquid."

Bert was on a small stage in front of a large screen with the words 'Nigel Hillman's retirement bash, 17th March 2023'. Bert was the production director for South African Breweries and my immediate boss. He'd been appointed to the role in 2017 shortly after SABMiller, as we were called at the time, had been absorbed by ABInBev in the third largest takeover in corporate history. That's the third largest corporate takeover in the world, not just in South Africa and not just in the brewing sector. ABInBev was already the world's largest brewing company, the result of a merger between three major companies, Anheuser Busch, Interbrew and the Brazilian brewer, Ambev. We weren't exactly small ourselves. We were the world's second largest brewing company, following our acquisition of Miller in 2002. However, our size didn't save us. We were swallowed whole, just like an anaconda swallowing a young piglet. We were now part of a brewing megalith with 630 brands in 150 different countries and a turnover in excess of fifty billion US dollars.

Before the takeover I was confident of being offered Bert's current job with responsibility for all seven of the company's breweries in South Africa. After all, I had an impeccable record as head brewer of Newlands Brewery. I had 25 years of dedicated service behind me and there'd been no zymomonas infections at the brewery on my watch. Zymomonas is the scourge of the brewing industry. Once established, it is a devil to get rid of as it leaves beer cloudy and smelling of rotten apples. The management at our breweries in Gauteng and KwaZulu-Natal had major problems when they got infected with it in 2009. Both sites had to close for a month for a deep clean and over 3,000 barrels of beer were tipped down the drain.

But my hopes were dashed once the takeover was completed and, as a result, I've been reporting to Bert for the past six years. There are currently rumours doing the rounds that he's going to be promoted again soon and his job will become vacant once more. However, it's too late for me. Even if it wasn't, they'll almost certainly give it to some youngster in a sharp suit, someone from human resources perhaps, who's never brewed beer in his life. They'll probably say he'll bring cross-functional skills to the role, when what they really mean is that he's a right bastard whom they've brought in to reduce headcount.

Thinking back, it was no surprise that Bert was appointed instead of me. After all, he ticked all the boxes where the new company was concerned. Firstly, he is Belgian and ABInBev is a Belgian company listed on the Brussels stock exchange. His parents moved to South Africa when he was little and he was brought up in Pretoria where he went to the same school as Elon Musk. It's rumoured that Bert was amongst the group of boys who hospitalised the young Musk after throwing him down a flight of stairs at Pretoria Boys' High School. He has never confirmed this, of course. But he's never denied it either.

When he was fifteen, he returned to his home country with his parents. Six years later, he graduated from the University of

Antwerp with a first-class honours' degree in Molecular Biology. He considered staying on to do a PhD but eventually decided to join Interbrew as a graduate trainee. Progress up the career ladder was swift and ten years later he found himself working for the company in the UK after being appointed as head brewer at the Samlesbury Brewery near Preston. Three years on, he was promoted to production director for the UK and Ireland.

That's why I say it was no surprise that he got the job instead of me. He was younger than me, better qualified, better connected and destined to rise even further up the greasy pole. He was also fluent in English, Dutch, Flemish and Afrikaans. Not that there's much difference between the last three languages, even though my wife would beg to differ. It's a bit like saying you're fluent in English and American just because you can say either petrol or gasoline dependent on who you're talking to.

Do I envy him? Of course I do. Do I hate his guts? Not really. He's quite a nice bloke when you get to know him. Having said that, I'm always careful to avoid crossing him on the stairs.

One other change that came about when we were taken over was that the retirement age for the new company was reduced to sixty. At least that's what it is in countries without strong labour laws. Retirement at sixty is now compulsory rather than an option. There are exceptions, of course. It wouldn't be the case if I worked for the company in either the UK or Belgium. Over there you have the legal right to continue working for as long as you like. But not over here, which is why this is my last day at work. I have to retire, even though I don't want to. Not only that but Bert doesn't want me to either. Retirement is what old people do and I'm not old. That said, I can at least retire on a full pension as I've got more than thirty years' service behind me.

There was still plenty of chatter going on in the room despite Bert's request for silence. He banged a spoon on the table.

"Ladies and gentlemen, dames en here," he said. "If I could just have some hush. I want to get this presentation underway."

The room we were in was usually the brewery hospitality suite and the assembled multitude were making full use of its free bar. I was pleased that the attendance was so good, although I suspected that some of the people were only there to get their fill of the massive finger buffet on offer. Why do people always over-cater for events like this? I've never been able to get my head around that. Perhaps catering firms do this deliberately so that their staff have plenty to take home for their families. It might save them from having to cook for the rest of the week. It's probably one of their perks.

It wasn't just the food that was in plentiful supply that night. The free bar might not have had any spirits on offer but there was an unlimited supply of lager to wash down the buffet. You wouldn't expect anything less in a brewery.

On reflection, I was perhaps just being pessimistic when I thought people were only there for the free food and drink. I guess that the majority were really there to say goodbye to me. I did consider most of them to be my friends.

"Nigel, if you would like to come and join me," said Bert.

I got up and went to stand next to him at the front of the room. I could feel fifty pairs of eyes focused on me and it made me feel slightly queasy. Unlike Bert, public speaking had never been one of my strengths, which was probably another reason why he was given the job instead of me.

A few seconds later, Bert started his presentation.

"As you are all aware," he said, "we are here today to say farewell to Nigel after 31 yeas of dedicated service to the company. Let's look back to 1992, shall we? This was the year when the European Union was brought into being by the Maastricht Treaty, the year that the Cold War officially ended, and Bill Clinton, remember him, was elected as the 42nd president of the United States. However, what was far more important than any of these things was that it was the year when a fresh-faced, long-haired 29-year-old called Nigel Hillman joined us as a brewer. This photo was taken of him shortly after he joined us."

A picture of Cousin It from the Addams family was projected onto the screen behind him. Nobody has ever seen what Cousin It looks like because he's got ankle length hair. I'm presuming he's male but he could be female for all I know. Anyway, it caused much amusement amongst my work colleagues, poking fun at me for shaving my head for the past ten years in an attempt to look cool and trendy, despite going bald. It was definitely one of my better decisions, far better than if I'd decided to go for a comb-over. That's despite getting a bad sunburn in the first week after I did it. It was a lesson I would never forget. It taught me to put sunblock on and wear a hat whenever I went out during the heat of a South African summer's day.

"Sorry," said Bert as the picture behind him changed to that of a young-looking me from the days before I shaved my head. "I seem to have mixed up the photographs."

"It doesn't look that different from the last photo," shouted Henk Bierman, one of the production workers.

Henk must have been destined to end up working in a brewery with a name like Bierman. It was a bit like me being destined to buy a Hillman Avenger as my first car. I couldn't continue buying Hillmans, of course, as they were discontinued in 1976. These days I drive a Mitsubishi pick-up truck or a bakkie as they are called over here. Sometimes I think everybody in South Africa owns a bakkie.

Henk was a member of my team and a bit of a joker. Back in the early '90s, I still had a full head of flowing locks and Henk's comment drew yet more laughter from the audience.

"As you know, Nigel joined us from the UK," Bert continued. "Prior to that, he'd been working at Shipstone's Brewery in Nottingham, which he joined straight from university. It was where he perfected all the modern methods of brewing."

The picture on the screen changed to show a black-and-white photo of the inside of an ancient brewery. Judging by the clothing of the men in the picture and the fact that they were all smoking clay pipes, it must have been taken during Victorian times. In the background was an enormous steam engine with several wooden casks at the front. These were massive hogsheads, each one containing 540 pints of beer. Once again this caused much laughter from everyone in the room.

"I believe his first job at Shipstone's was in the fermentation room," Bert added.

The picture changed to a drawing of a medieval brewer dressed in leather britches. There's a well-known myth in brewing circles that, back in the dark ages, brewers used to test their beer by pouring it onto a wooden bench before sitting on it. If their backside stuck to the seat, the beer hadn't fermented enough and wasn't ready to drink yet. The story wasn't true, of course. They simply tasted it instead but the myth has persisted. In any case, Bert's reference to it caused more laughter.

"Then after he arrived here at the brewery in Newlands, I understand people didn't really know what to make of Nigel, as this short film reveals."

The film consisted of interviews with people who'd been working for the company back in 1992. They'd all been asked what their first impression had been when they met me for the first time.

"When I heard he'd been appointed I wondered what the English know about beer," said one of the men. "Absolutely nothing is the answer to that. Otherwise, why do they serve it warm? Haven't they heard of refrigeration over there?"

"I remember saying let's give the bloke a chance," said another. "My dad always said that the English can do most things. Then I remembered what his three exceptions were to this rule – playing cricket, playing rugby and brewing beer."

"When I first saw the young man from England," said one of the brewers, "I thought, hello, we've got a right one here. He'll not last long. In fact, we christened him Nigel Hillman OBE, OBE for 'out before Easter'."

"And yet he lasted," Bert added. "So much so that he's still here 31 years later. It seems the only way to get rid of him is to drag him screaming out of the brewery gates."

A caricature of me appeared on the screen. I was wearing a Chesterfield football shirt and was desperately holding on to the brewery gates whilst two security guards were trying to throw me out of the building. This caused the biggest uproar so far.

"In 1995, Nigel was promoted to second brewer," added Bert. "Then three years later he took over as head brewer following the departure of Cobus Engelbrecht."

A picture of Cobus appeared on the screen. It wasn't really Cobus. It was a picture of Jacob Marley complete with chains and

Cobus's head photoshopped onto his body. Since the photo was in black and white, I presumed it was from the 1951 version of *A Christmas Carol* in which Alistair Sim played Scrooge. It was quite cruel really, as everyone knew that Cobus had only left because he'd landed in prison. It provoked more laughter though.

Cobus had been my first boss at Newlands Brewery. In April 1998, he was involved in a pile-up on the M5 near Rondebosch in which two people died. It transpired that he was more than three times over the drink-driving limit, and he received an eight-year sentence for manslaughter. This was in spite of the fact that he hadn't even caused the crash. It was a huge scandal at the time, especially since there was a feature about him in the *Cape Times* a few days later exposing the drinking culture at Newlands Brewery.

I was temporarily placed in charge after Cobus's arrest and given the job permanently after he'd been convicted. I was considered to be a safe pair of hands, especially since I never drank more than two pints before getting behind the wheel of a car. That was 25 years ago and I've been in charge ever since. It turned out that I really was a safe pair of hands. I was the Peter Shilton of the brewing world.

"Actually, Cobus wanted to be here today to say farewell to Nigel," added Bert. "But unfortunately, the electronic tag he's now forced to wear wouldn't allow it."

There was more laughter after that statement by Bert. This time it was more of a nervous laugh. People were obviously thinking, 'there but for the grace of God go I'.

"After 31 years with the company, Nigel is now hanging up his hydrometer and taking a well-deserved rest," Bert continued. "And where is he thinking of spending his retirement? No, it's not going to be on the sun-drenched beaches of the Western

Cape. Instead, he's decided to go back to England, which is why we've bought him this to keep the rain out."

Bert was holding up a Driza-Bone coat, which got a cheer from the room as a picture of London during a thunderstorm was projected onto the screen behind him.

"This isn't all we've got you, of course. There's also this tantalus and a rather special picture."

Bert held up the caricature that had been on the screen a few minutes earlier. He'd had it framed, which was a nice touch.

"We never could convert him to rugby," shouted Piet van der Merwe, our distribution manager, referring to the fact that I was wearing a football shirt in the picture.

"In addition to that, I'd like Nigel's long-suffering wife Monica to come up here as we've got a bouquet of flowers to present to her," Bert continued.

Monica went up and was handed one of the largest bouquets I'd ever seen. It was full of proteas, Barberton daisies and cerise roses. She also got a round of applause from the room and a peck on her cheek from Bert.

I met Monica shortly after I arrived in Cape Town. She was the girl next door I'd always dreamt of marrying, quite literally, as it turned out. She rented the flat next to the one I had taken. Our relationship started when she made me a coffee as the international removals firm unloaded my possessions from the container they had arrived in. Thirty-one years and two children later we are still together. She's threatened to strangle me on a few occasions, but other than that it has been a happy relationship. Next year will be our pearl wedding anniversary and I was thinking of buying her some earrings as a present. I don't want to tempt fate by buying her a necklace that she could use to garrotte me.

If I was honest, I was a little bit worried about whether she would adapt to living in England. It wasn't that she was leaving her parents behind, as both of them had died during the past decade, her father of a heart attack in 2015 and her mother from cancer two years later. Also, both of our sons were working abroad these days. Ben is a doctor in Canada, whilst Johannes is working for a computer software company in Japan.

"At least by living in the UK we'll be equidistant from the two of them," I'd said to her when I first broached the subject of moving to England. "We'll not be showing any favouritism to one or the other."

"If you wanted to be equidistant, then Hawaii would be far more convenient and you'd have better weather," she replied. "Also, the Hawaiian flag has a Union Jack on it, so you could always pretend you'd gone home."

She didn't mean it, of course. Not the bit about the flag of Hawaii having a Union Jack on it but her suggestion that we move to America. In fact, the USA was close to the bottom of the list of countries she wanted to move to. It was just above North Korea but below Afghanistan. That was probably because you were far more likely to be shot by a madman carrying an automatic weapon in America than you were in Afghanistan.

To be honest, Monica's ties with South Africa were as loose as mine these days. She has a brother who lives in Durban, and a few friends and former work colleagues. But many of her closest friends had emigrated during the past few years. They'd been forced out by rising crime and a lack of career opportunities. In fact, her best friend Sylvia now lives in Bakewell, which was probably the final thing that convinced her to move to Chesterfield with me.

After Monica had received her flowers, it was my turn to speak. I moved to the microphone that Bert had recently vacated and began my pre-prepared speech.

"Friends, colleagues."

"Countrymen, lend me your ears!" shouted Henk, which got him a few more laughs.

"To say I am going to miss you all is an understatement and, believe it or not, I'm also going to miss coming to this place every morning. In that respect, the caricature you've had done is quite apt. They really are kicking me out screaming and yelling. I've never told any of you this but when the closure of Shipstone's Brewery in Nottingham was announced back in 1991, I didn't know what I was going to do. Breweries in the UK were closing on what seemed like a daily basis back in those days and I was just another person joining the ranks of fully trained brewers looking for work. Things were pretty desperate for me in the weeks between the announcement that production was going to end and the brewery closing. I was preparing myself either for a life on the dole or having to take up a completely different career. I applied for all types of jobs including head of production in a cheese factory and shift manager at a mineral water plant."

"Where was that?" said Henk. "Namibian Breweries?"

Namibian Breweries was our biggest competitor in Southern Africa, and the company had recently been taken over by Heineken. It was common practice amongst ABInBev employees to take the mickey out of them by suggesting that their beers were similar to water.

I waited for the laughter to die down.

"In total, I must have sent my CV to over fifty firms. That's how desperate I was. Then I happened to notice an advert in the brewer's journal for a vacancy here in Newlands. I'd never considered working abroad before. But desperate times call for desperate measures and despite my reservations I decided to apply. If I'm honest, it was more in hope than expectation. However, a few days later I had a telephone interview with Cobus, and I must have impressed him."

"He was probably pissed at the time," came a shout from someone at the back of the room.

"Well, pissed or not, he invited me to come to Cape Town for a personal interview, after which he offered me the job. That left me with a big decision to make. Should I move or should I continue to look for a job in the UK? This was 1992, Nelson Mandela had been released from prison but the first free elections had yet to take place in South Africa. At the time, nobody knew what direction the country would be going in. But despite all of this I decided to accept the offer and the rest is history. I've never regretted that decision and have thoroughly enjoyed the 31 years I've been here. I've also really liked all the colleagues I've worked with over the years. Well, most of them anyway."

I looked at Henk as I said it, which raised another laugh.

"I say colleagues but, in reality, I regard you all as my friends. You've all had a massive impact on my life and you will always have a special place in my heart. And whilst I'm on that subject I'd like to mention my wife, Monica. I would never have met her if I hadn't moved here and, for that reason, Cape Town will always hold special memories for me. Unfortunately, all good things must come to an end and it is now time to move on. Or in my case, to move back. Monica and I are moving to Chesterfield, the town where I was born and raised. And just for your information, it doesn't always rain there and the beer isn't always served warm. I even hear they've got condensation fonts for the draught lager these days. Anyway, I'm going to miss you all, even though most of you prefer rugby to football. Monica and I have many friends over here, both inside and outside of work. We don't intend cutting all our ties with Cape Town. Instead, we plan to come back every couple of years or so to see you all. Therefore, if you thought tonight was the last time you were going to see me, think again."

That raised a small chuckle from my colleagues.

"And that's all I've got to say apart from a big thank you to all of you and here's to the next time we meet."

After a round of applause, that was it. They gave me a huge card with 'Time to put your feet up' written on the front, which they'd all signed. Many of them came to speak to me and wished Monica and I all the best on our retirement. Someone even said he must pop over and see us when he was in London. I don't think he quite appreciated that Chesterfield is 150 miles from London. To a lot of people around the world, London is England and everywhere else is just a short drive away. Many people believe the same thing about Cape Town and South Africa. The truth, of course, is very different.

All the guests gradually drifted away until only Bert and a few hangers-on were left. Then our taxi arrived, Bert kissed Monica on both cheeks, we said our farewells to those who were still there and that was it. I'd walked out of Newlands Brewery for the last time. I may have been planning to return to Cape Town in the future but I knew I'd never return to the brewery again. It felt strange as the place had been so much a part of my life for the past 31 years and now it was all over, just like that. It seemed as though they really had dragged me screaming through the brewery gates.

The house was pretty depressing when we got back. We'd already packed most of our possessions into boxes waiting for the removals company. This included all the flower vases, so Monica gave her bouquet to the next-door neighbours. We had accepted an offer for our house from a nice young couple. Our sale was now in the hands of the solicitors and we'd provisionally agreed a completion date for the week after next.

Three days later, the international removals company came to pack everything into a shipping container and we moved into a hotel for our last few days. We'd sold the bakkie to a local garage by then and had rented a car, which we were going to return at the airport when we were on our way back to England. We used the time to say our final goodbyes to some of our best friends. A week later, we were checking in at the airport. After 42 years away, of which 31 had been in South Africa, I was finally going home.

Chapter 2

We arrived at Birmingham airport at one o'clock in the afternoon, having travelled with KLM via Amsterdam. It was both cheaper and more convenient than a direct flight to Heathrow. We had decided to rent a property in Chesterfield to begin with and had signed a six-month contract on a house on Storrs Road in Brookside.

It was close to my old school in an area of town I knew very well. Mind you, when I was at the grammar school, Storrs Road was in Brampton. Either the border had moved so that it was now in the more upmarket suburb of Brookside, or clever estate agents had decided to stop referring to it as being in Brampton to inflate the house prices. It must be a bit like Battersea, which estate agents in London now refer to as South Chelsea.

Either way, it didn't really matter as we weren't buying the house. We were only renting whilst we looked for one to buy. The house wouldn't be ready for another couple of days and we were going to stay in the Premier Inn in the centre of town until we could move in.

It's a fairly complicated thing moving to another country, even if it is the country where you were born and of which you are a citizen. For a start, you've got things to buy, like a house and a car. We'd picked up a hire car from the airport but buying our own was a priority.

And, whilst I am on the subject of cars, we had the small problem of sorting out our driving licences. Monica, of course, had always had a South African licence, whereas I had exchanged my British one for a South African licence thirty years ago. Fortunately for us, South Africa drives on the left and is a Commonwealth country. Consequently, the UK and South African governments have an agreement that meant neither of us had to retake our driving test. Instead, we are allowed to exchange our South African licences for British ones, which is relatively straightforward. That's as long as you can master all the paperwork involved.

Slightly more complicated, however, is the fact that Monica is a South African citizen and had to apply for indefinite leave to remain in the UK at the British Consulate before we left. This is no longer as straightforward as it used to be. For a start, she had to show that I earned more than £18,600 per annum. Fortunately, my pension from the brewery is quite a bit more than that. It's a good job that's the case, otherwise I would have had to leave her behind despite having been married to her for nearly thirty years. Mind you, this wasn't the only hoop we had to jump through. She also had to prove that she was proficient in English.

Monica was brought up in a bilingual household and is fluent in both English and Afrikaans. She also has a master's degree in English. However, in a country like South Africa where there are eleven official languages, she might have been a native Zulu speaker, which is why she had to prove her proficiency. Armed with her degree certificate from the University of Cape Town and a letter from my pension provider, she queued for three hours at the British Consulate before finally getting her residence permit.

After she's been in the UK for three years, she can apply for British citizenship, which I'd strongly recommend. A British passport makes foreign travel a lot easier. We may have left the EU these days but we Brits still don't need a Schengen visa if we want to travel to mainland Europe. South Africans do though, which makes foreign travel both more expensive and difficult to arrange. It also means you can't take advantage of any last-minute cheap holiday deals to Spain.

Applying for British citizenship won't mean that she'll have to give up her South African passport, of course. She can apply for dual citizenship instead. I did exactly the same thing myself in South Africa three years after moving there. At the time, there were rumours that the new ANC government might bar foreigners from owning property in the country and I decided it was better to be safe than sorry.

Another thing that we'll both have to do now that we are back in the UK is to open new bank accounts and arrange for my pension to be paid into mine. In addition, neither of us has a recent track record of renting a property. We bought our house in Cape Town just before we got married and paid the mortgage off four years ago. As a result, the letting agent insisted we pay six months' rent upfront for the house in Storrs Road. It wasn't a problem. It just made me feel like I was 21 again and renting my first flat in Nottingham. On that occasion, I had to get my dad to sign as guarantor.

As I drove up the M1, it somehow seemed strange to be heading back to Chesterfield. I hadn't been back for 35 years and Monica had never been to the town where I grew up. In 1987, my father had taken early retirement from his job in local government and he and my mother upped sticks and moved to live in Cornwall. They'd bought a property called Upper

Salting's in St Ives where they lived until my father died. It was in a fantastic location, close to the centre of town overlooking the sea. Dad really liked the view from his lounge and he installed a telescope, which he used to look at the ships heading to and from the docks at Avonmouth. The building had originally been a large stone barn where the local fishermen used to hang their nets. But it had subsequently been converted into two apartments and my parents had bought the one on the first floor. It had the best views over the bay from its balcony.

Because Mum and Dad lived in Cornwall during the time I was in South Africa, we always went there whenever we came back to the UK. After Dad died in 2017, Mum moved into a bungalow close to my sister in Peterborough where she still lives. She'll be 88 next month.

I thought about moving to Cambridgeshire myself to be close to my few remaining relatives in the UK. But I've always wanted to go back to Chesterfield. It was the town where I was born and brought up and went to school. It has the football team I still support and the cricket ground where I used to go and watch Derbyshire play. The commentators on the BBC used to say that Chesterfield had the prettiest county cricket ground in England. However, Derbyshire only play there for one week during the summer these days and it's never televised.

Chesterfield is also the town where I had my first girlfriend, my first kiss and my first teenage fumble in the back of my Hillman Avenger. Then there's the fact that it sits just outside the Peak District National Park with its moors, dales and beautiful villages. No, as long as I could convince Monica, there was only one place in the UK I wanted to live and that was in Chesterfield.

I was excited about going back at the same time as being really nervous. It was not going to be the same as before. For a start, none of my friends from school lived there anymore, which was another reason why I'd never been back. Quite a few of them lived abroad these days, just as I had done until recently. I hadn't seen most of them for years. In fact, the only ones I'd seen since moving to Cape Town were Dan and Bruce and I'd only met both of them once. These days my relationship with my old school pals was confined to cards at Christmas. With Steve and Martin it wasn't even that, since I'd lost touch with them many years ago.

Out of all my old friends, the one I knew the most about was Alex even though he lives in New York these days. He's the deputy editor of the *New York Times*, a paper he joined in 1998 after leaving his job at the *Observer*. He'd graduated with a first-class honours degree in journalism and had numerous job offers after that. He'd chosen the *Observer* because it was a quality newspaper. It stood out above all the red tops that had also been interested in recruiting him. He enjoyed working there, or so he told me, but could not resist the lure of the US when the *New York Times* came knocking.

"You know that you'll have to learn how to spell again," I said to him when he phoned to give me his good news.

"It's easy," he replied. "All I have to do is remember to leave out the letters e and u and I'll be spelling like an American."

He soon realised there was more to it than spelling. There were also differences in the meanings of words. This was something he discovered as soon as he arrived at the *New York Times* building on Eighth Avenue. The receptionist told him his office was on the first floor and so he got into the lift, only to discover that she actually meant the ground floor. I suppose it could have been worse though. He could have asked her if he could borrow a rubber.

It's odd to think that he's done so well for himself when you consider how totally devastated he'd been after failing to get into the University of Kent at Canterbury to study English. He was eventually offered a place via clearing on a journalism course at the University of Lancaster. He'd never considered a degree in journalism when he'd originally been applying to universities, so it's funny how things worked out. If he'd got his required grades back in 1981, he probably would have become an English teacher at a comprehensive school in Rotherham, rather than the well-known figure in international journalism he is today.

The reason I knew more about Alex than any of my other old school friends is because he sends out an account of all the things he's done that year with his Christmas card. In some ways it appears quite old-fashioned as most people nowadays post every single detail about their lives on social media. I'll never understand why people take photos of meals and place them on Facebook whenever they go to a restaurant. I always think they ought to take photos of the restaurant's toilets as well. In that way we could have the complete story, from plate to poo.

The process of sending out a photocopied letter each year may be quaint but it means that I know all about his son Archie who got into Harvard to study medicine. I also know about his daughter Laura who's studying to become a physiotherapist. I even know all about Woofles the dog and how he was neutered last spring. Then there's the fact that he's just bought a second home in Long Island, which he hopes to retire to one day with Kelly, his third wife, who's fifteen years younger than him. All this information comes from a man who's effectively been out of my life for over thirty years.

Other than Alex and Martin, I know that Dan has been working for the Foreign Office since leaving university. He is now the British High Commissioner to the Seychelles, which sounds like a real doddle of a job to me. He must be nearing the end of his career, so they probably decided to give him an easy post just before he gets his knighthood. All former ambassadors and high commissioners are given knighthoods, aren't they? It's a perk of the job, a bit like a company car or luncheon vouchers for someone in a normal job. He'll probably get it for services to arse-licking like all the other senior civil servants who are given a similar honour. I'm only jealous that there isn't a comparable award for brewers. If there was, I could be awarded a knighthood for services to getting people pissed.

Anyway, he's almost certain to become Sir Dan Podgorski, which will probably make him the first person from his village to be knighted. Dan originally comes from Grassmoor, a former pit village just outside Chesterfield. Actually, Dan's the first person from Grassmoor to do lots of things, like go to the grammar school, get a university degree and still have all his own teeth by the time he reached fifty. One thing Dan never did, however, was marry.

"I never met the right woman," he told me on the one occasion that we met whilst I was in South Africa. He was working at the British High Commission in Pretoria at the time.

"Or what's more likely is that you've never met a woman who could put up with you," I replied.

"There's also the fact that the Foreign Office keep on moving me all around the world," he continued. "What woman would put up with that?"

"Not many," I thought to myself. "If they sent you to places like North Korea or Somalia."

But since the most dangerous place he was ever sent to was Washington DC, that excuse didn't really hold water.

Over the years, Dan was posted to Paris, Reykjavik, Bangkok and Tokyo, as well as Washington, Pretoria and Victoria in the Seychelles. It's not a bad set of cities to live in and most prospective partners would probably jump at the opportunity to visit them all. They are the kind of places people put on their bucket lists. It would be a bit like a permanent holiday.

Dan's problems with women started at university. I told him he'd never find a girlfriend at Loughborough and I was right. I knew he shouldn't have finished with Maggie. In fact, everything that has happened to him since then has proved I was correct.

I sometimes wonder what happened to Maggie, Claire, Jessica and Martha, not to mention all the other girls I knew when I was a teenager. I haven't seen them for over forty years and haven't a clue what any of them are doing these days, which is probably a good thing. In my mind, they'll always be young, fresh-faced and carefree. Whereas the reality is that they'll probably all be grandmothers with several failed marriages behind them. Their fresh faces must all be wrinkled now due to forty years of worrying about their kids, their husbands and all the other disappointments they've experienced in their lives. Either that or they'll be sad old spinsters, their lives full of regrets that they were never able to settle down and start a family. Not everybody's like that, of course. I wouldn't want you to think I'd summed up the entire population of British women in their sixties, just ninety percent of them.

Part of me thinks I ought to look up my old female friends on Facebook to see what they look like these days but another part of me thinks it's a bad idea. If I'm honest, I probably won't look for them. It's far more difficult to find girls from your schooldays, because they'll almost certainly have different surnames. Even if they don't, I doubt if I would be able to recognise them from their photos. I guess I'm going to go to my grave without ever finding out whatever happened to any of them.

I'm still in touch with Bruce. He's the only of my schoolfriends who's still in the UK, and he lives with his wife Christine in Chipping Sodbury.

Bruce was always the most sensible one in our group. He got a 2:1 in Mechanical Engineering from Trent Poly and went to work for British Aerospace in Bristol. He now works for Airbus making wings for their commercial jets. I'm not a hundred percent sure what he does but I do know he's in a fairly senior position. He's certainly not the man who does the welding. Mind you, I don't think they do any welding these days. Aircraft wings are now made from composite plastic instead.

I last saw Bruce in 2012, when he and Christine came to Cape Town to travel down the garden route. We'll have to meet up again now that I'm back in England. I think his mother still lives in Chesterfield, so he must return home occasionally.

And whilst I'm on the subject, I wonder how many people refer to the town where they were born as home? I do in spite of the fact that I haven't lived there for forty years and haven't even been back for 35 of those. Perhaps Bruce refers to Chipping Sodbury as home these days. Personally, I never referred to Cape Town as home, even though I lived there for more than half my life.

Thinking about it, there must be two types of people in this world, people who never move away from the town where they were born and those who do. Then there are two types of people in this second group, those who want to move back again and those who don't. I guess those who never left and those who want to move back again will always refer to the town of their birth as home. I definitely fall into this category. Whether or not Bruce falls into it, I really don't know.

I say Bruce is the only one of my former friends who lives in the UK. Of course, Steve and Martin might still live here. But since I haven't heard from either of them for over thirty years, they could both be living in a yurt in Outer Mongolia for all I know.

What I do know is that Steve qualified as a barrister and went to the Inns of Court in London, where I lost touch with him. Martin, meanwhile, got a job working for Scottish Television after graduating with a 2:1 in Politics. I always thought he'd get elected as an MP eventually and go on to become a government minister one day. On reflection though, it wasn't very likely as he was a member of the Liberal Party when he was at university. Mind you, that was forty years ago and I haven't heard from him since 1989. Therefore, he might be a member of the Monster Raving Loony party these days for all I know. However, when I think about it, being a raving loony is probably more likely to qualify him for a place in the Cabinet than being a member of the Liberal Democrats. I mean, it worked for Jacob Rees-Mogg, didn't it?

Having said all that, I seem to remember Martin falling out of love with politics whilst he was at university, which was probably why he got a job working in TV instead. I think it was one of his lecturers who put him off. They say good teachers have a major impact on your life, which is why you'll always remember them. However, in my experience you're more likely to remember the really bad ones, if only for the negative effects they had on your life's choices.

The last I heard of Martin was that he was living in Macau and was chief executive of a company that makes cartoons. Dan told me this as he had stayed in touch with him longer than I did, although even he has lost touch with him these days.

Dan also told me that Martin was working on a cartoon series called *Ninja Rats from Saturn*. That was back in the 1990s and I don't have a clue what he's done since then. He might have changed career and returned to the UK, or he really could be a member of the Monster Raving Loony party living in Outer Mongolia.

Anyway, wherever my friends were, none of them lived in Chesterfield as far as I knew, and that was the main reason why I thought things would be different. There'd be no meeting with them in the Portland Hotel, no driving out into the Peak District looking for girls and pubs, and no high jinks. It was only to be expected, I suppose. I'm not a teenager anymore, I'm a pensioner and life has moved on. I know that retirement isn't anything like it's portrayed in *Last of the Summer Wine*. Mind you, quite a large part of me wishes it was.

Chapter 3

I realised that I would hardly know anybody still living in Chesterfield. But what I didn't know was how much the town might have changed since the last time I was here. What if I didn't recognise the place?

Driving down the dual carriageway from the M1, I shouted, "I can see it."

"Pardon?" said Monica.

"I can see the Crooked Spire," I replied. "Every time we went on holiday when I was a boy, we'd have a competition to see who was the first to spot the Crooked Spire on our return. Even if the whole town has changed, the Crooked Spire never will."

I told Monica all about the Crooked Spire. In fact, I'd told her about many things in Chesterfield, like the market with its town pump, the medieval shambles with the twelfth century Royal Oak and how you came of age by drinking in every pub on the Brampton mile. I even told her about how you knew it was nearly Christmas when Dents the chemist put an illuminated star on the roof of their building. I also told her about the campaign to save the market hall and the shops on Low Pavement from being demolished during the 1970s and how Chesterfield Football Club was the last club in the football league to get floodlights. Over the years, I'd told her most of the things I knew about the town and I didn't stop there. I also told her about the Peak District, the pubs I used to go to and the walks I used to take. I told her all about well dressings, about Chatsworth House and how the village of Eyam had survived the plague back in 1665. I ended up telling her so much that she said she knew Derbyshire as well as I did, even though she'd never visited the county. If the truth be told, I'd spoken so lovingly about the place that she was almost looking forward to living there as much as I was.

Although they'll never admit it, most people in the New World look at Europe and the UK in particular through rose-tinted spectacles. They only see the history and the culture. Many of them believe our education system and our national health service are superior to what they have in their own countries. However, reality soon sets in when they realise that we are well behind most Southeast Asian countries when it comes to education, and that we can't afford to train enough doctors anymore. It's ironic, really, when you think about it. Not long ago, we used to send foreign aid to India. Now they send aid to us in the form of all the doctors they've trained. It's just like nineteenth century missionaries, only in reverse.

I was still thinking about this as we approached Horns Bridge roundabout on the outskirts of Chesterfield.

"That's new," I said pointing to a sculpture in the middle of the roundabout. "There wasn't a sculpture there the last time I was here. Bryan Donkin's has gone as well. It used to be over there where the Ford garage is."

"What the hell was Bryan Donkin's?" asked Monica.

"It was an engineering factory," I replied. "I haven't a clue what they used to make there. The only thing I know about Bryan Donkin is that he built the world's first canning plant."

We made our way around the roundabout and followed the road into town.

"Nothing else appears to have changed that much," I continued as we headed towards the Crooked Spire. "Some of the buildings are used for different purposes but it's basically the same as I remembered it. See that Thai restaurant over there? It used to be a nightclub called the Adam and Eve. Then the owners changed the name to Pussy Galore."

"How very tasteful," replied Monica sarcastically.

Soon we were going past the Crooked Spire.

"It's impressive," said Monica. "I'll give you that. Can we go and look around it tomorrow?"

"No problem," I replied. "You can even climb the tower on certain days of the week."

As we rounded the corner, I shouted out, "Good God, I don't believe it. Eyres furniture store is still going."

However, as we drew nearer, I could see the shop was empty and deserted even though the sign was still there. It had closed down twelve months ago after 147 years.

"That's so sad," I added. "My granddad used to work at Eyres. He started in 1919 when he was fifteen and by the time he retired in 1969, he'd worked there for fifty years. Those really were the days when you had a job for life."

I was six at the time and I could still remember the day he retired. I'd gone with my mum to see my granddad being presented with a bureau by the shop's staff. I remember him as a smartly dressed old gentleman with a bald head. In all the years I knew him, I don't think I ever saw him wearing anything other than a three-piece suit. He even wore it to the beach. Fifty-four years later, it was my turn to retire and yet I didn't feel old. I didn't think I looked old either, although I realised that I probably looked like Methuselah to someone in their teens.

Okay, I did look a bit like my granddad, especially since, like him, I was follicly challenged. But I didn't dress like him. I wore jeans and a polo shirt most of the time. Perhaps the young people of today think the way I dress is old-fashioned. I wonder if it was the same when my granddad was a lad and his grandfather retired. Did he think he dressed oddly? I guess not. After all, things have changed at a much faster pace over the last forty years than they ever did in the past.

All this thinking about my granddad made me wonder if he had a plan for when he retired. Perhaps he had a list of things to do and places to see. I knew he didn't have a long retirement as he died of a heart attack three years after he received his bureau. My parents inherited it and it now sits in the hallway of my sister's house in Peterborough.

I truly hope that my retirement will be a little longer than my granddad's. It ought to be, bearing in mind that I've retired five years earlier than he did. That's why I think mine will be more like my dad's. He was retired for thirty years before he died and spent most of it looking through his telescope or travelling to foreign shores. But then again, my dad was able to retire when he was fifty, which was one of the perks of working in local government back in those days. Nowadays most people can't afford to do that. Instead, they have to continue working until they drop dead. At least I'm lucky because I'm financially secure for the rest of my life.

I can't help but feel that the world is going backwards. It makes me wonder if, in years to come, people in the UK will look back on the last quarter of the twentieth century as the time when they were at their happiest. It wouldn't surprise me as there were no internet trolls back then and most people were in final salary pension schemes. Moreover, there was no need to feel guilty every time you got on a plane or bought a diesel car.

The old Eyres building was soon behind us and shortly after that I pulled into a multi-storeyed car park on Saltergate.

"This car park has changed as well," I said. "There was one here before. But it wasn't orange. It looks as if the council demolished the old one and built an identical one in its place. Either that or they got hold of a cheap supply of orange paint and tarted the old one up."

The Premier Inn, where we were going to spend the next two nights, was close by. I hadn't spotted it yet but according to the website it was just across the road from the car park.

"It should be easy to find," I thought to myself as Monica and I took our cases from the boot and headed for the exit.

"Good grief," I said once we were outside. "The Premier Inn is in the old Co-op building. Mum used to buy my school uniform there."

Once we'd checked in and put our cases in the room, we decided to go for a walk around town. I was pleased to see that it was pretty much as I remembered it. Okay, quite a few shops around town had closed and the buildings were lying empty. But that's merely a sign of the times and was the same in every other town across the UK. It's the result of shifting consumer habits. Everybody wants to shop online these days, a situation that was made worse by the coronavirus pandemic. That said, there was a new shopping area that had been created on Vicar Lane where the old bus depot used to be. But that was about it. Not much else had changed, unless you included Primark replacing Littlewood's and Marks and Spencer moving to a new retail park behind the bus station. The town I'd come back to was basically the same as the one I'd left behind in 1981 and this made me extremely happy.

It was early evening by the time we'd finished looking around and we decided to find somewhere to eat. The last place we'd been to on our sightseeing tour was the park and we'd walked past the Portland Hotel to get there. It still looked pretty much as I remembered it. We decided to give the food there a try.

However, as we approached the Portland, I noticed something I had missed the first time we'd walked past it: Dents had closed down.

"Why would a chemist close?" I said. "Surely people will always need medicine."

Dents was a long-standing Chesterfield business. It had been on the same site in New Square since 1903, just across the road from the Portland Hotel. Dents and Eyres were Chesterfield's equivalent of the royal family, permanent features offering stability and a feeling that things would never change. In fact, Dents and Eyres were to Chesterfield what the Queen and the Duke of Edinburgh were to the UK. You think they're going to be there forever and then, just like that, they're both gone.

"I can't believe Dents has closed down," I added. "How on earth will people in the town know it's Christmas without the star of Dents?"

"Things never remain the same for ever," Monica said gently as we went through the door into the Portland Hotel. "It's a fact of life, I'm afraid."

The Portland was a Wetherspoons these days and, although the outside hadn't changed, it was a different story inside. It looked nothing like the pub where my friends and I used to meet. It had been completely remodelled when Tim Martin bought it. One thing that remained, however, was its popularity with groups of youngsters.

"We used to start our pub crawls here when I was eighteen," I said to Monica. "It doesn't look as if anything has changed in that regard."

I looked longingly at a group of teenagers at the bar. They had their whole lives ahead of them and didn't appear to have a care in the world. Later that evening, they'd move on to other pubs and bars, just like my friends and I used to do when we were their age. The boys would try to chat up girls and they would fail most of the time. So they'd get drunk instead and throw up in the toilets. I'd been there, done that, and had the T-shirt.

Suddenly, I felt really old. I wanted to be eighteen again and have Alex, Martin, Steve, Dan and Bruce walk through the door. We'd laugh and joke and eye up the sixth form girls from St Helena's before moving on to pubs in the Peak District to play pool and darts. Then we'd buy chips from one of our favourite fish and chip shops before returning in time for last orders at the Highfields Hotel.

But you can't turn back the clock. Those days are gone for ever. They are never going to return. That's the sad thing about old age. It's knowing that your best days are behind you, days of carefree fun, when the only thing you had to worry about was whether your friends had spiked your beer or not.

Chapter 4

We did quite a lot of things over the next few weeks. We collected the keys for our rented house even though we couldn't move in for another week and a half as the container with our possessions in it had been delayed. It was very frustrating but it made the people at the Premier Inn happy as we had to extend our stay there. I took Monica to see the inside of the Crooked Spire. The tower wasn't open on the day we visited, so we'll have to go back again at some point.

We were able to open bank accounts at Lloyds Bank. However, they would only let Monica open one if it was a joint account with me as she wasn't a British citizen and had only recently moved to the UK. We also bought a new car, a SsangYong Tivoli, which should make us stand out from all our neighbours with their Audis and BMWs.

I like to think of SsangYong as the South Korean equivalent of Morgan. In my mind it's a company owned by the fourth generation of the Yong family, with all their cars handcrafted by master builders in a small workshop in the Southeast Asian equivalent of Malvern. Maybe that's why you see so few of their cars on the road. But then again, when I looked them up on Wikipedia, I discovered they were now part of an Indian multinational. That said, perhaps I ought to change my name by deed pole to SsangYong, in which case I could continue our family tradition of having the same name as the car I drive. Mind you, I'd have to change it a second time if I ever bought another one. Two weeks after we bought the Tivoli, the company changed its name to KG Mobility, which made it sound like a company making disability aids for the elderly.

We've been for quite a few drives in the new car as I wanted to show Monica the Peak District. If I thought Chesterfield hadn't changed much, that was nothing compared to the Peak District. It must be in a time bubble because it's virtually the same as it was forty years ago. In fact, it reminded me of the musical *Brigadoon* starring Gene Kelly. If you've not seen it, it's the one about the village that disappears and then reappears totally unchanged every one hundred years. Mind you, it's hardly surprising that the Peak District hasn't changed much, as that was precisely what the establishment of national parks in the 1950s was supposed to achieve.

I showed Monica Chatsworth House, Haddon Hall and even the small National Trust property in Winster. We went to see the well dressing in Tissington and to the caverns in Castleton. We also went for walks in the dales and on the moors and, of course, we visited some of the pubs I used to know.

In contrast with most things in Derbyshire, the pubs had all changed quite a lot. For a start, several had closed down, including the Horseshoe in Matlock, which has been converted into flats. It's a pity really, since this used to be one of my favourites, if only for its outside loo and its excellent draught Bass. The Horseshoe might be no more but the chip shop across the road was still open.

I hadn't been in a fish and chip shop for over forty years and was looking forward to being reunited with this pinnacle of British cuisine. When we were in South Africa, Monica and I used to go to Ocean Basket in Cape Town or the Codfather in Camps Bay if we wanted a fish supper. You couldn't get saveloys or Pukka pies in either of them but you did get calamari steaks and tiger prawns the size of lobsters.

I was drooling as I looked through the window of the chip shop in Matlock. But then I noticed that they don't sell haggis anymore. So we wouldn't be going there for old time's sake. We may as well try a chippy nearer to home instead.

I soon began to notice that hardly any of the country pubs that were still open had dart boards, pool tables or jukeboxes in them anymore. Most of them had been gentrified and things like that didn't really mix with fine dining, craft beer and an excellent wine list. The snug in the Devonshire Arms in Beeley had been incorporated into the dining area and the Peacock in Barlow was now a very smart pub. It had obviously had a major amount of money spent on it since the last time I was there. There was a massive outside terrace, a microbrewery and several letting bedrooms, as well as a vast area for dining. But it didn't have a pool table or a jukebox with Motörhead on it anymore. Also, there were no MGAs or Lotus Elites in the pub's car parks, just the usual bland selection of Mercs, Audis and BMWs.

Having said that, I quite liked what the new owners had done to it, which was just as well since Monica and I would be living just around the corner very shortly. We were buying a house in Barlow about 200 yards away.

The village of Barlow is just outside Chesterfield. It's close enough for us to use the town's facilities but with all the advantages of living in a quiet country village on the edge of the Peak District National Park. It's great that we'd be living so close to a good pub as it means we'd be able to walk to it in future.

My dad once said to me, "If you're going to buy a house in a village, make sure you chose one with a good pub."

Dad was always full of good advice like that, not that I'd ever bought a house in a village until now. The one and only house I'd owned so far had been in the Bishopscourt area of Cape Town. Being within walking distance of a good pub wasn't on our list of 'must haves' at the time we bought it. Instead, it was more important for it to have an alarm system linked to armed response and a garden surrounded by razorwire.

As we were moving to live close to the Peacock, Monica said that I ought to tell them I'm a qualified brewer in case they needed help. She was clearly starting to get worried that I was running out of things to do and needed a hobby to keep me occupied. Not that I'd class brewing as a hobby. After all, it had been my job for 38 years. For me working in a microbrewery would be a bit like the captain of a super tanker retiring and buying a rowing boat in order to keep his hand in.

In many ways Monica was correct, though. I always thought that I'd be fine whereas she would struggle to find something to do after we'd moved to Chesterfield. She'd been a nursery nurse back in South Africa and for the past 26 years she ran her own business. She used to have five members of staff and was licensed to take 24 children under the age of five. However, when I suggested moving to the UK, she sold the business to one of her employees for a knockdown price. She thought it was only fair as the lady she'd sold it to had been with her from the start and she wanted to reward her loyal service.

Monica could always have established a similar business in the UK but she was not that young anymore. In fact, she was two months older than me. So it was no surprise when she decided she didn't really want to look after young children anymore.

Despite my fears she soon found a new interest making biltong and droëwors, which she sells online and at farmers' markets. Her friend Sylvia, who lives in Bakewell, joined her in this new venture, and they have established the business in an old stone barn at the back of Sylvia's house. It's early days yet but sales are already very good, at least they are for the biltong. Most people in the UK have never heard of droëwors but biltong is quite commonplace these days. However, that didn't stop one of her customers thinking it was a Chinese snack made by a man called Bill Tong. Bloody Chinese, they make everything these days! I wonder if Bill Tong is related to Ssang Yong. You remember him? He's the South Korean guy who used to make cars in his shed before he sold out to a big multinational company.

You could even buy biltong in Tesco these days. It's far more mainstream than it used to be. So it was only a matter of time before hipsters started demanding artisan biltong made in an outhouse in Bakewell by girls descended from Voortrekkers. The hipsters rave about it, of course, even if it did taste exactly the same as biltong made in a factory in Halifax, which they could have bought in a supermarket for half the price.

My theory about trendy products like biltong is that they need to have exotic foreign sounding names in order to become successful. Take for example that other South African favourite, rooibos tea. For years nobody in the UK would buy it, mainly because it was called red bush tea. Then clever marketeers started calling it by its original Afrikaans name and soon after that there was a whole aisle dedicated to it in Sainsburys. It was the same when Blue Spot car radios decided to revert to their

German name of Blaupunkt. Mind you, the Greek lager brand Vergina would never make it over here if the brewery used its original name. With a name like that, I wouldn't want to even hazard a guess what it tastes like.

So Monica has a friend and a hobby and will probably be the next Anita Roddick. I'm convinced she's going to do for South African snacks what Anita did for make-up that hadn't been properly tested on animals.

In comparison with my wife, I haven't really done anything. In many respects, Chesterfield was like an empty shell for me. It was basically the same town as the one I grew up in with the same buildings and the same general feel to the place. The people who live there have the same accents as they always did. They still greet people with "ay up duck" and use words like mardy, manky and nesh that nobody else can understand. Yet it was different in so many ways and not just because the football team now play in a new stadium. The main change was that none of the people I used to know still live here.

In days gone by most people wouldn't have moved very far from where they were born but not anymore. For a start, my parents moved to Cornwall when my dad retired. Then my sister moved to Peterborough when her husband got a job with Anglia Water. My mother eventually moved there as well, which at least meant that I could kill two birds with one stone when I went to visit. However, it wasn't my relatives I missed, it was my friends. They have all moved away, and the place just wasn't the same without them. I wasn't any different, of course. I'd lived in Cape Town for 31 years and even before that I'd lived in Nottingham.

Why do people move away from places where they were brought up? Sometimes it's because the place they've moved to was more appealing than the place they left behind, like people who moved from Scunthorpe to live in Tenerife, or people who moved anywhere to get away from Mansfield.

I thought the desire to trade up might have been behind Mum and Dad's move to St Ives. Mind you, most people in Chesterfield just moved to Ashover if they wanted to live somewhere more upmarket. It's posh and only a fifteen-minute drive away from Chesterfield's BMW dealership.

That wasn't why I left. It wasn't because I wanted to move to somewhere better. No, I moved, like most of my friends, to progress my career. In fact, I wouldn't even have had a career in brewing if I'd stayed in Chesterfield. When I left university in 1984 there were no breweries in the town. That's no longer the case, thanks to the high number of microbreweries that have opened since then. But no one could have seen that coming in the early 1980s.

Taking my friends individually, Alex could have become a journalist for the *Derbyshire Times*, except they no longer employ proper journalists anymore. The only things they publish these days are endless lists, which don't require a genius or a highly paid investigative journalist to compile. The last time I looked, their pages were full of things like the top ten walks in the Peak District or the ten most dangerous roads in North Derbyshire. Perhaps I ought to suggest they publish the top ten list of *Derbyshire Times* lists next. Even their sports page doesn't contain proper match reports these days, just ratings out of ten for all the Chesterfield players and they probably make those up so they don't have to send anyone to watch the game.

When I was a youngster, the *Derbyshire Times* was a local paper, with offices and a print works located behind Stephenson's place. Then it became part of JPI media who closed the print works, and then the offices a few years later. Nowadays all their so-called journalists have to work from home.

That doesn't stop me from buying a copy every week. I live in hope that it will improve, thereby proving that even in your sixties, optimism can still win out over experience.

Alex must have been able to see what was going to happen to journalism in the UK, which was probably why he went to New York instead of returning to his hometown.

Bruce, of course, makes planes for a living whilst Martin makes cartoons. They couldn't have got a job doing either of those things in Chesterfield when they graduated.

Then there's Steve, the barrister. Maybe he could have stayed in Chesterfield and specialised in conveyancing. But he had more ambition than that, which was why he moved to London and became a Queen's Counsel instead.

Finally, Dan joined the Foreign Office after university. The only way he could have worked in Chesterfield was if the town had declared independence and became the People's Republic of Northeast Derbyshire.

So that's why we all moved away. It wasn't because we didn't like our hometown or even because we wanted to. It was because we all pursued careers that we couldn't have had in Chesterfield. Personally, I blamed my school. It gave us too good an education and instilled in us all a sense of adventure and ambition that could never be satisfied without moving away. When you considered it like that, it was no wonder that Derbyshire County Council closed it down.

Chapter 5

Three months had passed since we arrived back in the UK. We moved into our new house in Barlow despite having several weeks left on the Storrs Road lease. I'd since run out of things to do. For the first few months I was in Chesterfield I'd had things to buy, solicitors to see and documents to sign. That was all done now and I was starting to get bored. It didn't help that Monica kept telling me that only boring people got bored.

I could tell she was beginning to get really worried about me as my day seemed to revolve around *Homes Under the Hammer* in the mornings and numerous programmes about antiques in the afternoons.

"Why don't you get a hobby?" she asked me when she returned from Bakewell one evening.

"Like what?" I replied.

"You could join a walking group for a start. You've always liked going for walks."

It was true that I did like country walks. Since our move to Barlow, my walks always started and ended in the village, as Monica used the car to go to work most days. Having said that, I had absolutely no desire to join a walking group. So I told her that it really didn't appeal to me.

"How about doing some voluntary work then?"

"What, like helping out in the Oxfam shop?"

"Not necessarily," she added. "You could always volunteer to work in the Chesterfield Museum, for example."

"That doesn't appeal to me either. Besides which, how would I get there?"

"You could get the bus or buy a bike. Then you could get fit in addition to having a hobby."

She could tell I wasn't interested.

"Why don't you contact some of your old friends and ask them if they want to go out for a drink?"

"Because none of my old friends live in Chesterfield anymore," I replied.

"Well, make new ones then," she added.

That was easier said than done. After all, where had my friends come from in the past? Either I'd been at school or university with them, or they'd been work colleagues. Now, however, I was no longer at school, university or work and that was why I wasn't making any new ones. Our neighbours on one side were a couple in their eighties and there was a single guy who worked on the oil rigs for ten months of the year on the other. I wasn't in a hurry to go to the pub with either of them.

"Are you sure all your old friends have left Chesterfield?" she asked me. "I mean, I know your five best friends are no longer here. But didn't you have any others?"

She was right, of course. There were other people from school I'd been friendly with and not all of them would have moved away. Some of them might have gone to work in local government or had a family business to join. In fact, I was sure that Geoff Brigstock now ran his family's double-glazing business in Hasland. Mind you, Geoff had been a fan of Rod Stewart when we were at school together. He wasn't really the type of person I'd wanted to hang around with back then or now come to that. My interest in him was limited to discovering if he still had a mullet.

"Some of them might still be around," I said. "Perhaps they're on social media, and I could track them down."

"There might even be a Facebook group for people who went to your old school," added Monica.

I'd never considered looking for a Facebook group for former pupils of Chesterfield School. But thinking about it, there probably was one. On the one hand, I quite liked the idea of renewing my acquaintance with Porky Pilkington, the fat kid who used to light his farts in the changing room. On the other hand, having a Facebook group for former pupils at my school was a depressing idea. The school had closed in 1991, ten years after I had left, and the number of former pupils was getting smaller by the day. I couldn't help but compare it with some ex-servicemen's groups that had been around when I was younger. When I first started watching the parade past the cenotaph on Remembrance Sunday, there were hundreds of soldiers from World War One taking part. Gradually their numbers decreased until there were only three of them left. The following year there were none. They had all died. Pretty soon, the same would be true of soldiers from World War Two.

Despite my reservations, I decided to have a look and soon found the Chesterfield School for Boys private Facebook page. I immediately sent an email to a guy called Neil Parsons who was in charge of admin for the group and waited for a reply.

It was a formality really. All I had to tell him was the years I was a pupil at the school and which house I'd been in. There was no need for any more details than that. I couldn't really imagine anyone lying about having gone there in order to get accepted into the group. It would take a special kind of a weirdo to do a thing like that. Later that day, my request for membership of the group was confirmed and I was in.

The first thing I noticed was that there were 683 members of the group. I started to go through the old posts. There were plenty of school photos and I even found a couple that I was in. I never realised my hair was so long back in those days. I'd have thought the headmaster would have threatened me with detention if I didn't get it cut. But for some reason I managed to get away with it.

I stared at the one of my class, which had been taken in 1979. Mr Yates had been our form master back then. Frank Alan Yates was his full name which was why we called him Fay. Oh, how I miss schoolboy humour! I was sitting in the back row, along with Alex, Steve, Martin, Dan and Bruce. We were in the fifth form when the picture was taken and none of us looked as if we had a care in the world with our tousled hair creeping just below our collars in breach of school rules. Despite our carefree appearance, I knew that the reality was slightly different. We were in our O level year and failure to pass at least five subjects would mean that we wouldn't get into the sixth form. Worse than that, it would mean we'd have to go and find a job, and none of us wanted to do that.

In the end, we all made it into the sixth form, even though Alex managed to fail Latin. It was the first time any of us had ever come under any pressure. We were part of that fortunate generation who didn't even have to pass our eleven plus to get into the grammar school. It had been abolished two years before we were due to take it.

I continued looking. There were many pictures of various football and rugby teams, most of them featuring a ball with the year the photo was taken written on it. I'd never been any good at sport, so I only gave them a cursory glance. There were photos going back to the 1950s, which made me realise that some of the members of the group had been at the school more than 25 years before I started there. In one post, there was a photo of a boy who'd been at the school between 1959 and 1966. It had been put on by his brother who hadn't seen him for fifty years. His brother hadn't disappeared. Instead they'd had an argument back in the 1970s and hadn't spoken to each other since. The Facebook message contained a plea for him to restore contact with his remaining family.

There were also quite a few photos of boys who had died. One of them was Peter Royce who had been in my class and who'd died after being knocked off his scooter whilst on holiday in Barbados. The post said he was a professor of inorganic chemistry at Aston University at the time of his death, which I found surprising. The only thing I could remember about him and chemistry was the time one of his experiments had gone wrong and we'd had to evacuate the entire science block whilst the fire brigade was called out.

Then there were the photos of school reports, usually bad ones saying that the boy who's report it was will never make anything of his life. Naturally, he'd then gone on to become a captain of industry, a surgeon or a politician. I seem to remember one of Dan's reports said something similar when he was in the second year, which probably explains how he ended up as a diplomat. There were also numerous photos of school uniforms including the obligatory school cap, which was something we all owned but never wore.

However, the thing I liked most were the funny posts recalling things like teachers' nicknames or some of their quirky habits. For example, Ivan Monk who taught Physics was known as Ivan the Terrible and Beaky King, who taught History was known for breaking into Gregorian chants during his lessons. Then there was the effete Colin Potter, the art master whom we used to call Pansy Potter after the character in the *Beano*. At least I think that was where his nickname came from. Finally, there was Crapper Goodyear, the Latin master, who'd blown his family fortune on wine, women and song. I never knew how he came by his nickname, as I seemed to remember he was quite a good teacher, not crap at all. Perhaps he was called that because he was crap at managing his finances.

I looked through the many comments made about the various teachers who'd been at the school over the years and noticed that one of them had been made by Martin Howarth. It was my old friend Martin Howarth, who I'd lost contact with years ago. I didn't even know he was on Facebook. But there he was, a member of the Chesterfield School former pupils' group, just like I was. I immediately sent him a friend request.

The next time I went on Facebook I noticed he'd accepted and so we shared contact details. Over the next few days, we exchanged numerous emails telling each other what we'd been doing since the last time we met. Martin still lived in Macau although he'd sold his business many years ago. He had a Chinese wife and two young children aged eight and six. It was his second family. He hadn't decided to wait until he was in his fifties to get married and have kids. In fact, he also told me he had a son aged 31 from his first marriage. He was a civil servant working for the Scottish Parliament and living in Falkirk.

Martin admitted that he rarely came back to the UK these days and hadn't been back to Chesterfield since his mother died in 2011. It was a shame as I would have liked to see him for old times' sake. But then again, I was someone from his past. His future was in Macau with his new family.

I eventually discovered that there were nine of my classmates who were members of the Facebook group. Including Martin, two lived abroad, three still lived in Chesterfield and the other four lived elsewhere in the UK. None of those who lived locally had been close friends of mine when I'd been at school, although I did remember them all. Then a guy called Richard Hobart, who was now the owner of a wealth management consultancy in town, suggested that we all meet up one evening.

If you had asked me whether there was enough wealth in a town like Chesterfield to warrant the establishment of a wealth management consultancy, I would have said no way. But that just proved how little I knew. In fact, Richard told me that there were three wealth management companies in Chesterfield. He claimed that neither of the other two were as good as his firm, which made me wonder how you judged success in his line of work. Perhaps fewer of his clients have declared themselves bankrupt.

Richard had obviously done well for himself. I remembered that his parents used to live in a council house on Baden Powell Avenue when we were at school. Quite clearly, they didn't need the services of a wealth management consultant themselves. In fact, he was one of the few pupils at our school who used to get free school meals. He'd obviously made the most of his grammar school education and risen way above his poor background. Good for him, I thought. I bet his children don't get free school meals. They probably have a chauffeur to take them to Fischer's in Baslow for a Michelin star meal instead. No doubt they would spend the entire meal listening to Richard telling them how poor his parents were when he was growing up.

Richard put out an invitation on Facebook to all the pupils who'd been in our class at school. He asked if we wanted to meet for a drink and I was one of the first to say I'd be going.

In the end there were five of us who met up in the Portland Hotel on Friday the 4th of August. As well as Richard and myself, there was Kevin Brock and Phil Brown. They were the other two former pupils who still lived in Chesterfield. I didn't know Kevin that well but Phil was the guy who'd never heard of the Dolomites until his dad bought a new car. However, that hadn't stopped him from getting into Keele University to study geography and graduating with a 2:2.

He told me that a 2:2 was known as a sportsman's grade as most of the people who got it spent more time playing football and cricket than studying. He is teaching geography at St Mary's School these days, where he's also in charge of the second eleven football team. If only he'd been in charge of the first team, he could have claimed that he once trained the future England and Manchester United centre back, Harry Maguire. He also could have been on TV with him when he went back to visit his former school. However, he wasn't. So I guess Phil is still waiting for his ten minutes of fame.

The final member of our group was Keith Arnold, who lives in Leeds, but had driven down to be with us. I remembered that Keith had always been the type of person who would be the first to join in any piss-up and I was glad to see he was still the same old party goer he'd always been. His parents still lived in Chesterfield, and he had combined the night out with us with a visit to see them. He told us he was staying in his old room that hadn't changed at all since the day he moved away in 1981. In fact, it still had his old Hornby train set complete with track, signal box and engines set up in one corner. All he needed to do was to plug it in and he'd be able to pretend he was the fat controller once more. It was as if his parents believed that one day he would move back and want to play with all his old toys again. They'd never liked the girl he married and on the day of the wedding had been overheard saying that the marriage would never last. Mind you, that was 35 years ago, and Keith and his wife had three grown-up children. As a result, it was highly unlikely that he would move back to live with his mum and dad again, especially since Keith was in his sixties and his parents were both in their late eighties.

I really enjoyed the night out. Okay, none of the people who were there had been friends of mine when I was at school. But I knew them all. We'd all shared many experiences together and we all had similar things to reminisce about.

We spent three hours discussing things, like which of the masters were gay and whatever happened to the various people who'd been in our form. Some of the things my former classmates had done since leaving school amazed me. For a start, a couple of them had been awarded MBEs. One, who I'd considered to be a right thicko, was a government advisor and a member of the SAGE committee. Another was currently serving a five-year prison sentence for insider trading. It made me wonder which one of them had led the most successful life.

Eventually, it was time to say goodbye. If we'd still been eighteen, we wouldn't have left before closing time and, even then, we'd have moved on to a nightclub so that we could continue until two in the morning. However, things are slightly different when you are in your sixties, which is why we decided to go home at ten o'clock.

It had been a good night and one I hoped we could repeat again in the near future. We all said it would be good to invite all the former classmates we knew to join the Facebook group and I told them that I would contact Alex, Bruce and Dan as soon as I got home.

Monica was pleased I'd had such a good evening even though she did have to pick me up from the centre of town when we were done, which made her miss *8 out of 10 Cats does Countdown*. She felt I was starting to make friends again, which she said would be good for my self-esteem. Not that I realised I had a problem with it in the first place. She also said that all I had to do now was to get myself a hobby and she could stop worrying about me.

Whilst we'd been in the Portland Hotel, Richard had persuaded someone at the next table to take a photo of the five of us on his phone. He'd told us that he was going to post it on Facebook along with one in which he would photoshop the heads from our old school photo. I wanted to see if he'd done it yet. Also, I wanted to tell Alex, Bruce and Dan about the Facebook group.

I switched my tablet on and went straight into Facebook. Richard hadn't posted the photo yet. But then again, I was being stupid. It would take him quite a long time if he was going to photoshop our old heads onto the photo. But there was something else. I stared at the screen in disbelief, for there was a post from beyond the grave. It was from Giles Harrington and simply said, YOU KILLED ME.

Chapter 6

"How can it be from Giles Harrington?" I asked myself. "He died in 1981. It must be someone having a joke and a pretty tasteless one at that."

Giles and his girlfriend had both died in a car crash on the night we had gone out to celebrate our A level results. The fact that the message had been posted by Giles must have meant that someone had joined the group pretending to be him. Why would anybody do that and who were they accusing of killing him? The message didn't say.

I decided to go to bed, although it took me ages to get to sleep. I kept wondering over and over what was meant by the message. Who had sent it and why? When I got up the following morning, I decided to take another look. To my surprise, the message hadn't been removed by admin. Not only was it still there, but there were seven comments. I read them all.

Titch Lewis
This must be someone having a joke. Dead people can't put posts on Facebook.

John Stinton
I remember this. The next term was full of rumours about what had happened. I heard that Giles got into a drinking game with Nigel Hillman in the Kelstedge Inn. They both

got extremely drunk and when they came out of the pub, they decided to have a race to see who could get to the Red Lion in Stanage first.

Ray Hoar

They didn't have a race. Giles tried to overtake two cars in one go, which is why he crashed. Nigel wasn't exceeding the speed limit and the people in the car behind him confirmed this.

Stewart Smith

I heard that the people in the other car were the parents of Nigel's girlfriend. They only said he wasn't racing because she pleaded with them to lie.

Peter Zenner

Everyone in my class reckoned they were racing. I believe that Nigel was in the lead, and he was weaving all over the road in order to stop Giles from getting past. But Giles tried anyway and crashed into a drystone wall.

Glen Robertson

I heard that Nigel forced him off the road. My dad used to work at Walton Motors and Nigel brought his car in the following week with a damaged front wing. Dad told me that he'd hit something red as there were red flecks of paint all around the damaged area.

Michael Hadfield

I'm sure that Giles crashed into an oncoming lorry. I know that Nigel was driving the other car and everybody in it was as drunk as a skunk.

I didn't know any of these people who were making comments, but it was obvious that they were all younger than me. I'd already left school on the night of Giles's fatal crash.

Furthermore, I had no idea that I would become the subject of so much gossip and speculation the following term.

I knew I had to respond to these wild accusations, which was why I wrote the following:

Nigel Hillman

In answer to all the comments regarding my involvement in the death of Giles Harrington, I would just like to say the following:

It is true that I was with him on the night he died but I did not race him either before or after we left the Kelstedge Inn. Also, I did not engage in a drinking game with him. In fact, I never even had a drink in the Kelstedge Inn as we had decided to move straight on to the Red Lion at Stanage instead. One other thing that I want to clear up is that at no time did I ever exceed the speed limit. This was confirmed by numerous witnesses at the time. The people in the other car Giles overtook were not my girlfriend's parents, they were my ex-girlfriend's parents, and they had absolutely no reason to back up my story. The reason they did so was purely and simply because it was true.

In addition, I had only drunk a small amount of beer that night and I was not over the limit. In fact, I passed a breathalyser test after the accident happened. Giles, however, was more than twice the legal limit according to the autopsy report, which was almost certainly why he crashed. There was also the fact that he was showing off to his girlfriend. He had already done an extremely dangerous manoeuvre earlier in the evening. This involved going around a roundabout the wrong way in order to overtake Steve Bowler.

With regards to the damage to the front wing of my car, this was done a few days later when I clipped a red gatepost at my parent's house.

The fact is that Giles was an inexperienced driver, driving a powerful sports car whilst under the influence of alcohol. It is this that got him killed and I had no part to play in his death. I was just part of a group who went out with Giles and his girlfriend that evening. All of the others who were there that night will back up what I am saying. My only other involvement was that I just happened to be the person he was overtaking at the time he was killed.

When making your comments please bear in mind that it wasn't just Giles who died that night. Sue Pearce, his girlfriend, was also killed. He didn't hit a dry-stone wall or a lorry. He hit another car, and two people were killed in that vehicle as well.

I didn't know who was pretending to be Giles Harrington and posting on Facebook, but it was the height of bad taste. I was going to ask Neil Parsons to take down this post.

I was pleased to see that my statement had put an end to the speculation and there were no more comments on the post. No more, that was, except for a brief one by Martin Howarth:

Martin Howarth

I can concur with everything that Nigel has said. I was in the car with Nigel that evening and neither myself, Nigel or any of the others who were present had anything to do with Giles's death. It was a tragic accident caused by Giles's inexperience, coupled with the fact that he'd been drinking, just as Nigel has stated.

I tried phoning Neil Parsons later that morning but he was out and I wasn't able to get hold of him until later that day.

"I've seen the post," he told me when we finally spoke. "And I can only apologise for not removing it. But I didn't realise it was a scam until you just told me."

Neil was eight years older than me. He'd left school a long time before Giles was killed and didn't know the story behind what had happened to him.

"Do you know who the person is pretending to be Giles?" I asked him.

"Unfortunately not," he replied. "I received a membership request from him the day before yesterday. It all seemed above board, as he knew Giles had been in Bradley House, and he'd got his school years correct. In fact, he had even known that he'd spent an extra year at the school in order to take his Oxbridge entrance exam. That was why I accepted his membership request without question. His first post was the one saying, YOU KILLED ME. He must be a prankster. I'll remove him from our group when I remove the post."

Neil might have thought he was a prankster but I was far from convinced. Something in the back of my head told me it was far more serious than that and I needed to be on my guard from now on.

Monica could tell things weren't right as I was still finding it difficult to sleep at night. She asked me if everything was okay, and I lied saying everything was fine. I told her I was just finding it difficult to adjust to my new life.

If the truth be told, the post by someone pretending to be Giles Harrington was playing on my mind. It made me completely forget that I was going to invite Alex, Bruce and Dan to join the Facebook group. In fact, I still hadn't invited them four weeks later when I met Richard, Kevin and Phil again for another drink in the Portland Hotel. Keith hadn't come on this occasion as he said he couldn't get away with leaving his wife at home by herself a second time in four weeks. This time there was only one topic of conversation: what had happened to Giles Harrington and who the person was pretending to be him.

They all remembered Giles and knew he had been killed in a car crash. But none of them knew about my involvement. Well, they didn't until they saw the post on Facebook. It appeared that the only people who'd made the connection between Giles's death and me were those pupils who'd been in the years below us.

"Giles and Sue, his girlfriend, came out with us that evening," I told them. "We didn't want them to but Sue was a friend of Jessica Stevens who was going out with Bruce Young at the time. Giles's parents had recently bought him a Triumph GT6 and he was showing off in it. His driving that night was appalling and he was drinking heavily as well."

"I remember that his driving was bad," said Phil. "And he always did like a drink."

"We were in three cars," I continued. "As well as Giles in his GT6, there was Steve driving his dad's Granada and me in my Hillman Avenger. Giles was getting more and more obnoxious as the evening wore on. So the rest of us decided to leave him in the Kelstedge Inn and move on to the Red Lion at Stanage instead. Of course, we didn't tell him that as we knew he'd probably follow us there. We waited until he went to the toilet before the rest of us shot off leaving Giles and Sue behind. However, we didn't get away quickly enough. When he came out of the gents a few seconds later and realised we had left, he and Sue set off after us. As I said, he'd been drinking, and he tried a wild overtaking manoeuvre to get past me. Only he didn't make it and hit a car coming in the opposite direction killing himself, Sue and two people in the other vehicle."

"Did you stop after the accident?" asked Kevin.

"Of course I stopped. We all went to see if there was anything we could do for them. It was horrible. I'll always remember it for as long as I live."

"And you weren't racing him and zigzagging all over the road?" Kevin continued.

"There was a car behind me that Giles had just overtaken before he tried to overtake me. That was probably why he misjudged his manoeuvre, that and the fact he was half cut. He was trying to overtake two cars at once, you see, which he wouldn't have done if he'd been sober. Anyway, the driver of the other vehicle confirmed that I wasn't racing Giles. I was just driving normally at about fifty miles per hour on a road with a sixty miles per hour speed limit. My old Avenger would have been hard pressed to even reach the speed limit, since there were four of us in it."

"And the people in the other car he overtook were your girlfriend's parents?" added Richard.

"They were Claire Banyard's parents. She and I had broken up earlier that year. As I said on Facebook, they had no reason to lie. If anything, they blamed me for breaking their daughter's heart, not that she seemed too upset about it at the time. In fact, she started a relationship with Dave Willis the week after we broke up."

"And what about the damage to your car?" asked Kevin.

"I hit the gatepost at my parents' house four days after the accident. I guess I was still in shock from what I saw that night. I wasn't concentrating properly."

"I remember the gates to your parent's house," added Phil. "They were so brightly coloured, you could hardly miss them."

"Well, I certainly didn't miss them that August. I hit the gatepost when I was reversing out of the drive. It cost me a month's wages to get my Avenger repaired, even though the garage gave me a staff discount as I was working there as a petrol pump attendant at the time."

"So who do you think put that post on the Facebook page?" asked Richard.

"I don't have the remotest idea," I replied. "I also don't know what the motivation could be for doing this."

"Giles had a younger brother called Barnaby," Richard continued. "He was in the same class as my brother and I've seen a few of his posts on the old boys Facebook page, so he must be a member. Do you think he's got anything to do with it?"

"I suppose it could be him. But if it is, then why didn't he post it in his own name?"

"Probably because he wouldn't want to put his own name to any comments he made if they were wild accusations," added Kevin. "Anyway, whoever it was, they weren't accusing you, Nigel. All they said was YOU KILLED ME. They didn't say who they were referring to. The only time you were mentioned was in the comments made about the initial post."

"Can you ask your brother what Barnaby was like when they were at school together?" I asked Richard.

"Unfortunately not," he replied. "George died in a motorbike accident back in 1992."

"Sorry about that, Richard," I added. "I didn't know."

"Well, I think it was just someone having a laugh," said Phil, "someone with a warped sense of humour. I wouldn't worry about it if I were you. Giles's death happened over forty years ago and life has moved on since then."

It was all very well and good for him to say that but I wanted to know who had posted the message and what they had meant by it.

Chapter 7

The next day I decided to tell Monica about the post. I hadn't discussed it with her before because it was just three words on a Facebook page after all. It wasn't anything for her to get worried about. Naturally, she didn't agree.

"You should have told me about it earlier," she said after I'd told her everything. "It would have explained why you were so down in the dumps the past four weeks."

"I guess it's just bringing back something I tried to bury years ago. My memories from that night are horrendous. It's something I've been trying to forget for the last forty years."

"Well, in all the years I've known you, you've never mentioned it to me."

"There was no need to. I barely knew Giles Harrington or his girlfriend and I had absolutely nothing to do with their deaths. As I said, it was something I'd rather forget."

"Who do you think put the post on Facebook and what do you think is meant by YOU KILLED ME?"

"I haven't a clue. Richard Hobart suggested it might be Giles's younger brother Barnaby."

"And why would he do that?"

"God only knows. I mean, I don't even know if the post was directed at me. But it must have been. I'm a member of that Facebook group and I was driving one of the cars Giles was trying to overtake at the time he was killed. Many of the other members of the group seem to think it was directed at me."

"I thought you told me that your friend Martin whatshisname is a member. Perhaps it was meant for him."

"His name is Martin Howarth and it's true that he's a member. Only he wasn't driving that night, he was in the back of my car."

"If you think the Facebook post was directed at you, why do you think you weren't mentioned by name?" asked Monica.

"I don't know the answer to that either."

"If I were you, I'd just forget it, Nigel."

"That's what everyone keeps telling me."

"If you're not going to do that, are you going to contact Barnaby Harrington?"

"Well, he's a member of the Facebook group and he didn't comment on the post. You'd have thought he would have done as it was supposedly from his dead brother. But then again, he might not have seen it, since it was taken down the following day. I don't think it would be him who posted it but I suppose I ought to contact him and ask him if he's got any idea who it might have been."

"Why don't you ask your friends as well?"

"Shit," I replied, "you've just reminded me that I was going to ask Alex, Bruce and Dan if they wanted to join the group. Also, I think I need to ask Martin if he has any idea who it might be. I'd better email him and see what he thinks."

The only communication I'd had with Martin since the flurry of emails between us after I'd initially discovered he was on Facebook had been when he'd sent me a photo of him and his wife. That had been the previous week and it had been taken in a restaurant. It had just said, "Amber and I enjoying a delicious meal of pufferfish to celebrate our wedding anniversary."

Amber wasn't his wife's real name. Chinese people sometimes choose an English name in addition to the name they were given at birth and Amber was his wife's English name. It was one of the first things Martin had told me about her. She'd chosen the name Amber because it sounded similar to her real name.

I could tell from the picture that she was a lot younger than him. But they both looked happy and very much in love. Or was it just that they'd drunk too much Tsingtao that evening? I'd replied saying, "I bet there wasn't Motörhead playing in the background."

I emailed him and asked him if he'd seen the post on Facebook. Four days later, however, he still hadn't replied, which wasn't like him. Ever since we'd re-established contact, all his replies to my emails were virtually instantaneous. It wasn't as if he had any work commitments to distract him anymore. Then the following day I received an email from Amber. The email was fairly brief and looked as if she'd circulated it to all their friends. It said:

> It is with great sadness that I have to inform you that my much-loved husband Martin was killed on Friday of last week. We are having a service of remembrance for him to which all his friends and former colleagues are invited. This will take place on Thursday the 21st of September at 11.30 am at the central crematorium in Macau. The funeral directors are Michael Tsin and Sons, Tel 0853 2609 4390, email mjtsinandsons@mac.com. If you are not able

to attend the funeral in person, please contact them as
there will be a live link to the service on Zoom.

Her email was like a sucker punch to my stomach. It
contained no details about how he had died. Had he had an
accident? None of his communications with me had intimated
that he was ill. Perhaps he'd suffered a heart attack. I really
didn't know. But one thing I did know was that the picture of
him and Amber that he'd sent me the previous week must have
been one of the last things he'd done before he died.

I might not have seen Martin for forty years but I could
remember the things we used to get up to as if it was yesterday.
I remembered how the six of us had gone youth hostelling in
the Lake District when we were fifteen and how Martin was the
only one who could get served in a pub as he looked the oldest.
The rest of us had stayed in the pub's beer garden whilst he
went and bought the beers. I remembered how we'd hired a
rowing boat on Derwentwater and had left him on an island in
the middle of the lake for half an hour. He was mightily pissed
off with us when we returned. The more I thought about my
old friend, the more upset I became. In the end, I couldn't help
myself. I burst into tears.

I wanted to find out more but didn't want to cause more
distress for Amber who had never met me and quite possibly
didn't know anything about me. After all, I'd only contacted
Martin six weeks previously after an absence of forty years.
Therefore, I just sent her a brief email, offering my condolences.
I also emailed the funeral directors and asked them for the code
on Zoom.

I knew that Martin had been a successful businessman in
Macau, and I suspected that his death would warrant a mention

in the local paper. So I had a look on the website of the *Macau Post*.

It didn't take me long to find an article about his death as it had been major news the previous week. It seemed that Martin had not died of natural causes. He'd been found, bound and gagged with a plastic bag over his head, in an Airbnb let he owned. The man who'd rented it had sent him a text saying he couldn't get the hang of the air-conditioning unit and he'd gone there to show him how it worked. When he hadn't returned three hours later his wife went to see if anything was wrong and discovered his body.

The newspaper report said that the man's name was John Smith but when the police checked with immigration, nobody by that name had recently entered the country.

Local police were struggling to find a motive for the killing as the only thing that had gone missing was Martin's mobile phone. They also hadn't any leads who the man might be or where he was from. All the information he'd given to Airbnb was false and they didn't even have his credit card details because payment had been made using an Airbnb gift card.

The police thought it was highly unlikely that the theft of Martin's mobile phone was the motive, since whoever had carried out the murder had gone to a lot of trouble to plan the crime. They also thought that the man responsible had left the country shortly after killing him. The paper said it was going to be extremely difficult to bring the culprit to justice, especially since nobody had seen the man who called himself John Smith.

I read the article in complete disbelief. Who on earth would want to murder Martin? He was a retired TV executive who had made cartoons for a living. Was there something about him that I didn't know? Could he have fallen victim to Chinese triads and if so, why? One thing that was perfectly obvious was that whoever had killed him was not called John Smith. That was clearly a made-up name.

Chapter 8

I had to let Alex, Bruce and Dan know what had happened to Martin. I emailed them and sent them the weblink for his funeral. I told them about the Facebook group and how it had led to me re-establishing contact with him.

They were all keen to find out as much as possible about Martin's murder, which was why we decided to have a Zoom meeting the following day to discuss things.

The call was scheduled for three o'clock in the afternoon as this suited both Alex who was five hours behind UK time and Dan who was four hours ahead of us. I wondered if I should tell them about the fake post from someone pretending to be Giles Harrington. But I decided not to in the end. The call was about Martin's death, and I didn't want anything to distract from that.

We began by discussing Matin's murder and progressed to reminiscing about what we got up to when we were at school. Finally, the conversation turned to what we could do for Martin's funeral, and we decided to send a joint card and a wreath.

"I'll arrange it," said Dan. "I know people in the British Consulate in Hong Kong who will do it for us."

The British Consulate in Hong Kong was responsible for anything to do with British citizens in Macau. It was something that was far easier now that a 34-mile-long bridge and tunnel link, the longest in the world, had been built between the two former colonies.

"Do you think anyone at the consulate would know something about Martin's death?" I asked. "Surely, they would have been informed about what had happened to him."

"That's correct," Dan replied. "The consulate would need to be informed of Martin's death as he was a British citizen. I'll get in touch with one of the diplomats I know in Hong Kong and see if he can discover more detail about what happened."

"We have a reporter in Hong Kong," said Alex. "I'll contact him to see if he knows anything. I don't hold out much hope though, as Martin was a British citizen living in a former Portuguese colony and the *New York Times* is American."

The Zoom meeting ended with everybody promising to stay in touch. Three days later, Dan got back to me.

"I've been able to discover one piece of evidence that was not released to the general public," he told me. "Martin was discovered with flunitrazepam in his bloodstream. It appears that the person who murdered him had drugged him first."

I didn't have a clue what flunitrazepam was and had to look it up on Google to discover that it was the generic name for Rohypnol, the date rape drug.

The following day, Alex also got back to me.

"Our reporter in Hong Kong couldn't tell me anything about Martin's death that we didn't already know," he said.

It was bad news. Apart from discovering that Martin had been drugged, we had drawn a blank, not that I'd thought anything would come of our enquiries.

The following week, I attended Martin's funeral. Just like my friends, I did it virtually via Zoom. I didn't fly out to Macau. I noticed that the flowers we had sent were alongside a bouquet from his wife and children on top of his coffin as it was taken into the chapel. Also on his coffin was his old school cap. He'd obviously kept it all these years, whereas I'd lost mine many moons ago. The cap looked in pristine condition, as good as the day his mother had bought it for him from the Co-op. Mind you, it should do. After all, he'd never actually worn it. His mother hadn't realised that wearing a cap was no longer compulsory when he'd started at the grammar school in 1976.

As his coffin was brought in, *Ace of Spades* by Motörhead was playing in the background. Martin had always been a big fan of Motörhead and this track was one of his favourites. However, it was a weird choice for a funeral, especially since the lyrics mentioned dying, death and not wanting to live forever quite a few times. Still, I guessed it was what he would have wanted.

All too soon, it was over. If I'd been at the funeral in person I could have gone to the wake, where I could have reminisced with all the others about Martin's life. I could have shared some funny stories about him whilst poring over old photographs. I could have given my condolences to his wife and family and met people who'd known him later in his life. But I wasn't there in person. Instead, I was thousands of miles away looking at a computer screen and when the funeral was over, so was my link on Zoom.

I may not have been able to go to Martin's wake but Monica suggested that we go out for a meal at the Peacock as a tribute to him. After all, it did harbour lots of happy memories of nights out together when we were eighteen.

I thought it was a good idea when she suggested it. But as we walked down the road at seven o'clock, I was beginning to have second thoughts. Martin's funeral seemed to have taken away my appetite and I was not looking forward to mixing with other people. Also, the venue was adding to my overall feeling of gloom. Forty years ago, it had been one of the main pubs my friends and I always visited. The intervening years had seen the building change substantially. These days the interior contained nothing that reminded me of the pub we used to visit in my youth. However, the exterior brought the memories flooding back. For a start, the building looked basically the same from the outside as it had back in the 1980s, even though it had been extended. The car park was in the same position, and you still entered the pub from the rear before going downstairs to the bar, just as we had on that fateful night in August 1981.

I began to regret my decision to go out that evening. I'd have been much happier if we'd stayed at home with an Indian takeaway and a box set of *Death in Paradise*. Well, perhaps not *Death in Paradise* as that would have been in bad taste. Perhaps a box set of *The Crown* would have been a more respectful choice.

The pub was quite busy and we were lucky to get a table by the window. As I sat down, I was drawn to a couple at the next table. At first there was just something vaguely familiar about them. Then it suddenly hit me. I might not have seen them for forty years, but there was no doubt in my mind. It was Steve Bowler and Jessica Stevens.

Chapter 9

They recognised me about the same time I recognised them.

"Good God, I don't believe it," said Steve. "I'd know that face anywhere, despite the fact you've lost your hair. It must be what, forty years? I thought you'd emigrated to darkest Africa."

"I did, but I came back again," I replied. "I thought you'd moved to London and yet here you are with Jessica. It's just as if I'd got into a time machine and gone back to 1981. Well, it would be apart from the wrinkles, the spreading waistline and the grey hairs."

"And that's just Jessica," he joked. "You're correct though. I did move to London but I moved back again."

"I never moved away," added Jessica. "And after two failed marriages and three kids, all of whom are grown up now, I'm still here."

I could hear Monica clearing her throat in the background.

"Sorry," I said. "Steve, Jessica, this is Monica, my wife. Steve and Jessica were friends of mine from school. Well, Steve was. Jessica was at the girl's high school but she was part of our crowd."

"I'm pleased to meet you at last," said Monica. "Nigel has told me many stories about the two of you."

"I bet he has," added Steve, "and I could tell you a few about him as well."

"I look forward to that," Monica replied.

"Why don't you join us?" said Jessica.

I didn't need to be asked twice and we got the waiter to move the two tables together.

"How come you two are here together?" I asked as we took our seats again. "Don't tell me you're an item again."

"We live together, and have done for the past three years," Steve replied. "I for one have never been happier."

"And he's just about tolerable," added Jessica. "Although I do keep warning him that if he doesn't stop snoring, I'll phone Bruce and ask him if he wants to go out with me again. Are you still in contact with any of the others?"

I went quiet.

"You haven't heard then?" I said eventually. "Martin died recently. It was his funeral today."

It was obvious that they hadn't, and it hit them like a bolt out of the blue. Naturally, they wanted to know what had happened and I spent the next half an hour giving them all the details, including telling them that Martin had been murdered. The whole atmosphere had turned from joy to sorrow.

"Did they catch the person responsible?" asked Steve.

"The police don't know who did it," I replied. "Martin's body was discovered in an Airbnb let he owned. The only clue they've got is that someone calling himself John Smith had booked it. They're pretty certain that he's the person responsible.

"You don't think it was our old deputy headmaster, do you?" said Steve. "Perhaps Martin had failed to complete a detention before he left school."

It was true. I'd forgotten that John Smith had been the name of our deputy head. He was not the most memorable of the

95

masters at our school. Unlike most of them, he didn't have any strange habits or a quirky name, apart from being named after a pint of bitter, of course.

"It couldn't be our John Smith," I replied. "Do you remember him? He wasn't exactly the type of person who would go around murdering people. In fact, he wouldn't say boo to a goose. Not only that but he's probably dead by now. How old do you think he'd be?"

"He'd be at least in his late eighties if not in his nineties," replied Steve. "Anyway, I wasn't being serious. I don't think Martin ever had a detention."

And that was it. After thirty minutes of being down in the dumps, the conversation moved away from Martin's death. I was quite keen to talk about something else. For a start, I wanted to find out what they had been up to since we last saw each other.

"I joined the Inns of Court in London after university," said Steve, "and eventually became a Queen's Counsel. I was involved in many high-profile cases, including as the main prosecutor in the trial of Rosemary West. I was earning a lot of money at the time, which enabled me to afford a Georgian house in Barnes, close to the River Thames. I was happily married with two sons and everything in my life was just fine. Then in 2015, Jimmy, my youngest son, was killed in a stabbing, and that started a downward spiral in my life. Eventually, my wife and I split up after I suffered a serious breakdown. My whole life was like a stack of dominos. When the first piece fell, all the others just followed."

"I'm sorry to hear that, Steve," I replied.

"I took early retirement in 2019, sold the house in Barnes and bought one in Cutthorpe," he added.

This meant that Steve only lived a mile away from Monica and me.

"One day when I was out shopping, I bumped into Jessica in Morrisons," he continued. "I couldn't believe it, she looked exactly the same as she did the last time I saw her in 1981. She was still as beautiful as ever and was single again."

"He's talking rubbish when he says I'm still as beautiful as ever," added Jessica. "I'm a sixty-year-old grandmother. Don't forget he dumped me in April 1981 so he could go out with Martha. She was always better looking than me."

"No, I didn't," replied Steve. "I think your memory of what happened has become distorted over the years. You dumped me so you could go out with Bruce."

All this talk transported me back to the summer of that year. We were all teenagers back then, exploring relationships and sex for the first time. Boys were getting off with girls and dumping them a few weeks later for the most trivial of reasons. The girls were doing likewise. Dan dumped Maggie because he had expected to find a better girlfriend at university, and I dumped Claire because of what she had said about me in the sixth form common room at St Helena's. Or was it she who'd dumped me for Dave Willis? I was never sure about that. Whatever had happened, we were all extremely immature. But life was so much fun back then.

"Whatever happened to Martha Whittaker?" I asked.

"She died of cancer back in 1995," replied Jessica.

That brought me back down to earth again with a bump. All of a sudden, the conversation had moved from teenage relationships back to death again. When you are young, you don't expect your friends to die. The odd person you know may die in an accident, like Giles Harrington, for example. You might even know someone who had died of an illness. In reality though, the numbers are pretty low, which is why most young people believe they are immortal.

Then as you start to get older, you realise that more and more of the people you know have died. Death creeps up on you like a pickpocket about to rob you and when it hits, it robs you of the most precious thing you have, your life.

Martha had been a pretty girl. The fact that she'd died at such a young age meant that she'd never have to suffer the ignominy of old age like the rest of us. She'd never have to go through the menopause or buy incontinence pads from the supermarket. She'd always be just as I remembered her, young, fresh-faced and carefree.

"Did Martha ever marry or have children?" I asked.

"She married a really nice guy called Roger," Jessica replied. "He was a freelance photographer and they decided to delay having children until he'd established himself. They needed Martha's salary, you see. Unfortunately, she died before that happened. It was tragic. She was only 32."

I wanted to steer the conversation away from death once more and decided to change the subject.

"Tell me what you've done since leaving school, Jessica?" I asked her.

I knew she'd gone to Newcastle University to study Chemistry but that was about it.

"My relationship with Bruce didn't survive the first term," she told me. "I made too many new friends at university, just as he did at Trent Poly. It was never going to last. I graduated with a 2:2. My mum always said I should have done better than that and I guess I could have if I hadn't been partying so hard. You know the saying that nobody ever wishes on their deathbed that they'd spent more time at work. Well, I guess it's also true that nobody wishes they'd spent more time studying when they were at university. Nobody, apart from people who didn't get their degrees, that is."

"Phil Brown told me that a 2:2 is called a sportsman's grade because it's what all the footballers and cricketers get," I added. "I guess it must be a party goer's grade as well."

"You're still in contact with Phil Brown, are you?" asked Steve. "Does his dad still drive a Triumph Dolomite?"

"His dad died six years ago," I replied. "But yes, I am still in contact with him. He lives in Chesterfield and teaches Geography at St Mary's School these days. I meet him, Richard Hobart and Kevin Brock once a month at the Portland Hotel. Keith Arnold sometimes comes as well, although he doesn't live here anymore. He lives in Leeds but his parents are still in Chesterfield. You'll have to come next time."

"I'd like that," replied Steve.

"I may have met Phil Brown," said Jessica. "I'm also a teacher these days, although I've never taught at St Mary's. After I graduated, I did a post-graduate certificate in Education at Nottingham University. In fact, I went there with Martha who was also training to be a teacher after graduating. We both got jobs teaching at St Helena's after we'd qualified. She taught History and I taught Chemistry. Of course, we had to find new jobs when the school closed in 1991. Martha got a job at Tupton Hall, whereas I transferred to Brookfield Community School."

Both the boys' and girls' grammar schools had closed on the same day. St Helena's had since been reborn as the Chesterfield campus of Derby University. The building that had housed Chesterfield School was now occupied by Brookfield Community School.

"She took me to look around the school last year," added Steve. "I barely recognised the place. The fives courts have gone for a start as has the running track."

"What the hell is fives?" asked Monica.

"It's a game similar to squash that originated at Eton College," said Steve. "The main differences are that you use a gloved hand instead of a racket, the court is on two levels and has a buttress on one side."

"A buttress?"

"Yes, it mimics the side of the chapel yard where the game was originally played."

I hadn't heard anyone talk about fives since I left school, and I was quite disappointed that the courts were no more. Unlike Steve, however, I had no desire to go back and visit my old school building. It wasn't because it held bad memories for me, quite the opposite in fact. The reason I didn't want to go back was because my memories were so good, and I knew I'd be disappointed with the changes that had taken place since the school had closed.

"Let me tell you about my marriages," said Jessica. "My first husband was a dentist called Geoff. He was in the right profession. Trying to have a conversation with him was like trying to pull teeth."

I later discovered that Geof was the father of her three children. I guess being a riveting conversationalist isn't a prerequisite for being good between the sheets.

"I eventually discovered that he'd been having an affair with his dental nurse," she continued. "It started when Geoff said open wide and she thought he meant her legs rather than the patient's mouth."

She'd obviously gotten over him many years ago, which was why she could now make jokes like that.

"After Geoff came Duncan," she added. "He was charming but he was a shagaholic and couldn't keep his dick in his pants. Duncan was a sales manager for Playtex, the company famous for its Cross Your Heart bras, and I started going out with him on the rebound after Geoff and I had split up. Six months after our divorce came through, Geoff married his dental nurse. I retaliated by persuading Duncan to marry me, which I soon realised was a mistake. I'd only done it to get back at Geoff. Looking back, I guess I should have known that Duncan was sex mad. That was the reason why he worked in women's lingerie. Most of the other people in the company were women and so were all his customers. Not that he did much work. I don't think he had much time for it as he spent most of his time screwing. Anyway, I came home early one day and discovered him in bed with the lingerie buyer from Debenhams and that was the end of our marriage. I've been single ever since."

"Jessica doesn't want to marry me because she doesn't want to put the kibosh on our relationship," added Steve. "I've told her that I'm too old for shagging around. So it will probably be third time lucky for her."

"And I've told you that I'm waiting for George Clooney," replied Jessica.

The banter continued for the whole of the evening. What had started as a night out that I'd not been looking forward to, had ended as the best evening I'd had since I'd been back in Chesterfield.

"Why don't you join the Facebook group for former pupils of Chesterfield School, Steve?" I asked him. "I'm a member and there are lots of other people on it you'll know."

"I'm not on any social media platform," he replied. "It's something I actively avoid."

"How about going for a walk in the Peak District then?" I asked.

"That's something we can definitely do," he replied. "What about next Monday?"

"Next Monday's good for me," I said.

"You must come around for dinner," said Monica.

"That would be lovely," Jessica replied. "Let me give you my phone number, so we can arrange a date."

All too soon it was time to go home. But we all knew that tonight wouldn't be the end of it. Instead, it was just the start of part two of our friendship after a break of forty years.

"I think your friends are wonderful," said Monica as we were walking home. "And it's done you the world of good seeing them."

She was right, of course. It's amazing how you may not have seen your old friends for years. Then when you meet again, it's as if the intervening years had never happened. You reminisce, you chatter, you tell stories, and everything feels good. I was so happy to see Steve and Jessica again, all the more because it was unexpected. I never thought I'd see either of them again and now that I had, I knew that we'd not lose contact this time.

It was great to see that they had rekindled their relationship and both of them looked really happy together. Mind you, I couldn't help but wonder if Jessica had really given Bruce a blow job in the back of his mum's Ford Escort in 1981. However, I hadn't asked her at the time and I definitely wasn't going to ask her now.

Chapter 10

I had a spring in my step in the days and weeks after meeting Steve and Jessica. It was great to be back in Derbyshire and discovering that two of my old friends were here as well. My life was starting to fall into a pattern. Every Monday, Steve and I would go for a walk in the Peak District, unless it was raining. We chose Monday because it was less busy than other days of the week and we weren't limited to Sundays like people who were still working. Once a month, we'd go to one of our houses for a meal and, on Friday nights, Steve and I would meet for a beer. Sometimes this would be in the Portland Hotel with Phil, Richard and Kevin. The rest of the time it would be just him and me. On Saturdays, Monica and I would always do the supermarket shopping. First, we'd go to Lidl and then to Morrisons to get the things that Lidl doesn't sell like papayas and mint jelly. It was all very typical of things that middle-class people living in middle England do. I would also buy a *Derbyshire Times*, even though it's nowhere near as good a newspaper as the one I remembered from my youth.

One day in November, there was a news item on page two that shocked me to the core. It was a story about Alex. He'd been murdered in his holiday home on Long Island.

The report contained scant details about what had happened. It appeared that Alex and Kelly had been redecorating their house and had run out of paint. Kelly had gone to a hardware store to get some more and when she returned, she discovered Alex lying dead in the hallway. He'd been killed by a lethal injection and whoever was responsible had dropped the syringe next to his body. The police seemed to think it was a mafia hit as Alex had recently written a feature exposing a local godfather. They thought he'd been subject to a revenge killing.

"I can't believe anyone would want to kill Alex," I thought to myself. "He was the happy-go-lucky kid whose drinks we always spiked, the guy who was never able to drink a gallon of beer due to the amount of vodka we'd spiked it with. He was also the guy who claimed he'd lost his virginity to an older woman on the island of Ibiza back in 1980."

But then again, did anyone need a motive to kill anybody in America? The only thing that surprised me was that he hadn't been shot. I always thought the Taliban were wasting their time fighting against the Americans. Instead, they would be far better off just sponsoring the National Rifle Association. Then all they'd have to do is to sit back and leave the gun-crazed rednecks to do the job for them.

"Poor old Alex," I muttered. "He'd still be alive if he hadn't moved to New York. In that respect he's just like John Lennon."

Despite numerous attempts, Alex had never managed to drink eight pints and now he never would. I contacted Steve immediately and he was as shocked as I was.

That afternoon I'd planned to have another Zoom meeting with Dan and Bruce. I hadn't told either of them that I had bumped into Steve again and was going to surprise them by sitting next to him. Now, however, there was another reason for the call. I was going to let them know what had happened to Alex.

It was a big surprise for them when I appeared alongside Steve. But their joy at being reunited with him was short-lived after we told them what had happened to Alex.

"Do you think Alex's death has anything to do with Martin's?" asked Bruce.

"I doubt it," replied Steve. "Martin was suffocated in Macau, whereas Alex was killed by lethal injection on Long Island. Surely, there can't be a connection between the two."

However, I wasn't as certain as he was. The fact that two of our friends had been murdered only two months apart was not a coincidence as far as I could see. That was despite the fact they had been murdered using different methods and on different continents. I decided to throw what had happened in the Facebook group into the mix.

"Are you saying that someone pretending to be Giles Harrington accused you of murdering him?" asked Dan.

"Not exactly," I replied. "Whoever it was didn't make it clear who he was accusing."

"And you think that whoever did this might have some connection with Martin and Alex's death?" asked Bruce.

"All I'm saying is that it's one hell of a coincidence that these three things have happened one after the other."

"Why don't we go and tell the police about it?" added Bruce.

"Come on," I replied. "Do you really think they'll be interested in linking something they will probably regard as a practical joke in the UK with a murder in Macau and another on Long Island? For a start, we've got absolutely no proof that the three things are linked and, secondly, they will say that the murders are outside their jurisdiction."

"If you want, I can contact the British Consulate in New York and ask if they know anything," said Dan. "They may know something that wasn't in the newspaper or even details that haven't been released by the police. After all, I managed to uncover things about Martin's death that weren't in the public domain."

We agreed this would be a good idea.

"We also need to send a card and wreath for Alex's funeral," I added.

It was becoming quite a habit.

The following Monday, Steve and I were due to meet for a walk. We'd decided to go to Hassop station and walk along the Monsal trail. It was an ideal walk to do in autumn since the trail was along the route of a former railway line and had a hard-core surface. You have to think about things like that when you're going for walks in the countryside in November.

However, just before Steve picked me up, Dan phoned from the Seychelles with the result of his call to the consulate in New York.

"I've discovered a couple of things regarding Alex's death that have not been released to the public," he told me. "The first is that he was murdered with an injection of tetrodotoxin."

"What the hell is that?" I asked.

"It's a poison that attacks the central nervous system," he replied. "In fact, it's one of the deadliest poisons known to man. It's over 1,200 times more deadly than cyanide. The police have deliberately kept quiet about this. Then there's one other thing they haven't released and it's the reason why they believe his death is linked to the mafia. It seems they discovered a plastic bag with an empty packet of Rohypnol in it on Alex's table. The bag also had a message in it, which said 'a present from Luigi'. The police were confused because the man Alex had written the article about was called Mario Carlotti, and there was no mention of anyone called Luigi. But I'm sure I don't need to tell you what that means, especially since Martin's death was linked to a man calling himself John Smith."

I knew exactly what he meant. Martin had been drugged with flunitrazepam, the generic name for Rohypnol, before he'd been suffocated with a plastic bag. John Smith had been the deputy headmaster of our school and Luigi was the nickname we used to call the headmaster. It was obvious to me that both murders were linked and that they were also linked to our old school. Furthermore, I strongly suspected that the ghostly posting on Facebook by Giles Harrington was linked as well. It may have been obvious to us but not to anyone else.

"There's one other thing," said Dan. "Only I didn't want to mention it the other day because Bruce and Steve were listening. It's just that I wondered if you think this has anything to do with what we did back in 1981."

"We didn't do anything back in 1981," I replied.

"Look, I know we agreed that we'd never talk about it," he continued. "But we both know what we did."

"Giles died because he was drunk and shouldn't have been driving," I replied. "It's as simple as that."

"If you say so, Nigel," said Dan before he hung up.

Chapter 11

As soon as Steve arrived, I told him about the phone call from Dan. We still went for our walk, although we spent all our time talking about what Dan had just told me.

"I'm frightened," I said to him. "If there is somebody out there killing all the people who were out that night in 1981, any one of us could be next. What do you think we ought to do?"

"Well, let's think about it," he replied. "Are you sure that the murders are linked to the post on Facebook?"

"It would be one hell of a coincidence if they weren't," I said.

"In which case, this whole thing must have started shortly after you joined the Facebook group. Tell me, when was the first time you posted something in the group?"

"I've never posted anything but I have replied to posts made by others."

"And when was the first time you did that?"

I thought long and hard before I answered.

"It was about three weeks after I became a member. I replied to Richard Hobart's post inviting people to the Portland Hotel that Friday."

"So that would be the first time you became visible in the group."

"I guess so."

"And how many days was that before someone posing as Giles Harrington wrote YOU KILLED ME in the post?"

"I think it was four days later that the post appeared. The Giles Harrington post was put on the website whilst we were in the Portland Hotel on the Friday. I'd replied to Richard's post on the Monday before we all met."

"Which points to a couple of things. Firstly, it was probably aimed at you as you'd only recently joined the group and had just put your head above the parapet. Secondly, it was probably a fishing exercise."

"How do you mean?" I asked him.

"Well, think about it. Whoever posted it didn't say who they thought had killed Giles, they just said YOU KILLED ME and then waited for the comments. They'd probably heard that you were somehow involved but didn't know precisely how. That was almost certainly why whoever it was did it. I bet he wanted to find out what happened and who was involved that night. Did anyone respond?"

"Yes, quite a few people did, including myself and Martin."

"And he's dead now. What did the others say?"

"They were all from people in the years below us and they said they'd heard rumours that I'd killed Giles by weaving all over the road, which was totally untrue, of course."

"And how did you respond to that?"

"I only stated what had really happened that night. I said that Giles had been drinking and acting like an idiot. I explained how he had ploughed headlong into another car when he tried a ridiculous overtaking manoeuvre."

"And what did Martin say?"

"Only that he'd been in the same car with me and that he agreed with everything I said."

Steve stopped walking, so I stopped as well.

"Do you know what I think?" he said. "I think that whoever is doing this is targeting the people who were out with you that night. I wouldn't be surprised if the reason they posted that message was to discover who those people were."

"I've just remembered something," I replied. "I said in the post that you were driving the other car that night."

"And nobody's attempted to kill me despite the person responsible knowing that I was out with you before he knew about Martin."

Steve stopped talking for a moment whilst he pondered what that might mean.

"You know, I think whoever is responsible for these murders has a more specific target than the people who were out with us that night. What if they are only targeting those people who were in your car? Martin admitted that he was with you when he replied to the Facebook post, which was probably why he was targeted first. Whoever killed him tied him to a chair and suffocated him. What's the betting they tortured him first in order to make him say who the other two people were?"

"But why not kill me, if that's the case? After all, he knew I was driving."

"If I'm correct, and I pray that I'm not, I think he wants to kill you last because you were the person who was driving that night. If I'm right his next target will be Dan."

"You think he's singled me out for some form of special treatment, don't you?"

"I didn't want to say it, but yes, I do. It fits a pattern that I've seen before with other serial killers."

"But why? I didn't have anything to do with Giles's death. It was his own fault. He was drunk and was trying a stupid overtaking manoeuvre. I was just driving the car he was trying to get past. The others weren't doing anything. They were just my passengers."

"I don't know. Maybe he believes the story that you were zigzagging all over the road."

"But I wasn't. That story was discredited by the others in my car. Even if I had been weaving all over the road, it still wouldn't explain why he killed Martin and Alex."

"Perhaps he believes that the others were lying to protect you. That could be why he's targeting them."

"But it wasn't just Martin, Alex and Dan who said I wasn't to blame. The people in the car behind me said exactly the same thing, as did all the newspapers and the news on the BBC."

"Just because something was denied in the papers doesn't count for anything these days. That's why people believe so many conspiracy theories nowadays. All you need to do is to look at the number of people who believe that Covid-19 was caused by 5G masts or people who think that vaccinations are a ploy by Bill Gates to inject the entire population of the world with microchips. Giles's death may have been more than forty years ago. But the rumours about how it happened have resurfaced recently. The world is a very different place to what it was in the 1980s. We live in a world of fake news, a world where people are more likely to believe what they read on social media than the things they hear on the BBC. In fact, most people don't even watch the BBC or any other reputable news broadcaster anymore. It's no wonder the world is so screwed up these days. But all is not lost. Let's think logically about all of this. The Facebook group is private, which means that people who aren't in the group can't read any of the posts. How many members are there?"

"At the last count there were over 700. But there were only 683 when I joined."

"In which case the person who's doing this must be one of these 683 people. Now let's turn to the type of person who would want to get revenge for Giles's death. It has to be a loved one, doesn't it? I mean, why would anyone else want to do it? If that's the case it's probably a relative or a former partner."

"The only partner Giles ever had was Sue and she died in the crash as well. However, Richard Hobart told me that Giles had a younger brother who was a member of the group. I meant to get in touch with him, but I haven't so far."

"Well, there's your prime suspect then," added Steve. "He's got both the motive and the opportunity."

"If he's doing this under some misguided pretext of revenge for his brother, why do you think he's doing it now?"

"It's probably purely because you joined the Facebook group. I guess he wouldn't have known where to look for you before that, nor any of the others, for that matter, as you all lived abroad. After you joined the group, you suddenly became visible. I bet that's why all of this started."

"But Martin was a member of the group before I was."

"However, if it is Giles's younger brother who is doing this, he probably heard the same rumours as all the others. He would have heard that you were involved in his brother's death but had no idea that Martin was in the car with you. He probably didn't realise that until Martin replied to your post."

"If Giles's brother was responsible for all this, are we saying he travelled to Macau and to Long Island to murder two people just because they happened to be in the car Giles tried to overtake on the night he was killed?"

"I'm not saying I know why he did it. But the fact is that it's perfectly feasible. It's a shrinking world, Nigel. It's quite easy to get on a plane and go anywhere you want these days. In fact, it probably suits him that they both lived in different countries. It makes it far more difficult to link one death with another. As I said, I don't know the motive behind him targeting Martin and Alex. But I guess he's got some reason for blaming the four of you, however bizarre that might be. It could be something just as stupid as blaming the mobile phone companies for Covid-19. Who knows?"

"In which case we need to warn Dan."

"We'll contact him as soon as we get back to the car," replied Steve. "Then we'll contact Giles's brother. If he's a member of the Facebook group, we'll be able to get hold of him using Messenger."

Chapter 12

We contacted Dan when we returned to the car. He didn't seem as concerned as we were. I guessed it was because he was in the Seychelles where most people were as laid-back as he was and the overall crime level was very low. However, it was also a place where, if you did commit a crime, you were highly likely to end up in prison.

"You probably don't know that the Seychelles has the highest rate of incarceration in the world at 800 people per 100,000," he told us. "That's despite the low crime rate. In comparison, we have a mere 130 people per 100,000 locked up in British prisons."

We managed to get the fact across that it wasn't worth taking a risk with his life. He promised to brief the military attaché at the High Commission who was responsible for his security. I still wasn't happy though. I presumed that the UK's military attaché in the Seychelles was not likely to be a grizzled war veteran from Afghanistan. He was more likely to have received his training in the army catering corps than the SAS. Still, at least Dan would have some form of protection, which was more than could be said for me.

After speaking to Dan, I sent a message to Barnaby Harrington. I had to be careful what I said to him. I didn't want to accuse him of anything at this stage. I just wanted to meet him and assess whether he was really responsible for the post or not. That was why I wrote the following:

Hi Barnaby,

You probably don't remember me from school, but I knew your brother and was with him on the night he was killed. I've noticed that you are a member of the Facebook group for former pupils of Chesterfield School and wondered if you'd spotted that someone has joined pretending to be your brother.

I don't know if you've seen the post that he put on the site but it led to a lot of wild speculation. Some of this speculation was very hurtful and untrue and a lot of it was about me. Therefore, I would very much like to speak to you so I can put my side of the story.

Barnaby replied before we'd even got back to Chesterfield, saying that he hadn't seen the post I was referring to as he didn't go on Facebook very often. He told me that he did remember me from school and was more than happy to speak to me. He suggested I go around to his house for coffee one morning and included his address at the bottom of the message. I immediately replied, suggesting we meet at eleven o'clock the next day. Then I told Steve what I'd done.

"I don't think we should go," he said. "I don't want to go to the house of someone we suspect of being a homicidal maniac. If you'd witnessed some of the cases I've been involved in over the years, you wouldn't want to go either."

"He's probably not our killer," I replied. "A killer wouldn't invite people around to his home for coffee."

"I wouldn't be so sure of that," added Steve. "You know I

prosecuted Rose West. Well, nothing would surprise me after that case, I can tell you. Let's take our evidence to the police and let them deal with it. Derbyshire police might not be interested because neither of the deaths took place under their jurisdiction. But we should be able to persuade them to involve Interpol."

I wasn't convinced that we'd be able to persuade the local police to get Interpol involved. I was determined to go and see Barnaby Harrington, with or without Steve's support.

As soon as I got home, I looked up tetrodotoxin on Wikipedia. I reckoned it wouldn't be easy to get hold of since it was extremely poisonous, but if that was the case it might give us a clue about the person doing this. However, I was disappointed to discover that tetrodotoxin is produced by the pufferfish, which is considered a delicacy in parts of Southeast Asia.

For some reason, the mention of pufferfish rang a bell in my head, but I couldn't remember why that was.

I clicked on the link that took me out of the Wikipedia page for tetrodotoxin and into the page for pufferfish. It informed me that chefs who wanted to prepare pufferfish for consumption had to undergo a minimum of three years' training. If they failed to remove only a tiny amount of the fish's organs containing the poison, the diner would be killed instantly. There is no known antidote for tetrodotoxin.

I thought about what I had discovered. It was undoubtably the same person who'd carried out both murders. So could the person who murdered Alex have bought a pufferfish in Macau after murdering Martin? I did a bit more research and discovered there was a fish market in Macau where pufferfish were sold. I was also amazed to discover that restaurants serving the fish were strictly controlled by law but there were no such controls for domestic consumption. That was why most instances of pufferfish poisoning occurred at home.

I phoned Steve and told him what I'd discovered.

"That's all very well and good," he said. "But Alex wasn't fed the toxin, he was injected with it instead. That points to our killer having some knowledge of chemistry and biology to be able to extract the poison from the fish."

"Perhaps Barnaby has a degree in one or both subjects from university," I added. "I can ask him when I go and see him tomorrow."

"You aren't thinking of actually going to his house, are you?" he replied. "If you must insist on meeting him, can I at least suggest that you change the meeting place to somewhere more public, like a pub for example?"

However, I was determined to visit Barnaby at his home. After all, his house may contain something that would back up my theory that he was behind the murders. It might also provide some clues about his reasons for doing this.

The following day, I arrived at Barnaby's house in Ling Road bang on eleven o'clock and knocked on the door. Fortunately, I now had full use of our car. Monica and Sylvia's business was expanding fast and they had recently purchased a van, which Monica used to travel to Bakewell and back.

After a brief wait, the door was opened by a thin man with a pale complexion and dark glasses. He didn't look like a serial killer. In fact, he didn't look as if he'd got the strength to murder anyone. But then again, if serial killers had a specific look, they'd be easy to detect.

"Mr Harrington," I said, "I'm Nigel Hillman."

"Come in and please call me Barnaby," he replied. "I really hope I'll be able to help you."

As we walked through the hall, I noticed a tank containing tropical fish. Was that the clue I'd been looking for? I looked at it briefly but couldn't see any pufferfish, only guppies, neon tetras and angel fish.

"You told me in your message that you remember me," I said. "However, I'm afraid I don't remember you at all."

"That's often the way in my experience," he replied whilst showing me into the kitchen. "The junior boys often remember senior boys because they look up to them. However, senior boys rarely remember those in the years below them. That's because to them they were just little oiks."

"That's very true," I replied.

Barnaby offered me coffee and whilst he was making it, we chatted about school. To be honest, it was more as if I'd come to visit an old school chum rather than a suspected murderer.

"So what did you do after school?" I asked him.

"I went to Reading University where I got a degree in Estate Management," he replied. "After that, I got a job in the Estates Department at Derbyshire County Council in Matlock. They always said that a job in local government is a job for life and so it proved to be for me. I took early retirement two years ago aged 55. I was hoping to go travelling and see a bit of the world. But unfortunately, I'm losing my sight. That put paid to any thought of world travels."

"I'm sorry," I replied. "Is there nothing they can do for you?"

"There isn't," he replied. "However, I've come to terms with it. I intend to make the most of things until my eyesight eventually fails me. At the moment, it's only my peripheral vision that's affected. I'm able to manage just fine."

Did the fact that he was losing his sight make it more or less likely that he was the killer? I decided to reserve judgement on that. At least his degree was in Estate Management not in Chemistry or Biology. That didn't mean he wasn't responsible for the deaths of my friends. It just meant that he probably wasn't the person who'd extracted the tetrodotoxin from a pufferfish.

"You didn't know my dad, did you?" I asked him. "He used to work for Derbyshire County Council in the Finance Department."

"I might have known him. I used to have dealings with the Finance Department over things like rent on the properties owned by the council. When was he there?"

"He started at the age of fifteen," I replied. "But, like you, he took early retirement. That was in June 1987 when he was fifty."

"I wouldn't have known him then. I only started in October of that year."

After we'd sat down at the kitchen table, he asked me to tell him what had been said on Facebook about his brother.

"I looked for it but I couldn't find it," he explained. "It must have been taken down."

I confirmed that was the case.

"As I said in my message, it was more than just about your brother. It was sent by someone pretending to be him and all it said was YOU KILLED ME."

"I wonder who would do a thing like that?" he replied.

"Well, I wondered if it was you," I said, coming straight to the point. "You see, whoever did it would have had to join the Facebook group pretending to be him. In order to do that, it would have to be someone who knew he was in Bradley House and knew the dates he was a pupil at the school."

"That could have been anyone who was in his year at school," he replied. "Or even someone like you who was in the year below him."

"That's true," I continued. "Except that your brother was one of the first to go to the school after the eleven plus exam was abolished. He would have started at the school when he was thirteen rather than eleven. He also stayed on for an extra year to take his Oxbridge entrance exams. His was not a typical number of years spent at the school. Most pupils who were older than him would have gone to the school for seven years and most of the pupils his age and younger would have gone for five. But your brother was there for six and, according to Neil Parsons who runs the Facebook page, whoever was pretending to be him knew that. That's why I don't believe that the person responsible for this was just a casual acquaintance of his."

"Well, I can assure you it wasn't me," replied Barnaby. "Why would I want to do something like that?"

"Because you blame us for killing your brother."

"No, I don't," he snapped back. "There was only one person who was responsible for my brother's death and that was my brother himself. Mind you, my dad always shared the blame. He regretted buying him a powerful sportscar as a present. He'd wanted to buy him a Ford Fiesta but Giles had gone on and on at Dad to buy him a two-seater sportscar. In the end, Dad caved in and bought it for him. He never forgave himself for buying that car. I think he went to his grave still rueing the day he bought it. I knew how my brother drove. He took me out in it once and I'd never been so scared in my life. He was overtaking on blind corners and exceeding the speed limit. Then there was his drinking. When you add it all up, I wasn't surprised that he crashed. With hindsight, I guess the best thing that could have happened to him was if he'd been breathalysed and they'd taken his licence away. Unfortunately for him, though, that never happened."

"If you didn't do it, can you think who did?"

"You say the post just said YOU KILLED ME. Well, I'll help you if I can. But that doesn't give me a lot of clues, does it?"

"A lot of the guys in the year below us thought it was directed at me," I replied. "Did you ever hear any rumours when you returned to school after your brother was killed?"

"I did and I told my parents what I'd heard. But they'd been to the inquest into Giles's death, so they were able to tell me that you were not involved. It was all just malicious gossip by lads in the school playground."

"Two of my friends who were in the car with me that night were recently murdered," I continued. "That is one hell of a coincidence. I think their deaths have something to do with that post. Do you know anything that might help me uncover what happened to them? Were you involved in any way?"

"Absolutely not," he replied. "Who were they?"

"Martin Howarth and Alex Singleton."

"I remember Martin but not Alex," he replied. "Martin was a school prefect, wasn't he?"

Martin had indeed been a school prefect. The reason he'd been made one was probably down to the fact that he was captain of the school hockey team. I was mightily jealous at the time. School prefects got to wear a special tie and had their own room where they could make coffee. They were also able to put the more junior boys in detention and to get them to report to the deputy headmaster's study. I'd always hoped that I'd be made a prefect myself. But in order to achieve that honour, it was important that you had a glittering history of sporting success. At the very least, you would have received your school colours in one of the team sports. For that reason alone, I was never going to be appointed. My main extracurricular activities at the time didn't involve sport. Instead, they revolved around trying to avoid paying my fare on the school bus and chatting up the girls from St Helena's, neither of which were considered to be appropriate qualifications.

"I might recognise a photo of Alex, of course," he continued. "But I'm sorry, I don't know anything about either of their deaths. I hadn't heard that they had died and even if I had, I wouldn't have linked their deaths to my brother. I can't think of any reason why anyone would want to kill them. Are the police linking their deaths?"

"No, they both died abroad," I replied.

"Well, perhaps they aren't linked. Perhaps their deaths are just a coincidence."

"I don't think so," I replied.

I was sorely tempted to tell him about the John Smith and Luigi link but I didn't want to tell him everything. He claimed not to have heard about either death and therefore there was a chance he would slip up and mention something that he shouldn't have known. Deep down, I doubted it though.

"You haven't been out of the country recently?" I asked.

"No, I haven't," he replied. "I've decided not to travel abroad due to my eyesight."

I could tell he was starting to get annoyed by the questions I was asking him.

"Look," he continued. "I really want to help you. But if all you are going to do is sit there and accuse me of somehow being involved in the deaths of your friends, I'm afraid I'm going to have to ask you to leave."

I apologised to him but it was clear that he'd had enough of me for one day. I got up and he followed me through to the hall.

As I was going through the door, he said, "Look, I can see why you're getting all worked up about this. Your friends were killed and it's upsetting you. I'd be worked up as well if I were in your shoes. Why don't you give me your telephone number and I will phone you if I remember anything that might help you?"

So that was what I did.

Chapter 13

When I got home I phoned Steve who wasn't at all impressed that I'd been to see Barnaby at his house. But he was still keen to see if I'd discovered anything.

"What did you think?" he asked me.

"I don't know," I replied. "He didn't strike me as a serial killer. Not only that but his eyesight is starting to fail."

"Perhaps he wants to carry out the murders before his sight goes completely?"

"I don't think so," I said. "He seemed like a nice guy. That said, I think he only told me what he thought I wanted to hear. When accused of a double murder by someone you'd invited into your house, most people would have thrown you out. But he didn't. Instead, he kept telling me he wanted to help me. Despite this, I'm not convinced that he isn't involved somehow."

"You should have been more subtle," added Steve. "You shouldn't have accused him of anything. It might have made him flip."

"But it didn't," I replied. "Maybe he isn't involved after all."

"Or maybe the fact that he kept his cool is an indication that he is," added Steve.

"What do you think we should do next?" I asked him.

"I think we should go through the other 682 names in the Facebook group and see if anybody stands out as a suspect."

It was not an easy task so we agreed to share it between us. I took everybody with surnames starting from A to M and Steve took the rest of the alphabet.

We began by looking at their profiles on Facebook to see if it told us anything. As soon as I started on my quota, I realised that I hadn't looked up Giles Harrington yet. In order to join the Facebook group, the person responsible must have set up a bogus Facebook account and I was curious to see what he'd said about himself.

It didn't tell me very much. He'd only got six friends and all of them were either eastern European prostitutes or weirdos. They were the type of people who would send out friend requests to everybody in the hope that one or two would accept them. If you did, they would send you a few friendly messages before eventually sending a few naked pictures of themselves and asking for some dick pics in return. If you were foolish enough to send them some, there were no prizes for guessing what would happen next. It involved demands for money coupled with threats to make the pictures public.

Presumably, the person pretending to be Giles Harrington had accepted their friend requests, because anybody looking at his Facebook page would consider it strange if he had no friends.

I looked at his profile and noticed that the picture was the one taken for our school yearbook in 1981. He was dressed in his school uniform, wearing a prefect's tie with a head boy badge on his lapel. Under education it said Chesterfield School 1975 to 1981 and Trinity College Cambridge 1981 to 1985. Trinity College was where Giles had been about to start his studies. Under occupation it said NASA scientist, Kennedy Space Centre, Titusville, Florida, USA. It was as if the person who set up the account was saying, "This is what I could have done, if only I didn't die."

It appeared that he'd only posted once more. As I scrolled down to look at it, my eyes nearly popped out of my head. It was a photograph of a piece of paper with the following words written on it:

Giles Harrington – Four sixth formers
Martin Howarth – Deputy Headmaster
Alex Singleton - Headmaster
Dan Podgorski – Economics Master
Nigel Hillman – Gym Master

Only one person had liked the post and that was a lady called Olga Alferov from Minsk. This didn't mean anything. She almost certainly didn't understand it and probably liked all her friends' posts.

The post was a list of everybody who'd been killed and those he was planning to kill in the future. It was also the first positive connection between the death of Giles Harrington, the post on Facebook, and the death of my two friends. If it was Barnaby, why would he put this on Facebook? It was as if he was just toying with me. He was suggesting that my friends and I had killed Giles Harrington, that Martin had been killed by the Deputy Head from our school and that Alex had been killed by the Headmaster. What was more concerning was that he was telling me that Dan would be killed by Cec Thompson, our old Economics Master and Alf Jephcote, the former Gym Master, would kill me. Except, of course, they weren't really doing the killing. For a start, most of them were dead themselves.

Whoever set up the account had provided just enough personal information to avoid suspicion. There were no posts other than this one, not even an amusing post of dancing dogs shared with friends. But then again, I doubt if Olga from Belarus was this type of person. Despite her pigtails and the innocent look on her face, she was almost certainly a prostitute or the front for an Eastern European criminal gang. Her kinds of posts were certainly not allowed on Facebook.

I immediately phoned Steve and told him to look at Giles's Facebook page.

"Why do you think he'd put a post like that on Facebook?" I asked him.

"It's probably because anyone else looking at it would think it's just a list of names," he replied. "But to you and Dan it represents a death threat. We'd better phone Dan again and tell him what we've found."

I promised to contact him immediately and that was precisely what I did as soon as I finished my call to Steve. Dan told me not to concern myself as he had a bodyguard. He seemed very relaxed about the whole thing, more concerned about me than he was about himself. It was alright for him to be relaxed. I wasn't relaxed in the slightest.

I tried not to worry that my name was on the list. Instead, I attempted to put it behind me and began looking at all the other names I had to work through. It was a big job since it involved looking at all the details of the people who were members of the group. For a start, I had to look at all their posts and see who their friends were. Each one took me a minimum of fifteen minutes, unless they'd restricted access by altering their privacy settings, in which case I had to give up and move on to the next person. With over 300 people to get through, it was going to take me about six days to complete the exercise, and that was only if I did it for twelve hours per day. Steve had a similar task to perform.

By day four, I'd got as far as letter H, which is when I realised that I hadn't looked at Barnaby Harrington yet. Of course, I should have looked at his page right at the start, at the same time as I looked at the person pretending to be his brother. But I hadn't and it had taken his name on the list of members of the Facebook group to remind me that I needed to look at him as well.

It was obvious that Barnaby Harrington didn't use Facebook very often as he hadn't completed any of his personal details. He also hadn't put a picture of himself on his page or had many friends. However, one of his friends leapt out of the page at me. She was a pretty, blue-eyed girl with her blonde hair hanging down in pigtails. She looked as if butter wouldn't melt in her mouth. But nothing could have been further from the truth.

"Got you," I said as I looked at the photo.

The girl he was friends with was Olga from Belarus.

I decided to confront Barnaby Harrington immediately about what I'd discovered. This time I didn't contact him in advance. I just turned up unannounced at his home.

"Oh, it's you again, is it?" he said when he opened the door. "I suppose you'd better come in."

He led me through to the kitchen where he put the kettle on. He didn't even ask if I wanted coffee this time. He just assumed I would.

"I'm sorry but I can't remember if you have milk or sugar," he said as he got a couple of mugs from one of the cabinets. "My memory's not as good as it used to be, I'm afraid."

I might have been about to tell him that I had evidence he was a serial killer but, being British, I remembered my manners.

"Milk and no sugar," I replied, before adding, "thank you."

If it had been a TV detective programme, it was more likely to have been a scene from Miss Marple rather than some violent American crime drama. That said, I'd come with a purpose so there was no point in shilly-shallying about. I decided that I might as well come straight out and confront him with what I'd discovered.

"Barnaby," I said," I've been looking through the Facebook profiles of everyone in the Chesterfield School old boys' group. When I was looking through your list of friends, I noticed that one of your friends is also friends with the person who is pretending to be your brother."

"Let me have a look," he said.

I showed him the page with all his friends and the same page for his brother.

"See this lady here, Olga Alferov from Minsk, she's friends with both of you."

"I've never heard of her," he replied. "I don't know how she came to be on there. I don't remember accepting a friend request from her."

"Well, you see how it looks," I replied. "A lady from Belarus appears on both your list of friends and the list of the man pretending to be your brother. I'll ask you again. Did you put the post on Facebook pretending to be your brother?"

"No, I didn't," replied Barnaby. "I haven't got the faintest idea how she got to be friends with me. I don't use Facebook very often and I've never checked who's on my list of friends."

"This can't be a coincidence, Barnaby," I continued. "There has to be a reason."

He went quiet as he thought about what I'd just said.

"Hold on a second, my computer was hacked a few weeks ago. Maybe that's how she got there."

"A likely story," I replied.

"No, it really happened. Not only that but I'm pretty sure I know who did it. I think it was Georgia Pearce."

"Who?"

"Georgia Pearce," he replied. "Sue Pearce's sister."

I suddenly recalled that Steve had said the person doing this was probably a relative or a loved one. It would make perfect sense if that person was Sue Pearce's sister.

"I didn't know Sue Pearce had a sister," I said.

"Oh, yes," he replied. "There were quite a few years between them. Georgia's parents were fairly old when they had her. I believe she was an accident."

"What makes you think she was responsible for hacking your computer?"

"Well, for a start she has a PhD in Computer Science. But that's not all. After my computer was hacked, I took it to the computer store on West Bars, the one that's called A Geek, and they were able to restore all my data and emails. Or that was what I thought. I didn't realise it at the time but the emails from Georgia were still missing. They'd all been permanently wiped."

"So you were in regular contact with her then?"

"Not regular contact. In fact, I've never met her. She first got in touch with me four years ago and we've exchanged a few emails since then."

"If you've never met her, how do you know she is who she says she is?"

"She mentioned that Sue and my brother used to babysit her when she was little. I know they used to do that but I doubt if anyone else does. That's the main reason why I believe that she really is Sue's sister. Georgia must have been about three at the time. I would have been fifteen and I remember Giles talking about her. She also sent me quite a few photos of my brother and Sue. They were all family photos. Some of them were taken when Giles went with them on holiday to the Gower. Only a relative would possess photos like that."

"I don't suppose you downloaded them on your hard drive or to the cloud, did you?"

"I did but they've disappeared as well."

"Okay, can you tell me why she made contact with you and what the emails were about?"

"She said she'd looked me up because I'd known her sister. Her parents were dead and there were very few people she could ask about Sue. I told her that I hadn't known her sister that well, as she was my brother's girlfriend and I was three years younger than him. But she insisted on asking me things about her."

As he was saying this, it suddenly struck me that there was one person who could confirm whether or not Sue had a younger sister and that was Jessica. I made a mental note to talk to her as soon as I got home.

"What questions did she ask you?"

"Well, to start off they were questions about her sister's relationship with Giles, like if were they in love. Did I think they would have married eventually? She said her sister was a very clever girl and had been hoping to go to Cambridge just like Giles. She told me that her parents had pushed her to do all the things that her sister hadn't been able to do, which was how I came to know that Georgia had a PhD in Computer Science. She told me she'd studied Computer Science because that was what Sue was hoping to study at university."

He took a sip of his coffee and continued.

"She asked me eventually what I thought of the crash that killed her sister. I apologised to her because I said it had all been down to my brother. But she wasn't sure it was his fault. Then she mentioned your name."

"And you didn't think to tell me this the last time we met?"

"This was four years ago and I'd forgotten about it. I told you that my memory's not as good as it used to be. Pretty soon after mentioning your name, she stopped emailing me. Then a couple of days after you came to see me, it came back to me what she'd said. I went into my mail file and discovered all the emails she'd sent me had disappeared. So had all the photos I'd downloaded, and various items from newspaper reports into the crash that she'd sent me. It wasn't just these but the emails I had sent her had been wiped as well and her email address had disappeared from my address folder. I began to suspect that she must have been responsible for my computer crashing."

"Why?" I asked.

"Because she was an expert in computers. But there was more to it than that. My computer crashed two months ago, and I hadn't heard from Georgia for four years. However, just before it happened, I received an email from her with an attachment."

"What did the email say?"

"That was what puzzled me. It didn't say anything. It just contained the attachment."

"And what was in the attachment?"

"I don't know. I couldn't open it. My computer crashed the following day and the reason for that has got to be down to the attachment she sent me. It couldn't have been caused by anything else. I think she wanted to destroy all records of her existence."

"Okay, let's go back to the conversation you had with her four years ago. What did she say about me?"

"She asked if I thought you'd killed her sister. I said of course not as you'd been completely exonerated at the inquest. She replied that she wasn't so sure of your innocence."

"I don't suppose you remember any details about her, do you? Like, for example, where she lives, where she works or even her email address?"

"Sorry, she never told me where she lives or works. As for her email address, it was georgiafomison followed by a number then @gmail.com."

"Georgia Fomison?" I asked. "I thought her name was Georgia Pearce."

"I presumed that Fomison was her married name. Of course, that made it easy to remember as it sounds like George Fomison. In fact, she told me that her friends all called her George, which I considered to be quite bizarre. You remember George Fomison, don't you? He used to be head of physics at our old school."

Chapter 14

"Can you try to remember the number that was part of Georgia's email address?" I asked Barnaby.

"Sorry," he replied. "I can't. The only reason why I can remember the first part is because of the similarity to George Fomison, and the last part is the same as my own email address."

Eventually, I had to concede defeat and left. I went straight to see Steve to tell him about my latest discovery. I also wanted to ask Jessica if Sue had a younger sister but she had gone to see a friend of hers who lived in North Yorkshire and was incommunicado.

"There's no mobile reception where her friend lives," Steve explained. "I'll ask her when she gets home."

I told him I'd seen Barnaby a second time. He was even more unhappy than he'd been when I went the first time.

"Do you have a death wish?" he asked me. "Why didn't you just phone him rather than going to his house?"

He calmed down eventually, which allowed me to tell him what had happened during my conversation with Barnaby. In particular, I told him about Georgia Pearce or Georgia Fomison as she was now known.

"That's another connection to our old school," I said. "Everyone who's involved with this has been given the name of someone from our school."

"What did you think of his story?" asked Steve. "Do you think he was telling the truth?"

"Well, it makes sense," I replied. "Sue's sister could be behind all this. Except that we know Martin was killed by a man who called himself John Smith."

"Do we?" he said. "Don't forget that nobody ever saw the individual who'd rented Martin's property. We know he wasn't really called John Smith and we've got no proof he was a man. Most of these Airbnb lets have a keypad system that allows guests to check in by themselves. I doubt if Matin had even met the person who was renting it before he went there to explain how the air-conditioning unit worked. That person could well have been a woman. Likewise with Alex's death. The police might have assumed he'd been killed by the mafia but that's only because he wrote a story in the *New York Times* about a mafia godfather and a note with the name Luigi was left by his body. However, we are pretty confident that refers to the headmaster at our school and there's nothing to suggest that the murderer wasn't a woman."

"Georgia Pearce must be involved," I added. "I bet that Fomison isn't her married name. She's only calling herself that to taunt us. It's another connection to our old school."

"Why should she taunt us and why should anyone put that list on Facebook of all the people who are being targeted? It's all a bit too contrived for my liking. In the real world, killers don't deliberately leave clues."

"They might if they're psychotic," I replied. "They probably want us to know it's them but not the police."

"And why would they do that?"

"I don't know why. Maybe it's because they want to frighten us. Anyway, do you think Barnaby is involved?"

"I'll reserve judgement on that for now," replied Steve. "In the meantime, you and I are going to try and track down Sue Pearce's sister."

We started emailing everybody using georgiafomison followed by a number and @gmail.com. We began with georgiafomison1@gmail.com and went right up to georgiafomison999@gmail.com. We used a new email address using Jessica's name to send the message. We thought she'd be more likely to reply to her as it was a female name of someone who hadn't been in my car on the night her sister had been killed. The email we sent said:

> Did you used to be Georgia Pearce from Chesterfield? If so, I might have gone to the same junior school as you. Do you remember me?

We decided to keep the message simple and non-threatening. It was highly unlikely that she'd see through it. After all, how many kids' names can you remember from your junior school?

A few of the emails were delivered, although the majority came straight back to us and the number of these started to rise substantially once we'd gone past number one hundred. Some people even replied but none of them were the person we were looking for.

Once we'd completed the exercise, Steve suggested that we try dates of birth. If Georgia had been about three years old when Giles was going out with Sue, she must have been born sometime in 1977 or 1978. We erred on the side of caution and started with 111977 and then we abbreviated it to 1177. We progressed through all the dates until the end of 1978. It was an even bigger job than just going through from 1 to 999 and yielded far fewer replies, none of which were the one we wanted.

In the end, I had to go home for my tea. Steve promised to complete the task that evening, which was a little optimistic. It took him until mid-afternoon the following day. As for myself, I combed the internet looking for a Georgia Pearce from Chesterfield. I also looked for a Georgia Fomison just in case her married name wasn't made up. But it was all to no avail.

Once Steve had finished sending out emails, he phoned and said that he hadn't been able to discover anything. I told him my internet search had yielded nothing as well.

"I also asked Jessica if she could remember Sue having a younger sister when she was at St Helena's," he said. "She couldn't and reminded me that she hadn't been that friendly with Sue. She'd never been to her house, had never met her family, and didn't know whether she had any brothers or sisters. But she did stress that this didn't necessarily mean that she didn't have one."

"What do we do next?" I asked him.

"There are some websites we can try," he replied. "There's a site called Chesterfield Folks Reunited for a start, plus quite a few others. Also, something may yet come out of all the emails I've sent off. Some people may not have read them yet."

We decided to try these websites. I wasn't going to get my hopes up and I was right not to, as we'd run out of ideas by the end of the week and hadn't made any progress in our search for Georgia Pearce.

On Friday evening, I put on the six o'clock news as usual and got the shock of my life. One of the headlines was that the British High Commissioner to the Seychelles had been murdered.

Chapter 15

I phoned Steve straight away.

"Have you seen the news?" I said.

"No," he replied. "Why?"

"Dan's been murdered," I replied.

My voice was trembling as I said it. Dan had been a great friend for the best part of fifty years. He'd been a lifelong bachelor and incredibly laid-back. I always told him that he should never have finished with Maggie. She'd never marred either, which just went to show how correct I'd been.

"If only they could have foreseen the future," I thought to myself. "I bet they wouldn't have split up. They'd probably have gotten married and had kids instead."

The things that went through your head when you've just learnt that someone important to you had died were sometimes strange. All I could think of at that precise moment was Dan and Maggie splitting up in the spring of 1981. At the time, it hadn't meant that much. After all, they were both only eighteen. They both had many future relationships to look forward to. Neither of them realised that their first loves would also prove to be their last.

"I think it's about time we went to the police and told them all we know," added Steve.

So that was what we did.

We made an appointment with a DC Gethin at ten o'clock on Friday at Chesterfield police station. The mere fact that we were seeing a detective constable told me that the police were not going to take our claims seriously. This was despite Steve being a former Queen's Counsel and one of the victims a British diplomat.

We trawled the internet in an attempt to find out what had happened to Dan and the only thing we could discover was that he'd been poisoned.

"What's the betting it was tetrodotoxin again?" I said to Steve as we were waiting in the reception area at the police station.

This time we knew we weren't going to be able to discover anything that hadn't been released to the press. It had been Dan who'd been able to find out that type of information for us in the past. So if the murderer had written Cec Thompson in biro on Dan's forehead, we wouldn't get to know about it this time, nor indeed if the murderer had left any other clues that he was pretending to be our old Economics master.

We arrived at the police station at ten minutes to ten and were waiting to be called. In the end, we waited for 25 minutes before DC Gethin eventually came and collected us. They always say that one of the signs of getting old is when the policemen appear to be getting younger. In which case I must be about 120 as DC Gethin looked to me as if he was about twelve. In reality, he was probably double that age and whilst he was keen to make a name for himself by solving a high-profile case, he also appeared to be very inexperienced, which didn't bode well.

Steve did most of the talking. He was far more used to dealing with the police than I was. To start off, DC Gethin thought Steve was my solicitor. He had to tell him that, whilst he had been a barrister, he was now retired.

We gave DC Gethin the reason for our visit. We started with the mysterious post on Facebook and how three of our friends had been murdered. We provided him with details of the link to our old school and the list we'd discovered on Giles Harrington's Facebook page. I described my visits to Barnaby Harrington and how I thought that either he or Georgia Pearce, or possibly both of them, were involved in the murders.

I could see that DC Gethin was getting less and less enthusiastic after Steve explained that all the murders had taken place overseas. It was quite clear that he was not interested in taking any further action as none of them had taken place in Derbyshire.

"I can't go interfering in investigations by foreign forces," he said.

"What, even though they are all British citizens from Chesterfield?" I replied. "The people who are responsible for their deaths are almost certainly from Chesterfield as well."

"Investigating their deaths will be down to local police forces in cooperation with representatives of the various British high commissions and consulates," he replied.

"The problem is that nobody is linking these three crimes," added Steve. "But eventually the penny will drop and when it does, the shit will really hit the fan. That's when the powers that be will look for a scapegoat and there are no prizes for guessing who they'll pin it on. It will be the person who was told that these crimes are linked and did nothing about it when all he had to do was to report it to Interpol. Don't forget that these were all high-profile deaths. One of them was even on the six o'clock news."

That made DC Gethin sit up and take note. However, he'd never had to contact Interpol before. It was very much outside his comfort zone. He decided to start on far firmer ground by going to interview Barnaby Harrington. At least it was something, and he promised to keep us informed of any developments.

The next day, he phoned me back after he'd been around to Barnaby Harrington's house to interview him.

"Unfortunately, Mr Harrington wasn't in when I called," he said. "His next-door neighbour told me he was on holiday, and she didn't know when he'd be back. She also didn't know where he'd gone but she thought it was somewhere in Devon."

DC Gethin told me he would try again next week.

"See," I said to Steve when we met up in the pub that evening. "What's the betting Barnaby Harrington is in the Seychelles?"

If truth be told, we didn't really know where Barnaby was or when he was going to come back. However, he phoned me out of the blue a few days later.

"Where have you been?" I asked him.

"I didn't realise I'd have to ask for your permission before going on holiday," he replied sarcastically.

"You haven't been to the Seychelles, have you?"

"I should be so lucky," he replied. "If you must know, I've been in Dartmouth. I've been going there since I was a boy. It's one of my favourite places in the UK and I usually go there at least twice a year. It brings back happy memories of summer holidays with my parents and Giles. I wanted to see it one last time before my eyesight completely fails me."

"He's spinning me a yarn," I thought to myself. "He'll have been out of the country."

"Anyway, I haven't phoned to tell you about my holiday," he continued. "I've phoned to let you know that I've heard from Georgia Pearce again. Only, given what happened on the previous occasion, I've printed her email this time. She goes into great detail about your involvement in the death of her sister. I think you ought to come and read it."

"I will be with you in about thirty minutes," I replied.

Barnaby was busy making coffee once more when I arrived and, after asking me again if I took milk and sugar, he gave me a mug. I took a seat at his dining table and started to read the email. The first thing I noticed was the email address, georgiafomison1981@gmail.com.

"Damn," I thought to myself. "We never tried 1981, the year when Giles and Sue died."

The text of the email said:

Hi,

Many apologies for not contacting you again until now. It was just that there weren't any developments regarding my enquiries into the death of my sister and your brother until recently.

However, new evidence has come to light which proves that their deaths were not an accident. Instead, they were killed by Nigel Hillman, Alex Singleton, Martin Howarth and Dan Podgorski and they have been covering up what really happened ever since.

Firstly, the only people who witnessed what happened that night were the four of them and the two people in the car behind them. What never came out at the inquest was that the two people in the other car were known to Nigel Hillman. They were the parents of his girlfriend and probably agreed to cover up what really happened that night in the same way that his friends did.

"That's rubbish," I thought to myself as I drank my coffee. "Yes, I did know the people in the other car. They were Claire's parents, and they were hardly my number one fans at the time as I'd recently split up with their daughter. The reason why they backed me up was because it was the truth, pure and simple."

I read on:

The second thing that never came out at the inquest was that Nigel Hillman's car was damaged on the night of the crash. He'd hit something and whatever he'd hit had left red paint marks on one of his front wings. A few days later he took it to the body shop at Walton Motors where they repaired the damage. I believe that the red paint came from your brother's car, which conclusively proves that Nigel Hillman was deliberately preventing your brother from overtaking him.

"That's yet more rubbish," I thought to myself. "Georgia Pearce must have read my reply on Facebook to know about Claire's parents being in the other car and the damage to my front wing. That damage had nothing to do with the night that Giles and Sue died."

My head was starting to spin by this stage and I wondered who had provided Georgia with all this information. After all, she couldn't be a member of the Facebook group herself. Chesterfield School was an all-boys school. I continued reading the email.

However, the thing that is the most damning is the fact that I now know...

I couldn't read anymore because I had double vision.

"What's happening to me?" I thought to myself. "Has Barnaby put something in my coffee?"

I tried to stand up but my legs were like lead. I looked up and saw him smiling at me.

"I know what you're thinking," he said. "You're wondering if I've drugged you. Let me put you out of your misery. I have."

"But why?" I asked him.

"I'd have thought it was obvious," he replied. "I put the post on Facebook and killed your friends. I went to Macau pretending to be John Smith. I tortured and suffocated Martin Howarth after drugging him first. He was very useful, was Martin. He gave me the names of the other people who'd been in your car that night. After that, I flew out to New York where I surprised Alex Singleton and injected him with tetrodotoxin before leaving him with a present from Luigi. Finally, I flew out to the Seychelles where I did the same to Dan Podgorski. I injected him in the gent's toilet at the restaurant where he was eating. His bodyguard didn't have a clue what had happened."

"Why would you do that?" I mumbled, barely able to get my words out.

"Because you all killed my brother," he replied. "All four of you. Martin admitted it to me before I killed him. He told me how you did it. How you were all guilty. All of you but especially you, Nigel. That's because it was you who came up with the idea of how to do it in a way that you'd get away with it."

I wanted to say, "No, we didn't kill your brother," but by this stage I couldn't speak.

"Yes, I know you've had forty years in which to convince yourself you weren't involved. Traumatic events like that can often play tricks on your mind, you know. You put them to the back of your brain in order to forget them. Then one day you say to yourself, did that really happen? And you answer your own question by saying no, it couldn't have, and the process is complete. You've convinced yourself that those events didn't take place. But deep down in your subconscious you know what really happened, don't you? That it was you and your friends who killed my brother. That's why I've drugged you, or rather it's Alf here who's drugged you."

He turned the mug around that I'd been drinking from. On the other side was a photo of Alf Jephcote, the gym teacher from school. I'd been so keen to start reading the email that I hadn't even noticed it.

"But don't worry," he continued. "I've only given you flunitrazepam. It won't kill you. You see, I wanted you to know it was me before I give you this."

I noticed he was holding a syringe.

"This will really kill you. It contains a lethal dose of tetrodotoxin. It's the same poison I used on Alex and Dan. I extracted it from a pufferfish I bought in Macau. It's odd, isn't it, that people should choose to eat such a deadly fish. Just one small mistake and the diner is dead, just like you're going to be in a few seconds' time. Don't worry, Nigel, you won't feel a thing. Unlike my brother and Sue Pearce's deaths, yours will be completely painless. They died in absolute agony, trapped in the wreckage of their car. But you already know that, don't you? After all, you were there, and you were the person who caused them to crash."

As he started to approach me, I passed out.

Chapter 16

I opened my eyes but was barely conscious.

"Is this the afterlife?" I thought to myself.

It wasn't, of course. Instead, I was in an intensive care bed in Chesterfield Royal Hospital with Monica sitting at my bedside. As soon as she noticed I was awake, she called a doctor.

"Mr Hillman," he said. "You've received a particularly high dose of flunitrazepam. You might know it by the brand name Rohypnol. It appears that you were injected with it."

"No, he put it in the coffee," I replied.

"You couldn't have ingested the amount of the drug that you've got in your system," he added. "You'd have thrown up. Besides which you've got a needle mark on your forearm."

"He put it in the coffee and must have injected me with more of it after I'd passed out. He told me he was going to inject me with tetrodotoxin."

"Well, it's a good job he didn't," replied the doctor. "Otherwise you'd be dead by now. As it is, you could have died as the dose he gave you was so high. You didn't just pass out, you know, you've been in a coma. However, we should have you back to normal in a couple of days. We will have to check for symptoms such as memory loss. But now that you're back in the land of the living, I'll let your wife tell you what happened whilst I continue my rounds."

"What does he mean, what happened?" I asked Monica. "Barnaby Harrington injected me with flunitrazepam after confessing to placing the post on Facebook and murdering Martin, Alex and Dan. I hope he's been arrested."

"Barnaby Harrington is dead," she replied. "The police discovered his body next to where you were lying unconscious on the floor."

"What?" I said incredulously.

"Nigel, what do you think you were doing by going to see him? I've been talking to Steve and I know you thought Barnaby Harrington was somehow involved in the deaths of your friends. He told me he advised you not to go and see him. But you still went and not just once. You went on three separate occasions."

"I had to find out what was going on," I replied. "Barnaby was the younger brother of Giles Harrington who was killed in the car crash I witnessed in 1981. I believed Barnaby was blaming me and my friends for his brother's death for some reason. A lady called Georgia Pearce, the sister of Giles's girlfriend who also died in the crash, had been in touch with him and was accusing me and my friends of all sorts of things regarding her sister's death. He showed me one of her emails. She is probably the reason why he began his vendetta against me and my friends."

"Are you quite sure that you had nothing to do with the death of Giles Harrington?"

"Please believe me, Monica. I had absolutely nothing to do with that car crash or any of the deaths that occurred as a result of it."

I'd known Monica for over thirty years and she had never before questioned anything I told her. She'd always known that

I would never lie to her. Well, she had up until now. It appeared that she wasn't so sure anymore.

"Do you know anything else that happened after I passed out?" I asked her.

"They believe Barnaby was killed by lethal injection," she continued.

"That's the same way Alex and Dan were killed," I replied, "and the same way he tried to kill me. What's the betting he decided to commit suicide after thinking I was dead?"

"It's a possibility," she replied. "But the police are still looking into it. They told me they want to interview you as soon as you regained consciousness."

"How long have I been out for?" I asked her.

"Just over 24 hours," she replied. "You could have died, Nigel."

Then Monica hit me. Not in a violent way. It was more of a gentle slap, and it was obvious that she was mad at me for taking such a risk with my life by visiting Barnaby's house.

Until that point, I had presumed that I'd only been unconscious for a couple of hours rather than for a whole day. It was quite a shock to learn that I'd been in a coma for that long.

Half an hour later, the police arrived and asked if they could interview me on my own. I didn't know how I was going to be able to help them. After all, I'd been unconscious for most of the time I'd been in Barnaby's house. I was hoping they would be able to fill in any gaps for me rather than the other way around.

Monica said she needed to do some shopping and kissed me before leaving. I wished I could just get up and go with her. But, of course, they had to keep me in for observation.

One of the two police officers who came to interview me was DC Gethin. The other was a DI Cowling. It was obvious that the police were taking the matter far more seriously this time.

"Mr Hillman," DI Cowling began. "Can you start by telling me why you were at Barnaby Harrington's house?"

"He phoned me and said he had some information regarding the person I thought was responsible for the deaths of my friends. So I went to see him."

"Well, that strikes me as odd," DI Cowling continued. "Because a few days earlier, you went to see DC Gethin here and told him that you thought it was Mr Harrington who was responsible for murdering your former schoolmates. Are you telling me that you now believe someone else was responsible?"

"Well, I did think it was him until I went to see him the second time," I replied. "That was when he shifted the suspicion for their deaths on someone called Georgia Pearce. He had information about Georgia or so he told me. But when I got there, he drugged me and confessed that he'd been the killer all along."

"Hang on," added DI Cowling. "You're telling me that Mr Harrington, who you had previously thought was a murderer, phoned you. He says he has some information about the person who you now think is a murderer. But when you get there, he tells you it was really him all along."

"I know it sounds far-fetched but that was what happened. The reason I was beginning to have second thoughts about his guilt was because of what he'd told me about Georgia Pearce. You see, back in 1981, I witnessed a crash in which Barnaby Harrington's brother and Georgia Pearce's sister were both killed. Barnaby had told me that Georgia believed my friends and I were responsible for the crash. We weren't, of course. The inquest into their deaths found that Barnaby's brother was responsible. He'd been drinking heavily and had tried a dangerous overtaking manoeuvre, which resulted in him hitting an oncoming vehicle. On my second visit to his house, Barnaby had intimated to me that Georgia was responsible for killing my friends in some bizarre quest for revenge. But she wasn't. Instead, she was responsible for filling Barnaby's head with the ridiculous notion that we were to blame for the deaths of their brother and sister, and that was why he killed my friends. I don't know whether Georgia manipulated him into doing it. Or maybe he just spiralled out of control after she'd shared her conspiracy theory with him. The only person who can answer that question is Georgia Pearce."

I could see that I was going to have to explain the whole background to what had been happening to DI Cowling. This was despite having already explained it to DC Gethin a few days earlier. When I had finished, he asked me how I knew that Georgia Pearce was involved and that it wasn't just a story made up by Barnaby.

"Because Barnaby showed me an email from her," I replied.

"Well, we can check that because we've got his computer."

"But he'd also printed the email. You should have found it in the house."

"We didn't find any printed emails," replied DC Gethin.

"Perhaps he destroyed it before he committed suicide."

"You think he committed suicide, do you?" asked DI Cowling.

"It's the only thing that makes any sense," I replied. "He must have injected me with the wrong substance and thought he'd killed me. I guess I must be extremely lucky. He probably decided to take his own life now that he'd killed all the people he was holding responsible for his brother's death."

"What did Sue Pearce say in this email?"

"She said that all the passengers in my car lied to the police back in 1981 and so did the other witnesses."

"And why would they do that?" asked DI Cowling.

"She said it was because the passengers in my car were all friends of mine and the people in the car behind me were the parents of my girlfriend."

"And were they?"

"They were the parents of a former girlfriend of mine called Claire Banyard. But they wouldn't have lied for me."

"I've read the report from the inquest into the four deaths. Mr and Mrs Banyard both gave evidence and neither of them said they knew you."

"They probably didn't think it was important. I don't know. You'll have ask them if they are still alive. I haven't seen them for over forty years. As I've already said, Claire's parents wouldn't have lied in order to protect me. Quite the opposite in fact. I wasn't exactly in their good books at the time as I'd just finished with their daughter."

"Did Georgia Pearce give any other reason why she thought you'd killed her sister?"

"She said that I had damage to my car and had some bodywork repairs a few days after the accident. She reckoned there were flecks of red paint on my front wing, which meant that I must have forced Giles's red GT6 off the road."

"That was not mentioned at the inquest," said DI Cowling.

"That was because the damage didn't happen on the night of the accident. It happened a few days later when I hit the gatepost at my parent's house."

"We don't call them accidents these days, sir," added DI Cowling. "We call them road traffic incidents. The word 'accident' implies that nobody was to blame and, in our experience, that is rarely the case."

"And it wasn't the case back then either. The inquest found that Giles was to blame because he was drunk when he tried a stupid overtaking manoeuvre."

"How do you think Georgia Pearce found out about the damage to your car and the fact that you were known to the other witnesses of the crash? This all took place 42 years ago and it wasn't reported at the inquest."

"A few weeks ago, there was a post on the Chesterfield former pupils Facebook page, which simply said YOU KILLED ME. Both the damage to my car and the fact that the other witnesses to the crash knew me were mentioned by people who commented on the post. One of them was by someone whose father worked at the garage where my car was repaired. Another was by someone who'd heard that Claire's parents were in the other car. The Facebook post purportedly came from Giles Harrington but one of my friends suggested it had come from Barnaby. He admitted he'd posted it just before he drugged me. Steve Bowler thinks that Barnaby's post on Facebook was a fishing exercise, and I must say I agree with him."

"Mr Bowler is a friend of Mr Hillman, sir," added DC Gethin. "He accompanied Mr Hillman to the station when he came to see me to raise his concerns about Mr Harrington."

"We'll need to interview Mr Bowler," said DI Cowling before continuing. "Surely non-members of that Facebook group can't see any of the posts. Bearing in mind that Chesterfield School was single sex, how would Georgia Pearce have seen it?"

"I presume that Barnaby Harrington showed it to her," I replied. "Look Inspector, I'm not trying to hide anything from you. Georgia Pearce also had a supposed third piece of evidence against me. But I passed out before I could read it. If you find the email on Barnaby's laptop, you can tell me what it was and hopefully I'll be able to explain it to you."

"We'll do that, Mr Hillman," replied DI Cowling. "I think that's about all for now but we may need to speak to you again. In the meantime, we want to take a look at any laptops or tablets you own."

"Why would you want to do that?"

"To see if there's been any communication between you and Barnaby Harrington."

"The only written correspondence between us was when I messaged him asking if we could meet and he agreed. Other than that all our communication was all face-to-face."

"Unfortunately, we can't just take your word for that, sir."

"I've got nothing to hide, Inspector," I replied. "You can take them if you must."

"Thank you, sir," replied DI Cowling. "I'm sure we'll be able to clear this whole thing up very shortly."

It had been a tough interview with the pair of them, especially considering that I had just regained consciousness. I couldn't help thinking that they were accusing me of somehow being involved in Barnaby's death. I was glad it was over and I tried to put it behind me as I turned over and went back to sleep again.

The following day the doctors gave me the all clear to return home. I was very grateful as I've never liked hospitals. I thought they were mind-numbingly boring as you've got nothing to do most of the time.

Monica came to collect me and she brought a fresh set of clothes for me to put on. But as we exited the front of the hospital, two gentlemen approached me. It wasn't until they got nearer that I recognised them.

"Nigel Hillman," said DI Cowling. "I'm arresting you for the murder of Barnaby Harrington. You do not have to say anything. But it may harm your defence if you do not mention when questioned something which you later rely on in court. Anything you do say may be given in evidence."

Chapter 17

I was in complete shock. Why did the police think I had murdered Barnaby Harrington? Surely, he had tried to murder me. Monica couldn't believe what was happening either. But she fortunately had the presence of mind to phone Steve who agreed to act as my legal representative. I was lucky to have him as a friend as he'd previously been one of the top barristers in the country. He was a far better person to have in my corner than a duty solicitor whose normal brief was to act on behalf of people accused of shoplifting or exposing themselves. He was bound to get me released from police custody. After all, I hadn't done anything wrong, and he was a former Queen's Counsel.

Before the police started interviewing me, they had taken my fingerprints and a sample of my DNA. Once they'd done this, Steve asked to have a word with me in private.

"Why do they think you killed Barnaby Harrington?" he asked me.

"I don't know," I replied. "He tried to kill me."

"Is there anything you can think of that might give us a clue about what led them to arrest you?"

"I've racked my brain and I can't think of anything."

"Okay, they haven't charged you yet. We are going to have to find out what evidence they've got against you. My advice is to answer all their questions as honestly as you can. If you are in any danger of saying anything that might harm your defence, I will step in and answer on your behalf. Are you ready?"

"Yes," I replied.

Steve knocked on the door signalling that DI Cowling and DC Gethin could enter. We all took a seat at the table and DI Cowling switched on the tape.

"Interview with Nigel Hillman on Tuesday the 19th of December 2023, at 14.06," said DI Cowling after switching on the voice recorder. "Also present are DI Keith Cowling, DC Anton Gethin, and Mr Steven Bowler, Mr Hillman's legal representative. Mr Hillman, I'd like you to start by telling me why you suspected Mr Harrington of murdering your friends."

"I've already told you the reason for that," I replied.

"Yes, but you weren't being interviewed under caution on that occasion. Tell me again, this time for the tape."

Steve gave me a nod.

"It started with a Facebook post, which was purportedly from Barnaby's brother Giles who was killed in 1981. It was posted on a closed Facebook group for former pupils of Chesterfield School. Barnaby and I were both members of the group. The post said YOU KILLED ME. One of my former classmates suggested that it might have come from Barnaby."

"How did you make the leap between a Facebook post and the murder of your friends?"

"Martin was murdered in a house he owned in Macau. It was an Airbnb let, which had been rented by someone calling himself John Smith. Alex was murdered in Long Island by someone who left a note saying, 'a present from Luigi'. John Smith was the deputy headmaster of our old school. Luigi was the nickname we gave our headmaster. That was why I thought there was a connection to our old school."

"If I could just stop you there for a moment," said DI Cowling. "The police in Long Island have emailed a copy of their findings into the death of Martin Howarth. The message left at Alex Singleton's house was never made public by them. How do you know about it?"

"My friend Dan Podgorski, who was the third victim, told me. Dan was the British High Commissioner to the Seychelles and he used his contacts at the British Consulate in New York to find things out that weren't in the public domain. You'll back me up on that, won't you, Steve?"

"Can we just stop there for a minute, Inspector?" said Steve. He started whispering in my ear.

"Nigel, I can't back you up as it was you who spoke to Dan," he said. "I got that information second-hand from you. It won't be admissible as evidence."

After a brief pause, DI Cowling continued.

"We'll be interviewing Mr Bowler separately as a witness in this case. What reasons did you have for suspecting Mr Harrington? You've explained why there was a link to your old school, but not to Mr Harrington."

"He had a friend on Facebook called Olga Alferov who was also a friend of the person calling himself Giles Harrington. It's too much of a coincidence that she should be friends with both Barnaby Harrington and the person claiming to be his brother. That was why I believed it was Barnaby Harrington who sent out the Facebook post in Giles's name. Barnaby admitted that was the case when I went to his house on the 17th of December. He also admitted to killing Martin, Alex and Dan. So why are you interviewing me? He was the guilty party, not me."

"Because, Mr Hillman, we only have your word for that. As well as speaking to the police in Long Island, we've also spoken to the police in Macau and the Seychelles, and all three forces believe that there is no link between their murder and either of the other two. In fact, the police in the Seychelles believe that Mr Podgorski was killed by a woman, whereas the police in Macau think Mr Howarth was killed by a man. The police in Long Island are keeping an open mind about the sex of the murderer."

"Dan couldn't have been killed by a woman," I replied. "Barnaby told me that he'd murdered him in a gent's toilet."

"Mr Podgorski was not killed in a gent's toilet. He was murdered whilst out shopping in Victoria market on the island of Mahe. It seems he'd given his bodyguard the day off in order to let him go and see his daughter in a play. The market was crowded, but despite this, someone caught sight of the killer and told the police she was a woman."

I was dumbstruck by this announcement. Dan had never taken the threat against him seriously and had paid the ultimate price as a result.

Eventually, I just said, "But Barnaby told me he killed him."

"It appears that you and Mr Bowler are the only people who believe that the three deaths are linked," DI Cowling continued. "Therefore, even if Mr Harrington did place the post on Facebook pretending to be his brother, and we haven't even proved that he did, then it would appear to be the only thing he did."

"No, they are linked. I discovered a list of all the people who'd been killed on Giles Harrington's bogus Facebook page, starting with Giles and ending with myself. Next to each person was the name of someone from our school. Martin had deputy head next to his name and Alex had the word headmaster next to his. Finally, when Barnaby Harrington tried to murder me, he drugged me using a mug with a picture on it of Alf Jephcote, our former gym master. My name had gym master written next to it on the list."

I missed out the fact that Dan had Economics Master next to his name as I had no evidence that his death was linked to Cec Thompson.

"Why did you drink from the mug if he'd already warned you that was what he was going to do?"

"Because when Barnaby gave me the coffee, the picture of Alf' was facing away from me. He turned the mug around and showed it to me after he'd drugged me."

"On the day we discovered Mr Harrington's body on the floor of his kitchen, we discovered two mugs containing a small amount of coffee in them. They were both on the table next to where we discovered you lying unconscious. They were the only dirty mugs in the kitchen and neither of them contained flunitrazepam. Can you tell me if they were the mugs you and he drank from that day?"

"For the tape, I am showing Mr Hillman two coffee mugs retrieved from Mr Harrington's house," added DC Gethin.

I looked at the mugs, which were in a plastic evidence bag. They were identical to the ones we had drunk from the previous Thursday, except for one thing. Instead of a picture of Alf Jephcote on the front, these mugs each had a picture of Wayne Rooney.

"No," I replied. "I told you that the mug I drank from had a picture of Alf Jephcote on it. These two have pictures of Wayne Rooney."

"But no other mugs were found at the scene other than clean ones in the cupboard and none of these had a portrait on the front. How do you explain that?"

"I can't."

"In addition, one of these mugs has Mr Harrington's fingerprints on it and the other has those belonging to you. How do you explain that?"

"I can't," I said for the second time.

DI Cowling continued the interview.

"Returning to the list that you claim to have seen on Giles Harrington's bogus Facebook page."

"My client did see it, Inspector," Steve cut in. "It was not a bogus Facebook page. I saw it myself as well. Not only that but I took a screenshot of the page and will be pleased to show it to you."

I was mightily pleased that Steve had done that. I hadn't even considered it at the time. But then again, that was why he was a retired Queen's Counsel, whereas I was a former brewer. I could tell that DI Cowling was taken aback by that piece of news.

"Okay," he said. "In which case we will assume for the moment that the list does exist. When you were telling me about it earlier, Mr Hillman, you didn't mention Dan Podgorski. I thought the list had all of you on it."

"It did. Dan had Economics Master written next to his name. I presume whoever killed him left the name of Cec Thompson, our former Economics Master, at the crime scene."

"Not as far as we're aware," replied DI Cowling.

"Perhaps the police in the Seychelles aren't as efficient as the police in the UK," added Steve sarcastically.

"You also mentioned that Giles Harrington's name was on the list," DI Cowling continued.

"That's correct. His was the first name on it."

"Who from the school was next to his name?"

"It just said four sixth formers."

"Which you took to mean your three friends and you?"

"That's correct."

"Okay. But the only thing you have that links Barnaby Harrington to the person pretending to be his brother was the fact they had the same friend on Facebook?"

"Yes, but as I've already told you, Barnaby admitted that he was the person who placed the post on Facebook and also murdered Martin, Alex and Dan."

"If I understand you correctly, you are telling me that Barnaby Harrington admitted to you that he murdered Martin Howarth in Macau, Alex Singleton in Long Island and Dan Podgorski in the Seychelles."

"That's correct."

"And how would he do that?"

"I presume he flew out to all three places."

"We've checked Mr Harrington's computer and as far as we can see he hasn't bought any airline tickets for more than two years."

"Well, perhaps he bought standby tickets at the airport."

"We've also checked Mr Harrington's bank account and credit card statements and he has never used any of his cards to purchase flight tickets."

"He might have used cash."

"In which case the cash withdrawals would show up on his bank statements."

"Perhaps he's got a secret account that you don't know about or had been squirrelling money away for years. Alternatively, Georgia Pearce might have given Barnaby the money."

"Perhaps indeed, but I'm struggling to understand why he would go to such lengths."

"To disguise the fact that he was the murderer."

"And why would he need to do that? Think about it logically. You told me that he must have committed suicide after thinking he had killed you. It wasn't as if he needed to cover anything up through a fear of having to go to prison. There'd be no reason to hide what had happened if he was going to kill himself. In my experience, serial killers don't try to cover up their murders before committing suicide. Instead, they like to boast about all the people they've killed. They want to be recognised and remembered for what they've done."

"I don't know how he paid for the tickets, or why he should wish to cover it up. But as I keep on saying, what I do know is that he told me he killed them."

"Even putting aside the credit card and bank statements, I still have difficulty believing that. You see, at the time of his death, Barnaby Harrington didn't have a passport."

I didn't know what to say to that. I looked at Steve and he looked back at me. Clearly, we needed to rethink what had happened.

Chapter 18

"Inspector," said Steve, "all your questions have so far been about whether or not Barnaby Harrington was a murderer. You have not given us one piece of evidence why you suspect my client of murdering him."

"Good point, Mr Bowler," replied DI Cowling. "And that is something I'm going to come to now. You see, all I've been trying to do so far is to establish your client's motive and I think I've done that. He wrongly believed that Mr Harrington had murdered his three friends and, fearing he was to be next, he decided to kill him first. Only, he'd got it wrong. Mr Harrington did not kill his friends. There is no connection between any of these murders. Even if there was, Mr Harrington could not have carried them out because he didn't have a passport."

"My client has already told you that there is a connection between them. There is the list of victims that was posted on Facebook. I have also seen that list and can concur with everything that my client has told you."

"We'll look into that," replied DI Cowling.

He looked at me before continuing.

"Before we do that, let me tell you what I think happened. You believed that Mr Harrington had murdered your friends as I've already said. This was no more than a conspiracy theory. You say it was Mr Harrington who thought there was a conspiracy. But it wasn't him, it was you. In fact, you were so convinced that you even managed to persuade yourself that a photo of Wayne Rooney on the coffee mug you drank from was really a photo of your old gym teacher from school."

"That's not true," I replied. "It really did have a picture of Alf Jephcote on it."

"So you say but the evidence tells me otherwise. I believe it was because you'd convinced yourself that you were next on Mr Harrington's list that you decided to murder him. The plan you had was a very clever one. You wanted to convince us that Mr Harrington was trying to murder you, whereas the reality was that it was you who wanted to kill him. During our search of Mr Harrington's house, we discovered two empty syringes on his kitchen table. Forensic analysis of those syringes has revealed that one of them had once contained flunitrazepam and the other tetrodotoxin. We also discovered a third syringe under Mr Harrington's kitchen table and this one still had tetrodotoxin in it. In total, there were two empty and one full syringe. Why do you think that was?"

"Barnaby Harrington must have used the one containing the flunitrazepam to put a small amount into my coffee. Once I was under the influence of the drug and unable to fight him off, he told me he was going to inject me with tetrodotoxin. The third syringe must have been there for him to commit suicide with. Only he obviously made a mistake and injected me with the syringe containing the rest of the flunitrazepam. That was why there was still a syringe full of tetrodotoxin under his table. It must have rolled off the table, which is why he made the mistake of injecting me with the wrong syringe."

"That is what you'd like us to believe. However, what really happened was that you injected Mr Harrington with tetrodotoxin and then injected yourself with flunitrazepam. You'd only taken the third syringe in order to convince us that it was Mr Harrington who was trying to kill you, rather than the other way around. That's really what happened. Isn't it, Mr Hillman?"

"No, it's not. He must have mixed up the two syringes,"

"Inspector, you do not have a shred of evidence to back up your theory," said Steve.

"Oh, but I do," replied DI Cowling whilst looking at me. "For a start, our experts have had a look at your laptop and they have found Google searches for both tetrodotoxin and flunitrazepam on your computer."

"I looked them up because they were the drugs used on Martin and Alex," I replied.

"So you say. However, both of these facts were never released by the police."

"But I told you. Dan was able to find this out using his diplomatic contacts."

"You know, Mr Hillman, in my experience it's quite common for criminals to blame a dead man, since they're not around to contradict them. But I congratulate you. This is the first time I've ever heard someone saying the dead man was their alibi."

"That's because it's the truth, Inspector," said Steve.

"Did your friend also provide this information to you, Mr Bowler?" asked DI Cowling.

"I'm not here to answer your questions, Inspector," replied Steve. "I'm here to represent my client."

"Well, let me tell you, even if your client did have that conversation with Mr Podgorski, it wouldn't make any difference. After all, what would be more apt than to use the same method to kill Mr Harrington as the one you believed he had used to murder your friends?"

"My client strenuously denies that he murdered Mr Harrington, Inspector."

"Is that Mr Giles Harrington or Mr Barnaby Harrington, sir?"

"Both, Inspector. Furthermore, my client would have no idea how to get hold of flunitrazepam or tetrodotoxin."

"Really?" replied DI Cowling. "In which case, can you please identify this? For the tape, I am showing Mr Hillman a credit card statement."

"Yes, it's a Visa statement."

"Can you confirm for the tape that it is yours?"

"Well, it's got my name at the top."

"And can you tell me what this item is that you purchased on the 1st of December this year?"

"I haven't got a clue."

"What does the statement say?"

"It says TZK Holdings and the amount of £297.50. But I have never bought anything from a company by that name. In fact, I don't even know this company."

"Are you telling me that you also don't know what you bought from TZK Holdings?"

"I haven't the faintest idea. I'm telling you, I've never heard of TZK Holdings. I haven't received that statement yet. If I had, I would have queried the charge."

"Well, let me enlighten you. TZK Holdings is a front for another company called Chemnico Ltd, which is registered in Nigeria. They sell drugs on the dark web. We've had a look on your computer and have discovered that you bought 50 mg of tetrodotoxin and 250 mg of flunitrazepam from them. What do you have to say about that, Mr Hillman?"

"I don't know anything about any of these companies. I've never purchased either of these drugs."

"In addition, we discovered this in the bin in Mr Harrington's kitchen. For the tape, I'm showing Mr Hillman a plastic bag. A forensic examination of the bag has shown minute traces of tetrodotoxin and flunitrazepam on the inside. I believe this is the bag that you used to transport the three syringes to Mr Harrington's house. The reason I believe this is because the only fingerprints we've found on the bag are those belonging to you."

"Inspector, can I suggest we take a break now?" said Steve. "I want to have a word with my client."

Chapter 19

"This isn't going as well as I thought it would," said Steve once DI Cowling and DC Gethin had left the room. "How do you explain the plastic bag with your fingerprints on it?"

"The only thing I can suggest is that somebody must have placed it in my hand after I passed out, in the same way that they transferred my fingerprints onto the Wayne Rooney mug."

"The trouble is that the evidence is starting to mount up against you," added Steve. "The most damning evidence they have come up with so far is the credit card statement. How do you explain that?"

"I can't. I've never bought anything from that company."

"But you can see what it looks like," replied Steve. "If it wasn't you, who do you think bought these drugs?"

"Barnaby told me that Georgia Pearce had a PhD in Computer Science and that she hacked his computer. I think she must have done the same thing to me."

"Well, that's the line we'll take then," said Steve. "I'm going to advise you to reply no comment from now on until we've heard all the evidence they've got against you."

"But in all the true crime programmes I've seen on TV, it's always the guilty who say no comment."

"Believe me it isn't just the guilty," Steve replied. "A solicitor will often recommend that their client says no comment until all the police evidence has been presented. All the evidence against you so far is circumstantial, except for the credit card statement. We need to think of a way to explain that and, at the same time, hope they don't have any other substantial evidence against you."

"I've been thinking about Barnaby's death. He might not have committed suicide. Perhaps Georgia Pearce killed him. She might have switched the mugs after pressing my fingers around it. She must have done the same with the plastic bag and took the piece of paper with her email on it."

"Well, that's something we can suggest. Are you ready to continue?"

I was. So Steve knocked on the door again and DI Cowling and DC Gethin entered the room.

"Interview recommencing at 15.01," said DI Cowling.

"Inspector, I've been speaking to my client," said Steve, "and I have instructed him to say no comment from now on. However, with regards to the purchase of goods from TZK Holdings, he wants to reiterate that he has never bought anything from this company. He believes he is being framed for the murder of Barnaby Harrington and that the person responsible for framing him transferred his fingerprints to both the mug and the plastic bag after he passed out."

"And why should anyone want to frame you?" DI Cowling asked me.

"No comment," I replied.

At no time had I ever envisaged that I would be sitting in a police station being cross-examined by two police officers accusing me of murder. Even worse was the fact that I was saying no comment. It made me feel guilty, even though I knew I wasn't.

"Inspector, my client thinks the person who is trying to frame him is called Georgia Pearce. He believes she hoodwinked Barnaby Harrington into murdering Martin Howarth, Alex Singleton and Dan Podgorski by convincing him that Mr Hillman and his friends killed his brother. My client also believes that it may well be Miss Pearce who murdered Barnaby Harrington. She must have switched the coffee mugs after ensuring that my client's fingerprints were on one of them and did the same with the plastic bag. She would also have taken the missing email. Mr Harrington told my client that Miss Pearce has a PhD in Computer Science and that she had hacked his computer. My client believes she may also have managed to access his computer in order to throw suspicion on him."

"Your client says quite a lot for a man who's making no comment," added DI Cowling. "However, let me debunk this myth straight away. Sue Pearce was an only child. There is no Georgia Pearce. Whoever this person is, she couldn't have hacked either Mr Harrington's computer or the one belonging to your client. As I have already told you, Barnaby Harrington couldn't have murdered your friends because he didn't have a passport. In addition, Georgia Pearce didn't murder them because she doesn't exist."

DI Cowling turned away from Steve to look at me instead.

"I'll repeat what I told you earlier, Mr Hillman," he continued. "There is no connection between any of your friends' deaths. You wrongly believed a conspiracy theory that linked their deaths, which is why you murdered Barnaby Harrington, didn't you?"

"No comment," I replied.

"Inspector, my client is a man of impeccable character," said Steve. "He has stated that Mr Harrington told him he murdered his friends. However, even if Mr Harrington didn't carry out the murders personally, he could have had an accomplice. If that accomplice wasn't Georgia Pearce, it must have been somebody else."

DI Cowling was not in the mood to speculate, which is why he just ignored Steve's theory.

"Mr Hillman, I want to show you another piece of evidence," he said whilst putting another plastic bag on the table. "For the tape, I'm showing Mr Hillman a printout of an email received at Beetwell Street police station. The email was sent by Barnaby Harrington on the morning of his death. But it was not read until the following day as emails to the police are not considered to be emergencies. DC Gethin, would you mind reading out the email, please?"

DC Gethin picked up the evidence bag.

"This is an email dated Sunday the 17th of December 2023. It was sent at 13.46 by Mr Barnaby Harrington to Derbyshire Constabulary:

Dear Sir,

I am getting increasingly concerned over a spate of visits to my house by a man calling himself Nigel Hillman. Mr Hillman seems obsessed with a conspiracy theory that I am responsible for the deaths of his three friends. This is a ridiculous accusation and is totally groundless. This is all the more so since his friends were all killed abroad and I am not currently in possession of a passport. Mine was stolen on 31st July this year, a fact that was reported to the police at the time, crime number 21000865717. Despite this, Mr Hillman believes that I travelled overseas to murder his friends and has accused me of targeting him next. I am extremely worried that Mr Hillman may want to cause me physical harm. I have already thrown him out of my house on two separate occasions, the last time after he threatened to kill me. Mr Hillman is not a well man. I believe he is mentally unstable and a risk to both himself and the general public. I hope you will take what I say seriously and will take some form of action against him before he hurts somebody."

I couldn't believe what the email said. It was a wild distortion of what really happened. I wanted to explain, and Steve knew I wanted to. But he just shook his head at me as DI Cowling asked, "So what do you say about that, Mr Hillman?"

"No comment," I replied.

"It's a pity he sent us an email rather than dialling 999," said DI Cowling. "If he'd done that he'd probably still be alive. Still, someone else had at least the presence of mind to do just that."

"I'm now going to play you a tape," said DC Gethin. "This is the recording of a 999 call received on Sunday the 17th of December 2023, at 14.54. It was made by Mrs Abigail Booth, Mr Harrington's next-door neighbour:

Emergency, which service please?
Police.
Putting you through, caller.
Derbyshire constabulary. How can I help you?
I'm really worried about my neighbour. I think he may have been attacked.
Can you give me more details please?
I heard shouts and screams coming from next door after a man went into the house. Mr Harrington, my next-door

neighbour, had already told me about a man who had been threatening him. He was extremely concerned that he might come back and attack him.

Are the shouts and screams still happening?

No, it's gone quiet, which is why I think something terrible has happened.

Can you give me the address of the property where this took place, please caller?

Yes, it's 123 Ling Road, Chesterfield.

I'll send a squad car around straightaway. In the meantime, please stay in your house and lock all the doors and windows. Also, can I have your name, address and telephone number?

Yes, it's Mrs Abigail Booth, 125 Ling Road, Chesterfield, telephone number 01246 278905."

DC Gethin switched off the recording.

"I don't need to tell you what we discovered when we arrived at the house," added DI Cowling. "Do you have anything to add?"

"No comment," I replied.

Chapter 20

After the interview, I was taken back to the cells where Steve was allowed to have some time with me.

"What happens next?" I asked him.

"They will speak to someone at the Crown Prosecution Service who will decide whether there is enough evidence to charge you."

"And do you think there is?"

"I'm afraid that the CPS solicitors will almost certainly think that the case against you passes their threshold. They'll believe they have a reasonable chance of a conviction. I'm sorry, Nigel."

"But I didn't do it, Steve. How the hell did I manage to end up in this situation?"

"It's as I said to the inspector. The reason behind all of this is probably because someone wants to frame you."

"But why?"

"That's the sixty-four-thousand-dollar question. However, if I were to hazard a guess, it would be because somebody believes you were responsible for the deaths of Giles Harrington and Sue Pearce. Both you and I know that isn't true, as did the police at the time and everyone involved in the inquest. But it's immaterial. Someone believes you were and we have to find out who that person is if we are to unlock this case."

"And do you think that person was Barnaby?"

"It could be or, as I said to the police, it's highly probable that he had an accomplice. If I was to hazard a guess, I think he made up the Georgia Pearce story to hide the identity of his real accomplice."

"What I don't understand is why Barnaby confessed to me that he murdered Martin, Alex and Dan. He couldn't have killed them if he didn't have a passport. However, he must have been involved somehow. He knew a lot of the detail that wasn't in the public domain. For a start, he knew that a note saying 'a present from Luigi' was found at Alex's house. He also knew that Dan had been injected with tetrodotoxin, even though he lied to me about the place where he'd been killed."

"It all points to him having an accomplice," replied Steve. "And whoever that is must have told him how he had carried out the murders."

"And do you think Barnaby was murdered by this accomplice, or do you think he committed suicide?"

"Don't forget that Barnaby was going blind. I think the most likely scenario is that he couldn't face up to what was going to happen to him and decided to commit suicide. That said, his accomplice may have assisted him in killing himself. I'm keeping an open mind about that for now. But to make sense of this whole thing, I think you and I need to go back through the police evidence with a fine-toothed comb. We need to look for anything that might tell us who is doing this and why. The police think you concocted a conspiracy theory that Barnaby was going to kill you. One of the things we are going to have to demonstrate is that it wasn't a theory and that he was somehow involved in the post on Facebook and the three deaths. The first piece of evidence they've got against you is that you googled the two poisons that were used."

"But you know that was after Dan told me about them and I wanted to find out what they were."

"I know that and I would have been able to back up your statement to that effect if I had been with you at the time Dan told you. But unfortunately I wasn't. However, what I will try and do is to find out the names of the people from the consulates in Hong Kong and New York who provided Dan with this information. If I can speak to them, we should be able to prove that this was the reason why you looked those poisons up on Google. Let me move on to the next thing raised by the police and that was the mug you drank from in Barnaby Harrington's house. Are you certain it had a picture of Alf Jephcote on it?"

" I'm one hundred percent certain it was him."

"Even though you'd been drugged with flunitrazepam?"

"I'm totally sure."

"Well, since that mug was never found, we must assume that either Barnaby or his accomplice substituted it with the Wayne Rooney mug after you passed out. That would explain why it had your fingerprints on it. Whoever did it must have wrapped your hand around it whilst you were unconscious and done the same with the plastic bag. Now, I'll tell you one thing. If it had happened the way DI Cowling thinks it did, Barnaby Harrington's fingerprints wouldn't only be on one mug and yours on the other. Your mug would have two sets of fingerprints on it, yours because you drank from it and Barnaby's because he made the coffee."

Steve was right, of course, and his observation at least gave me some hope. It was the first time we'd been able to prove that there was something wrong with a piece of evidence. It was the first mistake the real killer had made.

"Barnaby's accomplice was also probably responsible for removing the printed copy of the email from Georgia Pearce. Just think about it. If it had been found, the police would have had to admit that someone was falsifying emails, in particular that someone was pretending to be Sue Pearce's non-existent sister. That would drive a coach and horses through the evidence they've got against you."

"They may not have the hard copy," I replied. "But they've got Barnaby's laptop. They should find it on there."

"I wouldn't hold out much hope about that. Whoever is doing this is extremely cunning. Barnaby told you that Georgia Pearce had a PhD in Computer Science, which we now know was not true. However, I bet whoever is really behind all of this has a good knowledge of computers. That would also explain the order to TZK Holdings. If someone was able to gain access to your computer, they would have been able to place the order on the dark web."

"I wouldn't even have a clue how to get onto the dark web," I added.

"And neither would most people," replied Steve. "If your computer has been hacked, we need to try and prove it. Can you remember recently receiving any unsolicited emails or any emails with attachments?"

"I get phishing emails all the time, just like most people. God only knows where these people get your email address from. But I'm always very careful not to open any attachments from someone I don't know."

"The problem is that you might have clicked on an attachment infected with a virus from someone you do know. Barnaby told you he had clicked on an attachment from Georgia Pearce, which we now know wasn't true. But he could have based that story on something either he or his accomplice had done to you. Can you think of anything that might help me?"

I racked my brain but still couldn't think of anything. But then again, I received hundreds of emails every week. It was quite conceivable that I'd missed something.

"How far back do I need to go?" I asked.

"That's the problem. Normally, when your computer has been hacked, you find out what has happened pretty quickly. Your computer might freeze and the hacker demands a ransom, or you notice your bank account has been cleared out. However, on this occasion someone might have hacked your computer and then waited until he ordered those drugs from the dark web."

"But if he did order something for me from the dark web, shouldn't I have received it?"

"He would almost certainly have used a false address. It could even have been his own address if he needed more supplies of the drugs. In fact, that was probably how he got flunitrazepam and tetrodotoxin in the first place. We assumed that he'd extracted the tetrodotoxin from a pufferfish but it was a lot simpler than that. He must have just purchased it from the dark web instead."

"Barnaby told me that he'd extracted it from a pufferfish he bought in Macau."

"Which we know was a lie, because he was never in Macau."

"What I don't understand is why a credit card company would even deal with a company on the dark web?"

"They wouldn't. But Chemnico has TZK acting as a front for it. I looked TZK up on my phone and it is a legitimate company operating pharmacies in Nigeria. The two companies probably have the same directors and that's how they are able to process credit card transactions. Now, think again, Nigel, can you think of any suspicious emails you've received over the past few weeks? If I'm correct about when they identified you, it wouldn't have been before you joined the Facebook group."

"The only thing I can think of was that I received an email from Martin the day he was killed. Initially, I thought he must have sent it to me just before he died. But what if whoever had murdered him had sent it after he'd killed him? Martin's phone had been stolen, so whoever did that would have had access to all his contacts' email addresses including mine."

"And did the email have an attachment?"

"Yes, it had a photo of Martin and his wife. They were having a meal together to celebrate their wedding anniversary."

I went quiet, before shouting out, "Jesus Christ, I've just remembered that the caption under the photo said they were eating pufferfish."

"That's it then. Whoever is doing this must have gone through Martin's photo album and chosen a photo where he was in a restaurant. He added the caption about the pufferfish and sent it to you along with a virus that would allow him to take over your laptop remotely. You know what this means? Martin's death involved flunitrazepam, a plastic bag, pufferfish and someone pretending to be a master from our school. So did Alex's death and so did Barnaby's. The only death where there isn't a similar pattern is Dan's."

"We don't know that though. We just haven't got access to all the evidence in the same way as we have with all the others.

"You haven't deleted the photo of Martin in the restaurant, have you?"

"No."

"Good. Can you remember what time you received it?"

"I just know it was the same day Martin was killed."

"In which case, I need to get hold of your laptop which is currently with the police. Bearing in mind that Martin was killed on the 1st of September and there is a seven-hour time difference between the UK and Macau, we should be able to work out if the email was sent before or after he was killed."

"You can always look at my emails on the cloud," I replied. "Monica knows my password, it's saved on her computer. Talking about passwords, how would the murderer have known Martin's password for his phone?"

"He might have forced Martin to tell him. But he wouldn't have needed to do that. His phone probably had either fingerprint or facial recognition software on it. With Martin tied to a chair, the murderer could easily have used him to access the phone and once he'd done that, he could change the password to anything he wanted. He might even have done it after he killed him."

"Why didn't he just send the email and leave the phone on Martin's body?"

"I'm speculating but I would say it would have taken him some time to set up the hack. Also, he would have had to go through all of Martin's photographs until he discovered one that was suitable. There was bound to be one as everybody takes photos of their meals these days. However, he must have gotten lucky and discovered one of Martin and his wife at a table in a restaurant, which was far better than just sending you a shot of a plate of food. It's almost certain that he would have wanted to get away from the murder scene as soon as possible. Therefore, it would be far less risky just to take the phone and do all that later."

What Steve was saying made perfect sense. But it worried me at the same time. Whoever was doing this appeared to have planned everything down to the finest detail. It was not going to be easy for us to prove that the case against me was based on a pack of lies.

"Let's move on now to the email that Barnaby Harrington sent to the police."

"It's all made up," I replied. "I never threatened to kill him."

"Well, it's your word against his. A jury is probably going to believe his version of events as he's dead and his body was discovered next to you lying unconscious on the floor. When you add that to the other evidence, it doesn't look very good."

I put my head in my hands. The evidence against me was mounting up.

"As I said before, somebody is trying to frame you and that person is almost certainly Barnaby's accomplice. Can you think who this person might be?"

"If Georgia Pearce doesn't exist, then no, I can't," I replied.

"If Sue Pearce was an only child as DI Cowling said, would she have had anyone else who would have enough motive to do this?"

"Only her parents and I don't know if they are still alive. Even if they are, they'd probably be in their late eighties or nineties by now. They're hardly the type of people you would associate with being serial killers."

"Well, I can certainly look into it," added Steve. "What about Giles Harrington, did he have any siblings other than Barnaby?"

"I don't know," I replied.

"I'll see if I can find out and I'll also check to see if his parents are still alive."

"Barnaby told me his father was dead," I added.

"We don't want to take the things that Barnaby said at face value. I mean, he could have been lying when he told you that his father was dead. Don't forget that he's lied about other things, for example, that he murdered Dan in the toilet of a restaurant. The reality is that I don't believe Barnaby killed anyone, apart from himself. But let's put that to one side and move on to the last piece of evidence the police have against you, the 999 call made by the next-door neighbour, Abigail Booth."

"I can't understand that," I replied. "There was no screaming and shouting."

"Are you saying she's lying?"

"She must be."

"Why would she do that?"

"I don't have a clue."

"Perhaps she was just exaggerating. Barnaby could have told her that he was afraid of you and when everything went quiet, she just panicked. She might have thought that the police wouldn't come out unless she said she heard raised voices. I'll check out her statement to the police. It might differ from the 999 call. I presume she and Barnaby lived in adjoining semi-detached houses?"

"Well, Barnaby's house is semi-detached. I don't know if her house is attached to his or whether she lives on the other side of him."

"That's something else I can check out, just in case she lives too far away for her to claim she heard shouting. Anyway, I've got plenty to be getting on with for now."

The cell door opened and DI Cowling entered the room.

"Mr Hillman," he said "I have spoken to the Crown Prosecution Service, and they've informed me that we have enough evidence to charge you with the murder of Barnaby Harrington. Consequently, you will be remanded in custody until your trial. You can apply for bail. If you decide to do that you will have to go in front of a judge who will hear your application and decide if it will be granted. DC Gethin will now take you to the desk sergeant where you will be formally charged."

"Don't worry," shouted Steve as I was led away. "I intend to file an application for bail with the court as soon as possible."

Chapter 21

My bail hearing was set for Thursday the 21st of December at Derby Crown Court. I had presumed it would be heard at Chesterfield Magistrates' Court but discovered that the offence with which I'd been charged was too serious for a lower court. It had to be heard in the high court instead.

"Aren't most people who are charged with murder refused bail?" I asked Steve as we were sitting in the holding cell below the courtroom on the day of my hearing.

"That's correct," he replied. "But it's not always the case. I'm optimistic about your prospects. You need to be as well because I think we've got a very strong case. For a start, you've no history of any criminal activity and you intend pleading not guilty."

"But I thought most people charged with murder plead not guilty because they face life in prison."

"That's true. However, most people accused of murder have overwhelming evidence against them. Besides which, many of them pose a threat to the public, which isn't true in your case. There's another reason why I think you'll be granted bail."

"Which is?"

"All our prisons are full at the moment, so there's never been a better time to be accused of murder. The judge will almost certainly be looking for a reason not to remand you in custody."

I'd been hoping that Steve would say the reason the judge would grant me bail was because he thought I was not guilty, rather than it being down to prison overcrowding. But at least it was something.

"Have you been interviewed by the police yet?" I asked him.

"I have and I gave them a copy of the screenshot I took of the list. I also had to admit that it was you who told me about the flunitrazepam and tetrodotoxin Although I added that I was in no doubt that you got that information from Dan. Other than that, there was very little of note to come out of my interview. But let me tell you what I've managed to find out since the last time I saw you. For a start, I've discovered that Abigail Booth does indeed live in the semi-detached house that is joined to Barnaby Harrington's house. Unfortunately, this gives credence to her 999 call as the houses were built in the 1960s and have paper thin walls. I've also checked her statement to the police, and it's identical to her 999 call."

"Jesus Christ," I said. "It's not looking good, is it?"

"Don't worry about that," he added. "If I'm honest, I was expecting them to be the same. The police officer who took her statement would have written it for her and he almost certainly based it on the tape of her call to the emergency services. As well as that, I've discovered that the Giles Harrington Facebook page has been taken down. However, this might help our cause, as I took the screenshot of the list that had been on there. It should help me to prove that somebody was trying to cover something up."

"That's something at least," I replied.

"However, I've some bad news about the photo that Martin sent you. It has also been removed, which means that we can't prove it was sent after Martin had been killed. The fact it has been removed may indicate that your computer has been hacked but, at the same time, it removes all evidence of the hacking."

"That's typical. Every time we take a step forward, we take two steps back."

"I also found out that both Claire's parents are dead," he said. "So we won't be able to ask them why they failed to say they knew you when they took the stand at the inquest. Personally, I think it was because they didn't want to throw any suspicion on you."

"But I'd just finished with their daughter," I added. "Why would they do that?"

"Well, I think I may have the answer to that. You see, I've managed to track Claire down and she told me that they liked you more than you realised."

"You've spoken to Claire?"

"I have," he replied. "She lives in Matlock and she reckons her parents were really upset when you two broke up. She said they never liked Dave Willis as much as you and they always hoped that the two of you would get back together one day. You never did, of course, and Claire eventually married Dave, which she told me was a mistake. Three years later, he announced he was leaving her for his gay lover. They got divorced the following year."

I couldn't help but remember what Claire had said about Dave shortly after she'd started going out with him. She had described him as being like a Saturn rocket, which I presumed was a description of his performance in bed. Who'd have thought he would turn out to be gay?

"She's since remarried," Steve continued. "She's Claire Pilkington these days."

"She didn't marry Porky Pilkington, the guy who used to light his farts in the changing rooms, did she?"

"She certainly did, although she tells me he's not that porky anymore. It seems he goes to the gym regularly these days."

"That's amazing," I replied. "Who'd have thought that Claire Banyard would marry Porky Pilkington. We'll have to meet up with them when this is all over. Mind you, Monica might not like the idea, being as though Claire is an ex-girlfriend of mine."

"I think we've got more pressing matters to sort out first," added Steve.

Shortly afterwards, a court usher came and told us that my bail hearing was about to begin. Steve went and took his place in court whilst I was led into the dock.

I took up my position behind a bulletproof screen and a few minutes later, the clerk of the court read out the details of the charge against me. I could see Monica sitting at the back of the court with an anxious expression on her face. Once the clerk had finished, it was Steve's turn to say why I should be given bail.

"My Lord, my client has an impeccable record as a law-abiding citizen," he began. "Until this point, he has never been charged with so much as a parking offence. In addition, he strenuously denies the charges against him and looks forward to proving his innocence at the forthcoming court hearing. My client does not represent a flight risk and he doesn't pose a threat to members of the public. He and his wife have recently bought a house in the county and were looking forward to spending their retirement there. In addition, his life has been a model of stability. He was with his last employer for 31 years. Consequently, I see absolutely no reason why bail should not be granted."

That was all Steve had to say and so he sat down. Next, it was the turn of the barrister representing the Crown Prosecution Service to say why she thought I should be refused bail. Steve had said there was absolutely no reason why bail shouldn't be granted despite the seriousness of the charge against me. Even so, I was extremely nervous that the judge would refuse our request and I'd be spending Christmas on remand in prison. I was praying that he would grant me bail and was quite prepared to report to the local police station every day and to surrender my passport if necessary.

To be honest, I didn't like the look of Miss Cartwright, the prosecuting barrister. She looked threatening and had an aggressive manner about her.

"I bet she's a lesbian," I thought to myself.

Then I felt bad for thinking that. After all, the barrister's sexuality had absolutely nothing to do with my predicament.

"My Lord," she said. "The Crown strongly objects to the granting of bail. For a start, the charge facing Mr Hillman is extremely serious, that of premeditated murder. It is a charge for which, if convicted, he will face a mandatory life sentence. For this reason, we believe that Mr Hillman does indeed represent a flight risk. He holds dual British-South African citizenship and has lived in South Africa for more than half his life. Consequently, the prosecution believes it would be the height of folly to release him on bail."

The judge considered the arguments from both sides before delivering his verdict.

"I have to say, I am leaning towards agreeing with the prosecution's argument," he said.

He looked at the prosecution barrister, who smiled back at him. However, if she thought she was going to get her way, she was soon to be disappointed. The judge had not taken too kindly to Miss Cartwright's statement that it would be the height of folly to release me. It was his decision whether I was granted bail or not and he would not be bullied into making the decision preferred by the prosecuting barrister.

"But given Mr Hillman's previous unblemished character, I am going to grant bail," he continued while still looking at Miss Cartwright. "Bail will be set at £100,000 and Mr Hillman will have to surrender all his passports, be restricted to his house and garden and made to wear an electronic tag."

I was ushered away from the dock by an officer of the court. It was all very well and good being granted bail but how was I going to raise £100,000? All of a sudden, I was facing the prospect of spending Christmas in prison.

As I walked down the steps, I could see Monica with her head in her hands. Steve was trying to console her.

"We don't have £100,000," she sobbed.

"You don't physically have to come up with the money," Steve replied. "You just have to provide surety and since you own your house, you merely have to sign the papers with the clerk of the court and Nigel will be able to go home with you. You'll only have to pay £100,000 if Nigel absconds."

An hour later, I was a free man again, albeit one who was still facing a murder charge and was wearing an electronic tag.

"How on earth am I going to explain this to my mother?" I thought to myself.

Chapter 22

Time seemed to drag on during the weeks awaiting trial. Between Christmas and New Year, Bruce came to see me. He was in Chesterfield visiting his mother and wanted to show that he wasn't ignoring me because of the charges against me. However, he didn't bring his wife with him, which made me think that she didn't want to spend part of the Christmas holiday with a man awaiting trial for murder. This was despite him reassuring me that the only reason why she hadn't come was as a result of work commitments. Steve and Jessica came around as well and the five of us had quite a good evening together, despite the sword of Damocles hanging over my head. Everyone was interested in my electronic tag.

"Can you get it wet?" asked Bruce. "Will you get an electric shock if you have a bath?"

I assured him that it was perfectly safe.

"I read in the paper about a man who had one fitted to his false leg," he continued. "Every evening, he used to unscrew his leg and leave both it and the tag behind whilst he went to the pub."

"Did he get legless?" joked Steve.

For a brief second, I forgot about my problems. It was good to have two of my oldest friends in my house, laughing and joking.

"It's ridiculous that they think you committed murder," said Bruce, which brought me back down to earth again. "Everyone who knows you would tell them that. If you need a character witness, I'm prepared to be one."

I thanked him but told him it wouldn't really help. After all, he'd only seen me once in the past thirty years.

The evening ended far too soon and as the three of them left, Steve promised to come around the following day to update me about some of the issues he was looking into that might have a bearing on the trial.

Steve was doing his best to help me and kept his promise to visit me the next day. He'd tracked down Sue Pearce's mother and she'd confirmed that Sue had been an only child. So that didn't help. He'd tried to trace Giles and Barnaby's parents even though I'd told him that Barnaby said his father was dead.

Steve reminded me that most of what Barnaby had told me had turned out to be a pack of lies. However, on this occasion, it appeared he'd been telling the truth. His father had died sixteen years ago, and his mother had passed away in 2015. Barnaby and Giles did not have any other siblings.

Steve had also managed to track down the officials Dan had spoken to in the British Consulate in Hong Kong and in New York. They confirmed that they had given details of both deaths to him, including what kinds of drugs were used. Most importantly, they both provided written testimony to that effect. However, Steve pointed out that this information didn't get me off the hook. The prosecution would almost certainly say the reason why I decided to kill Barnaby Harrington with the same poisons was exactly because I'd been given this information.

Two weeks before my trial was due to start, however, he made a real breakthrough. He'd been to visit A Geek, the shop in West Bars where Barnaby had supposedly taken his computer to be repaired after it had been hacked. The guy behind the counter, whose name was Andy, had laughed out loud at the thought of Barnaby's computer being hacked.

"He told me that Barnaby had never been to A Geek but he knew him," said Steve. "He said they used to be quite friendly back in the 1990s before he came off the rails."

"What did he mean by that?" I asked.

"According to Andy, Barnaby Harrington is notorious in the world of computers. In 2001, he hacked into the mainframe computer of Northern Rock Building Society and stole eight million pounds. He was arrested and given a sixteen-year jail sentence. Andy said Barnaby would never have been hacked and he wouldn't have needed to bring his computer into his shop. It seems Barnaby was one of the world's foremost computer experts. He was virtually unrivalled when it came to hacking."

"This information could turn out to be extremely helpful in trying to prove my innocence, couldn't it?"

"It could and there's more. Andy also told me that Barnaby was a flawed genius. He dropped out of Cambridge when he was two years into a degree in Computer Science, which he was expected to pass with a first. After leaving university, he had a series of jobs in IT, none of which lasted very long, mainly because he found them mind-numbingly boring. His jobs were punctuated by periods on the dole and bouts of depression. Then in 1999, he hacked into the mainframe at the Kremlin looking for suppression of information about the existence of UFOs. The Russians soon discovered it was him, and they charged him with espionage. He was tried in absentia as there's no extradition treaty between the UK and Russia. So he was okay as long as he never tried to travel there."

"Unless he'd found himself bound and gagged in the back of a lorry one day heading for Moscow in the company of several heavies from the FSB," I added.

Steve nodded before continuing.

"Andy told me that Barnaby had been surprised at just how easy it was to hack into the Kremlin's mainframe. That was why he decided to hack into the computer at Northern Rock. Unfortunately, he hadn't learnt anything from his Russian exploit and was soon tracked down again. This time he did go to prison, where he completed his degree and then did a PhD. He'd obviously learnt his lesson by then as he was never caught again. Andy said he didn't know if Barnaby had done other hacks after he was released, but he wouldn't be surprised if he had. Barnaby left prison in 2013 after serving twelve years of his sixteen-year sentence and hasn't worked since. Mind you, he didn't need to. His mother had died whilst he was locked up, and she'd left her entire estate to him. He used the money to buy his house and still had a substantial amount left over."

As Steve was telling me this, everything suddenly started to become clear. Barnaby had never done a degree in estate management as he'd told me. He'd also never worked for Derbyshire County Council. Instead, he was the computer expert who had hacked my computer.

"Andy also told me that he wasn't surprised Barnaby had told you that he'd taken his computer into his shop. He reckons he was a compulsive liar. When he was friendly with him, he used to lie all the time. On one occasion, he told him his father had been awarded the Victoria Cross during the war. When Andy reminded him that he'd told him on a previous occasion that his father was born in 1929, Barnaby said he meant the Korean War. Andy checked this and he discovered there were only four VCs awarded during the Korean War and none of them were to anyone called Harrington."

"I've met people like that before," I added. "They keep on lying even when it's blatantly obvious they aren't telling the truth."

"Anyway," continued Steve. "Andy is prepared to come to court and give evidence for the defence. He's given me his card."

Steve showed me Andy's business card, which had A Geek printed on it alongside the picture of a man with ginger hair and glasses. Underneath was his name, Andy Geek, managing director. Despite the seriousness of the situation, I couldn't help laughing.

"Surely that's not his real name?"

"It is now," replied Steve. "He said he used to be Andy Galbraith but he changed it to Andy Geek to make him stand out in his line of work. I had a friend at university who did something similar. He changed his name from Howard Smith to Howard You-like-to-go-out-for-a-drink. He reckoned it was a name and a chat-up line all in one. Only it didn't work as none of the girls he fancied took him seriously when he told them what his name was."

I laughed again. More importantly, I was starting to believe that we were gathering enough evidence to disprove the case against me. However, there was still the two most damning pieces of evidence, the email sent by Barnaby Harrington and the statement by his next-door neighbour. I asked Steve what we could do to counter them.

"I need to give some thought to both of those if I am to cast doubt on them in court," said Steve. "There must be a way. I just haven't thought of it yet."

If anyone could do it, it was Steve.

"You know, the more I think about the three murders, the more convinced I am that they were committed by a woman," he continued. "I believe there is little doubt that there were two people involved. Barnaby did the computer hacking and someone else carried out the murders. If that's the case, it's highly likely that his accomplice was the woman spotted in the Seychelles. We've got no evidence that Martin and Alex were killed by a man or a woman. But if the witness in the Seychelles is to be believed, Dan must have been killed by a woman. If this is correct it was almost certainly the same person who was responsible for killing the others."

"What about the next-door neighbour? Could she be involved? After all, she's lied in her statement to the police and during her 999 call."

"Well, I can't go and see her," replied Steve. "I'd be accused of interfering with witnesses for the prosecution. But I can try to find out something about her. I also thought I'd go and speak to Barnaby's neighbours on the other side and see if they can shed any light on what has happened."

That was it for the time being. But three days later, Steve came back to see me again and this time he was quite excited.

"I've been to see a Mrs Carol Parker who lives at 121 Ling Road," he told me. "She was at home on the day Barnaby Harrington was killed and for part of it she was out at the front of her house cleaning her car. Anyway, she says she never heard any screaming and yelling coming from his house that afternoon and she's agreed to testify on your behalf."

"That's good news," I replied.

"I also asked her about Abigail Booth who lives at number 125. She told me that Mrs Booth moved into the street three years ago after her latest divorce. She said that Barnaby had been quite friendly with her and there were rumours they were romantically involved. Mrs Parker pulled his leg about him becoming her next husband. He'd replied that he didn't think Mrs Booth would want to get married to him as she'd already been divorced three times and had no desire to tie the knot for a fourth time."

"If Abigail Booth was quite friendly with Barnaby Harrington, perhaps she's the mystery woman who killed Dan and probably Martin and Alex as well. He might have manipulated her into carrying out the murders for him."

"She'd have to be pretty weak-willed if that's the case," added Steve.

"It sounds like she may have been having a relationship with him," I added. "And if that's the case, she might do anything for him."

"That could well be true," replied Steve. "After I'd been to see Mrs Parker I contacted Barnaby's doctor. I wanted to ask him whether it was true that he was going blind and if there was an underlying reason for it. However, he quoted patient confidentiality at me and wouldn't tell me anything even though his patient was dead. I've summoned him to appear as a witness for the defence. He'll have to tell me in court."

For the first time in ages, I was feeling optimistic. After all, we now had quite a lot of evidence to back up the fact that I was being framed. That didn't stop me from continuing to worry about the forthcoming court case.

Chapter 23

On the day of the trial, Steve collected Monica and me and drove us to Derby Crown Court.

"Have you been able to find out anything else about Abigail Booth?" I asked as we headed down the A61.

"I phoned Carol Parker who told me that Mrs Booth was adopted when she was a baby. Her original name was Abigail Miles. Does that ring any bells?"

"I'm afraid not," I replied.

"Also, I've discovered that Mrs Parker was correct when she said Abigail Booth had been married three times. At various stages, she's been known as Abigail O'Neil and Abigail Steen. I don't suppose any of those names ring a bell either?"

"Unfortunately, they don't," I replied.

As soon as we arrived, Steve was called into a meeting with the prosecuting barrister. It seemed that new evidence had come to light that they had to disclose to us. Half an hour later, he returned to the lobby where I was waiting to tell me what it was.

"They've discovered a letter whilst searching Barnaby's house," he said. "It doesn't directly impact the trial. But the prosecution intends using it as background to the case. They want to use it to damage your character. They had to disclose it as it is probably going to help our case more than theirs. It adds credence to our argument that Barnaby really believed you killed his brother. It might help us to convince the jury that the threat against you was real, not just based on a conspiracy theory."

"But even if we are able to do that, the prosecution will still say it's my motive for killing him."

"That's true. But you have to remember that the prosecution will be building the case against you brick by brick. We need to cast doubt on whatever they're saying. By itself, this won't be enough to make the jury find in your favour but it'll certainly help when combined with the other pieces of evidence we've got."

"What does the letter say?" I asked.

"Here, have a look," he replied whilst passing a copy to me.

43 Brassington Lane
Old Tupton
Chesterfield
S42 6LA
3rd June 1995

Dear Danica

You may already have heard that my diagnosis is not good, and I know that I don't have long to live. I would have liked to return to school one last time to say farewell to the students in my class. But unfortunately, I am too weak to do that now.

The reason for this letter is that there has been something I've wanted to get off my chest for some time now and it involves the death of your parents. You see, I was there on the night they died. I was with a group of my friends, and we had been out visiting some country pubs. There were ten of us that night in three cars. One of these, the car I was in, was driven by my boyfriend, and there were two of our friends in the back. Nigel Hillman was driving one of the other cars and he had three passengers with him. Finally, Giles Harrington was in his sports car along with his girlfriend, Sue Pearce. We'd just called at the Kelstedge Inn where we decided to play a trick on Giles and Sue.

As soon as Giles went to the toilet, the rest of us dashed off leaving him and his girlfriend behind. Giles must have finished sooner than we thought he would. He'd probably worked out what we were doing and followed us at speed. It was his car that ran into your parents' vehicle. He was overtaking Nigel's car when he drove straight into them.

At the time of the crash, we were so far ahead of the rest of the group that I didn't know he was following us and I didn't see what happened. We drove to the Red Lion at Stanage and waited for our friends in the other car. But they never turned up and it wasn't until the following day that I heard what had happened. I discovered that Giles, Sue and your parents were all dead.

I hope you can forgive me and my friends for the trick we pulled that night. If we hadn't done it, your parents may not have been killed and you wouldn't have been orphaned.

But that's not all I've got to tell you. There is something else, and it involves what I saw as we pulled out of the car park of the Kelstedge Inn. You see, I caught sight of our four friends from the other car. They were all gathered around Giles Harrington's Triumph GT6 and from their body language it looked as if they were up to no good. I was convinced that they were doing something to his car.

However, the coroner said that the car was mechanically sound when it crashed, so I must have been mistaken. But I've always had this nagging doubt at the back of my mind about what really happened that night. I have never told anyone what I suspected and, to be honest, it may have been nothing at all.

If you want to talk to me about what I saw, please give me a call. At least by telling you this, I am not going to go to my grave with it still on my conscience. I guess I ought to have confronted my friends with what I saw that night, but I never did. Please believe me, Danica, when I say that I am extremely sorry for that.

Yours truly,
Martha Cook

I put the letter down and looked at Steve.

"I presume Cook was Martha's married name," I said.

"I phoned Jessica after they gave me the letter," Steve replied. "She confirmed it and told me that Martha went into Ashgate Hospice on the 4th of June and she died on the 7th. Therefore, I doubt very much that Danica was ever able to contact her and find out any more details about that night."

"What kind of a name is Danica?" I added. "I've never heard anybody called that before. Is it a man's name or a woman's?"

"I'm pretty certain that it's a woman's name," Steve replied. "At the back of my mind I'm sure there was an American racing driver called Danica something or other. I think she was the only woman ever to win a NASCAR race."

"Do you see what this means?" I added. "It must be this Danica who was Barnaby's accomplice. It must have been her parents who were in the car that Giles hit. She must have blamed us for killing them after she received Martha's letter."

"What were the four of you doing to Giles's car?"

"Absolutely nothing," I replied. "We were only looking at the interior and we only did that for a couple of seconds before we all got into my car and set off for the Red Lion. I can appreciate that it might have looked suspicious. But there was nothing to it. We didn't do anything to his car. As Martha said in her letter, the car was examined after the crash and was found to have no mechanical defects. Besides which, the only person who knew anything about the workings of cars was Bruce and he was with you. Martha must have just looked around whilst we were looking through the window. You, Jessica and Bruce never saw anything suspicious, did you?"

"No. But I was driving and Bruce and Jessica were snogging on the back seat. None of us would have seen anything anyway. Martha must have been the only one who looked back. She must have got the wrong idea about what was happening."

"Jesus Christ, Steve. All this has probably happened just because Martha happened to catch sight of us admiring Giles's leather seats and misinterpreted what we were doing."

"It's important that we find out who this Danica is," added Steve. "She is almost certainly the person trying to frame you. From the tone of the letter, she must have been in Martha's final class when she was a teacher at Tupton Hall School. I'll phone them and see if they've still got records for 1994/95."

The news about the letter gave me some hope. We were a long way from finding out who was trying to frame me. But there was now at least light at the end of the tunnel.

Chapter 24

I was wearing my best suit for my appearance in court. As I waited to be called, I couldn't help but be reminded of the old joke. What did you call a Liverpudlian in a suit? The answer, of course, is the accused.

Whilst I was waiting, the jury were being sworn in. Steve was already in the courtroom ensuring that there were no hanging or flogging types amongst their ranks. I had told him that these were the least of my worries and what he really needed to ensure was that there were no teetotallers or Mansfield Town supporters on the jury.

After what seemed like ages, I was eventually led into the dock. It was just as if I was appearing in an episode of *Crown Court*, although I wouldn't be appearing in *Coronation Street* the following week if I was found guilty. Instead, I'd be slopping out in Wormwood Scrubs or somewhere equally grim for the next twenty years.

Whilst I was thinking this, I suddenly realised that, if I was found guilty, I'd probably be in my eighties by the time I was released. I might even die in prison, just like Peter Sutcliffe and Myra Hindley. Even if I didn't, would Monica wait for me? Would she come and visit me in prison? I couldn't imagine her being checked for drugs by the prison guards before each visit and then sitting opposite me at a small table in a room with fifteen other women doing the same thing. The only difference would be that she was the only one without tattoos and piercings.

I tried to put these thoughts out of my mind. After all, I was innocent and the only thing I had to focus on was proving this to the jury.

As I stood in the dock waiting for proceedings to start, I looked around the court and saw Monica sitting in the public gallery. Next to her was my sister and my mother, who had told me they were going to drive to Derby every day while the trial was on. They all looked tense and nervous. However, I was far more nervous than they were.

"Nigel Sebastian Hillman," said the judge. "You are hereby charged that on Sunday the 17th of December 2023, you did murder Barnaby Harrington, contrary to common law. How do you plead, guilty or not guilty?"

"Not guilty," I replied.

Once I'd entered my plea, I sat down and Miss Cartwright rose to her feet and began making the opening address for the prosecution.

"My Lord, on the face of it Mr Hillman appears to be a mild-mannered, clean-living man who wouldn't hurt a fly. But the reality is that this is a mere front. I will show that he is a cold, calculating killer, a man who, in 1981, got away with murder and thought he could do the same in the present day. The prosecution will show that Mr Hillman, along with three of his friends, was instrumental in the death of Mr Giles Harrington during a night out together in August 1981. Giles Harrington and his girlfriend, Sue Pearce, were killed in a head-on crash after Mr Hillman and his friends played a trick on them."

I could tell that all eyes in the courtroom were on me as she spoke.

"More recently, he has become obsessed with a theory that Mr Barnaby Harrington, Giles's brother, was wreaking revenge on him and his friends by murdering them in retribution for killing Giles. He'd even convinced himself that a lady called Georgia Pearce, who supposedly was the sister of Giles Harrington's girlfriend, was also involved. However, this was pure fantasy. Sue Pearce never had a sister and Barnaby Harrington was not responsible for the deaths of his friends. But Nigel Hillman believed he was, and he also believed that he was next on Barnaby Harrington's death list. In fact, Mr Hillman was worried on two fronts. He was worried that the truth would come out about his involvement in the fatal crash that killed Mr Harrington's brother back in 1981 and he was worried that he was the next to be killed. That was the reason why he devised a scheme to murder Barnaby Harrington. After all, he'd got away with killing his brother back in 1981. So why shouldn't he get away with murder a second time?"

She paused and took a sip of water before continuing.

"The prosecution will demonstrate that on Sunday the 17th of December last year, Nigel Hillman went to Barnaby Harrington's house. He'd already been there twice before and had threatened him. In the meantime, he'd devised a plan that involved poisoning Mr Harrington before injecting himself with flunitrazepam, which is also known by the brand name Rohypnol. He did this so that he could claim it was Mr Harrington who had tried to kill him. We will show that Nigel Hillman is a ruthless killer who believed he could outfox the police. However, his arrogance was his downfall. The police weren't fooled in the slightest, which is why he's ended up in the dock today. Furthermore, I believe that once you've heard the evidence against him, you won't be fooled either."

Having completed her opening address, Miss Cartwright sat down. It was now Steve's turn to make his opening address for the defence.

"My Lord, learned counsel mentions that Mr Hillman appears to be a mild-mannered, clean-living man who wouldn't hurt a fly. Instead, she would have you believe that if you probed underneath this, you would discover a cold, calculating killer. However, I have a much simpler explanation. The reason why he appears to be a mild-mannered man who wouldn't hurt a fly is because that is precisely what he is. Nigel is not just my client. He is a personal friend of mine. I have known him since we met on our first day of senior school back in 1976. In all these years, has he ever displayed any violent tendencies? No, he hasn't. Has he ever hurt a fly? Well, I do remember him swatting one with his textbook during a Maths lesson in 1977. However, I can honestly say that said fly was dispatched swiftly and efficiently and did not suffer in the slightest."

There was laughter from the public gallery.

"Over the course of this trial, I will demonstrate that Nigel Hillman is not responsible for the death of Barnaby Harrington. Instead, he was lured to Mr Harrington's house in an attempt to frame him for murder. The prosecution will seek to demonstrate that Mr Hillman was fixated on a conspiracy theory that Mr Harrington was going to kill him, which is why he killed Mr Harrington first. However, this was not a conspiracy theory. It was a very real threat. In fact, three of Mr Hillman's friends had already been murdered and both he and I saw a list of victims' names on Facebook. His name was next on this list."

Steve was doing a good job. I'd been very concerned when Miss Cartwright was giving her opening address. I felt a lot happier now.

"The prosecution also alleges that Mr Hillman was responsible for the death of Mr Harrington's brother back in 1981. But this is not true. The inquest into the deaths of Giles Harrington and the other three fatalities in this terrible crash back in that year apportioned no blame whatsoever to my client. Yes, he had consumed a small amount of alcohol but he was under the legal limit. His involvement in the crash was purely that he just happened to be driving one of the cars that Mr Harrington was overtaking when he drove into an oncoming vehicle. If any new evidence has come to light about his involvement, then you need to ask yourselves, why hasn't he been charged?"

I looked at the jury and was pleased to see that several of them were nodding.

"We're going to win this case," I thought to myself.

"We will demonstrate that it was Barnaby Harrington, not my client, who believed in a conspiracy theory," Steve continued. "We will show that Mr Harrington and a fellow conspirator was responsible for the deaths of Mr Hillman's friends and that on the day of Mr Harrington's death, they lured him to the house in Ling Road. Did they intend to murder him there or did they intend to frame him for murder instead? The only person who can answer that question is Mr Harrington's accomplice. However, there is one thing that I can definitely tell you. My client did not go to that house intending to commit murder. Once you have heard all the evidence in this trial, I believe that there is only one verdict that you can possibly come to and that is to find my client not guilty."

Steve sat down. The opening addresses by the two barristers were now completed. But the judge had something to say.

"Mr Bowler is correct when he said that the inquest into the death of Giles Harrington apportioned no blame to Mr Hillman.

Miss Cartwright, I am instructing you not to suggest that Mr Hillman was responsible for the death of Giles Harrington. Mr Hillman is on trial for the murder of Barnaby Harrington, not his brother."

"Very good, my Lord," she replied.

Chapter 25

The real trial was about to begin and it was the turn of the prosecution to call their witnesses. The first one called was DC Gethin.

"Please state your name for the record," said Miss Cartwright.

"Detective Constable Matthew Gethin," he replied.

The clerk of the court produced a card, which he held up in front of DC Gethin.

"Please recite the words on the card, DC Gethin," Miss Cartwright added.

"I swear by Almighty God that the evidence I shall give shall be the truth, the whole truth, and nothing but the truth."

"DC Gethin," she continued. "Please can you tell the court when you first met the accused."

"It was on Friday, the 1st of December last year."

"Would you tell the court what the circumstances were?"

"He and his friend, Mr Bowler, had arranged to see me at the police station regarding the deaths of their three friends overseas."

"And for the record, can you confirm that the Mr Bowler who accompanied the accused that day is the learned counsel for the defence"

"It is."

"So what was the theory that Mr Hillman and Mr Bowler wanted to put to you?"

"They wanted me to get Interpol involved in the deaths of their three friends. They were Martin Howarth, who was killed in Macau, Alex Singleton, who was killed in Long Island in the USA, and Dan Podgorski, who was killed in the Seychelles where he was the British High Commissioner. They believed their murders were connected and that they were linked to a Facebook post that had been placed on the Chesterfield School former pupils' page. They said they suspected that Barnaby Harrington was involved in all these deaths as well as the Facebook post."

"And did you contact Interpol?."

"No, I did not. I wanted to speak to Barnaby Harrington first and to the three foreign police forces before I contacted Interpol. But Mr Harrington was on holiday at the time and not contactable. However, I did manage to speak to the three police forces involved and they told me that the deaths were not linked. The police in Macau said the murderer was a man, the police in the Seychelles said their murderer was a woman, and the police in Long Island said they were keeping an open mind about the sex of the killer."

"What did you think of Mr Hillman and Mr Bowler's theory that the three deaths were somehow linked?"

"I thought it was just a conspiracy theory," said DC Gethin.

"I've no further questions for the witness," added Miss Cartwright.

It was Steve's turn to cross-examine him.

"DC Gethin, can you tell the court why the police in Macau thought the murder of Martin Howarth was carried out by a man?"

"They told me their main suspect was a man called John Smith who rented the Airbnb where Mr Howarth's body was discovered."

"And did anybody see this John Smith character? Were there any witnesses?"

"Sorry, I don't know the answer to that."

"Well, let me enlighten you. Nobody saw him and nobody called John Smith entered or left Macau on the three days before and the three days after Mr Howarth was killed. John Smith is a made-up name. It could be a woman who used that name instead of a man, couldn't it?"

"I can only go on what the police in Macau told me as I wasn't there."

"Let's move on to the murder of Alex Singleton in the USA. You said the police were keeping an open mind about the sex of the killer. Can you expand on that a little?"

"They said they suspected it was a mafia hit. So they thought it would be a man. However, it was not unheard of for the mafia to use a woman as an assassin."

"Did they say why they thought it was a mafia hit?"

"Yes. Mr Singleton had recently written a newspaper article about mafia activity in New York. In addition to that, whoever had carried out the assassination had left a note with the words 'a present from Luigi' written on it in the room where his body was found."

"And was the person who Mr Singleton wrote about in his article called Luigi?"

"No, he was called Mario Carlotti. Although, I believe that Mr Carlotti has quite a few known associates called Luigi."

"How stereotypical of him," added Steve. "Are you saying there was no link between Mr Singleton and anyone called Luigi?"

"No, direct link, no."

"Finally, I'd like to move on to the murder of Dan Podgorski in the Seychelles. You said that the police thought this attack was carried out by a woman. Can you tell me why they said that?"

"Because they had a witness to that effect."

"Only one witness?"

"I believe so."

"Nobody else saw this woman?"

"I believe that is the case, yes."

"Do the police have a description of her or indeed do they have any suspects?"

"They told me that their witness had only seen her from behind."

"But they were convinced she was a woman?"

"Yes, they were."

"So we have three murders, two where nobody could tell what sex the murderer was and one where someone has confirmed it was a woman."

"It would appear that way."

"Do you know what the odds are of three school friends being randomly selected by different murderers and killed within three months of each other?"

"I wouldn't know anything like that, sir."

"It's about one in fifteen million, which is about the same as winning the jackpot in the National Lottery. Are you telling me that you don't believe these murders are linked and my client and, indeed myself, were just the self-deluded victims of a conspiracy theory?"

"I can only go by what the local police forces are telling me and all three have said that the murders aren't linked."

"You see, I believe that all three victims were killed by the same person and that person was a woman, the same woman who was reported to the police in the Seychelles."

"As I said, I can only go by what the local police forces are telling me."

"I would like to show you exhibit one," said Steve as he passed an A4 piece of paper to DC Gethin. "This is a screen shot that I took of a page on Facebook. Can you please tell me what you see?"

"It's a list of names."

"And who posted the list?"

"It says Giles Harrington."

"That's Giles Harrington, the brother of Barnaby Harrington who we know died in 1981. Furthermore, the Facebook page of Giles Harrington has now been taken down. In your opinion, why do you think that was?"

"I wouldn't really know."

"Well, I suggest it was done so that your computer experts wouldn't have the opportunity to examine it. Would you not agree that whoever said he was Giles Harrington and put the post on Facebook was playing a cruel trick on people?"

"It would appear that way."

"Yes, it would. Now please read out the list of names in the first column."

"Giles Harrington, Martin Howarth, Alex Singleton, Dan Podgorski, Nigel Hillman."

"Thank you. You will see from the date I took this photo that it was nine days before Dan Podgorski was killed. Would you not think that this is a list of people who have either died or were about to die, written in the order of their deaths?"

"It would appear that way."

"Can you read the second column, please?"

"Four sixth formers, Deputy Headmaster, Headmaster, Economics Master, Gym Master."

"Thank you. I believe that this is a list of the people who the killer is saying either carried out the murders or was about to commit murder. He or she must have believed, quite wrongly, that four sixth formers murdered Giles Harrington. He is also saying that Martin Howarth was killed by someone posing as the deputy headmaster, Alex Singleton was killed by someone posing as the headmaster, etc, etc. This all goes back to the year 1981 when Giles Harrington was killed. Giles was the head boy at Chesterfield School. At the time the Deputy Headmaster was a man called John Smith and the headmaster, although his real name was Geoffrey Price, was known as Luigi by all the boys in the school. Do those names mean anything to you, Detective Constable?"

"They are the names associated with the murders of Martin Howarth and Alex Singleton," he replied.

"Also, as this Facebook page was subsequently taken down, it's a good job I took a screenshot of this list. Otherwise, we would never have been able to prove it existed. I suggest to you that whoever is responsible for the deaths of Martin Howarth, Alex Singleton, Dan Podgorski and indeed Barnaby Harrington was responsible for taking it down. Do you not agree?"

DC Gethin hesitated for a brief second before finally saying, "Yes."

Chapter 26

There was a ten-minute comfort break between DC Gethin and the next witness, which gave me time to speak to Steve.

"It seems to be going pretty well so far," I said.

"We've still got a long way to go," he replied. "Also, the police knew that I'd taken a screenshot of that post on Facebook. I'd have thought they would have had better answers to my questions."

"But that's good, isn't it?" I replied.

"I think we may have to wait a bit until we know the answer to that one," he added. "I can't help but feel that they've got something up their sleeves."

Soon the court was back in session and the next witness was called. His name was Max Bracher and he was the police's computer expert.

"Mr Bracher, you examined the computers and tablets belonging to Barnaby Harrington and the accused," said Miss Cartwright.

"That's correct," he replied. "I did it as part of my role as a forensic computer expert attached to Derbyshire constabulary."

"I understand from the statement that Mr Hillman gave to the police that he claims Mr Harrington had shown him an email purportedly from someone called Georgia Pearce. Can you tell me if you discovered any emails from anyone by that name?"

"No, I did not."

"Is it possible for someone to delete such an email?"

"Even if they had, it is not possible to completely obliterate all traces of an email. If there had been one, we would have found it."

"So in your opinion this email never existed?"

"That's correct."

"If we now turn to Mr Hillman's laptop. Can you tell the court what you discovered when you looked at it?"

"The first thing I discovered was that he had made two Google searches of interest prior to Mr Harrington's murder, one for flunitrazepam and the other for tetrodotoxin."

"I understand that flunitrazepam is the generic name for Rohypnol and that tetrodotoxin is a deadly poison, more deadly even than cyanide."

"That's correct."

"As we will show later," added Miss Cartwright, "tetrodotoxin was the drug used to kill Mr Harrington and flunitrazepam was the drug found in Mr Hillman's body after he was discovered at the scene of the crime."

"We also discovered that someone had used Mr Hillman's laptop to access the dark web," Mr Bracher continued. "On the 1st of December it was used to order 50 mg of tetrodotoxin and 250 mg of flunitrazepam from a company called TZK Holdings."

"Would you mind telling the court what TZK Holdings is?"

"It is a front for a Nigerian company called Chemnico that sells illegal drugs on the dark web."

"Could you deduce from this that someone who had access to Mr Hillman's laptop must have ordered tetrodotoxin and flunitrazepam?"

"That's correct."

"And would you mind telling the court what security software you found on Mr Hillman's laptop?"

"It uses facial recognition software."

"And was Mr Hillman's face the only one that could gain access to the computer via this software?"

"It was."

"And from that did you deduce it must have been Mr Hillman who ordered these drugs?"

"That's correct."

"Moving on to the Facebook page that was established in the name of Giles Harrington. I understand you looked into this."

"That's correct."

"Can you tell the court what you discovered?"

"Although the Facebook post was taken down, I was able to discover that the page in the name of Giles Harrington had been established on the 3rd of August last year. I was able to trace the IP address of the computer used to set up the page."

"And do you know whose computer it was."

"Yes, it was Mr Hillman's laptop."

"Shit," I thought to myself. "He's just destroyed all the good work that Steve did about the list. Now the jury will believe it was me who put the post on Facebook and me who took it down again."

"Thank you, Mr Bracher," said Miss Cartwright, before she sat down.

Steve stood up.

"Mr Bracher, you said you discovered that my client used Google to search for flunitrazepam and tetrodotoxin on his computer, and yet my client has an innocent explanation for that. He says he looked up both of these substances in order to

216

find out what they were after being told they were involved in the deaths of two of his friends."

"I understand that the involvement of these two drugs in the death of Mr Hillman's friends was never released by the police in either Macau or New York though."

"You've obviously been well briefed by your police colleagues, Mr Bracher. However, this information was passed to my client by Dan Podgorski, who at the time of his murder was the British High Commissioner to the Seychelles. He was able to obtain the information from his colleagues in the British Consulate in Hong Kong and in New York. I have sworn affidavits to that effect from both the diplomats involved. Would you not agree that there was no malicious intent when my client looked up these two chemicals on the internet?"

"He could have been looking them up because he wanted to use the same chemicals to kill Mr Harrington as the two that were used on his friends."

"In which case, wouldn't you think that he'd look them up on the same day?"

"I suppose so, yes."

"Would you mind telling the court when precisely my client looked up these two substances?"

"He looked up flunitrazepam on the 13th of September and tetrodotoxin on the 30th of November."

"Two dates, both one day after the two diplomats say they passed the information to Dan Podgorski, which I think proves my point. Mr Bracher, can you tell me if you had ever heard of Barnaby Harrington before this case?"

"Yes, I had."

"Would you mind telling the court the circumstances under which you had heard of him?"

"Mr Harrington was notorious in the world of computers. He's on the list of the world's most infamous hackers. In 2001, he hacked into a computer at Northern Rock and stole eight million pounds for which he received a sixteen-year prison sentence."

"I also understand that Mr Harrington hacked into the mainframe computer of the Kremlin in 1999. Is that correct?"

"I believe so, yes."

"In fact, is it not fair to say that Mr Harrington was one of the world's foremost experts in computer hacking?"

"I don't think there's a league table for computer hackers."

"However, Mr Harrington studied Computer Science at Cambridge University where he was predicted to get a first-class honours degree until he dropped out in 1986. He subsequently hacked into the mainframe at the Kremlin, one of the most secure servers in the world. Then two years later he hacked into the computer of Northern Rock, even though it had an extremely advanced firewall. I put it to you again, Mr Bracher, do you not think that Mr Harrington was one of the world's foremost experts in the field of computer hacking?"

"Well, when you put it that way, I suppose he was."

"Of course, the two examples I've just given you are the only two we know of. Mr Harrington completed his degree in prison and then got a PhD. He was probably even more proficient in the world of computers when he was released than when he was jailed. Would you not agree that it's perfectly feasible that he carried out many more hacks over the years even though he never came to the attention of the authorities again?

"That's speculation, my Lord," said Miss Cartwright.

The judge gave Steve a stern look.

"Mr Bowler," he said. "Counsel for the prosecution is quite correct. Please refrain from asking the witness to speculate."

"Sorry, my Lord," said Steve. "Returning now to the answer you gave earlier to one of my learned colleague's questions. You said, and I quote, 'it is not possible for someone to completely obliterate all traces of an email'. Would you mind telling us why?"

"If a computer file is deleted, the data lingers for some time on the hard drive. Instead of actually deleting the file in its entirety, the computer simply marks that section of storage to be rewritten when more space is needed."

"Very interesting. So if I was to send you an email, could you delete it without leaving a trace?"

"I could because I've been trained to do it."

"If you could do it, would it not be possible for Barnaby Harrington, a man with a PhD in Computer Science, also to have the skills necessary to delete an email and leave no trace?"

"It is feasible, yes."

"My client thinks that his computer was hacked when he received a photograph of his friend Martin Howarth attached to an email he was sent on the same day that Mr Howarth was murdered. Did you find any evidence of this when you examined my client's computer?"

"No, I did not."

"But given that Barnaby Harrington was an excellent computer hacker, would it not be possible for him to hack into my client's computer and leave no trace?"

"It would be possible, yes."

"And given Barnaby Harrington's expertise in hacking computers and the fact that he is central to this case, would you not say that it was highly likely that any hack was carried out by him?"

Miss Cartwright immediately stood up.

"My Lord, I object. My learned friend is asking the witness to speculate again. There is no evidence whatsoever that Mr Hillman's computer was hacked."

"Objection sustained," said the judge before turning to the jury. "You will ignore the last question."

"Mr Bowler, I've warned you once. You will refrain from asking the witness to speculate."

"Sorry, my Lord," Steve replied.

He continued his cross-examination.

"My learned friend said earlier that unless someone else had access to my client's computer, we must conclude that it was Mr Hillman who ordered the drugs from TZK Holdings. However, knowing what we now know, is it not possible that Barnaby Harrington took control of my client's computer remotely and placed the order? I mean, you were able to access my client's computer by bypassing the facial recognition software. If you could do it, then surely Mr Harrington, a man with a PhD in Computer Science, could do it as well."

"It's a possibility. But it is far more likely that Mr Hillman ordered them himself."

"Except that my client wouldn't know how to order anything from the dark web."

"We only have his word for that."

"That's true. But we do know that Barnaby Harrington was a computer expert and would have known how to access the dark web and place an order with one of the companies on it. Tell me, Mr Bracher, do you have any proof of the address the flunitrazepam and tetrodotoxin were delivered to?"

"Companies like Chemnico are very good at covering their tracks. They don't issue delivery notes or receipts."

"Which is not surprising as the products they supply are all illegal. However, that means there is not a shred of evidence that these drugs were delivered to my client."

"As I said, companies like Chemnico are very good at covering their tracks."

"If we can now move on to the Facebook page that was set up for Giles Harrington. You said that you traced the IP address of the computer that established the page back to the laptop belonging to my client."

"That's correct."

"But we have already ascertained that Barnaby Harrington was an expert hacker. What's to stop him from hacking into my client's computer and setting up the Facebook page remotely?"

"Nothing," he replied. "But if Mr Hillman's computer was hacked on the same day Mr Howarth was killed, it means it must have been hacked on the 1st of September. The Facebook account was set up on the 3rd of August, which is four weeks before then."

As soon as he said it, I realised it must be true. The Facebook message saying YOU KILLED ME had been placed on the 4th of August, so the account must have been set up before then.

Chapter 27

Once Max Bracher had finished giving evidence, the judge ordered a one-hour break for lunch.

"How do you think it's going?" I asked Steve as he sat down with Monica and me.

"I thought it was going pretty well until they threw in the hand grenade about the IP address," he replied. "All we can do is to hope Andy can come up with a rational explanation about the dates."

"Nigel wouldn't know how to set up a bogus Facebook account," added Monica. "I had to set up his Facebook account for him."

"Andy won't be giving evidence until tomorrow morning. I'll phone him and tell him what the expert witness for the prosecution has said. It will give him a bit of time to think about it."

Steve had half an hour between finishing his lunch and the court proceedings recommencing. He used the time to phone Andy Geek and the headmaster of Tupton Hall School. By two o'clock, we were all back in court again. The next witness called by the prosecution was Dr Angus Fletcher, the pathologist who'd examined Barnaby Harrington's body.

"Dr Fletcher," said Miss Cartwright. "For the benefit of the court, can you please explain what your role is in this case?"

"I'm a Home Office pathologist working at Chesterfield Royal Hospital. I'm head of the team that carried out the autopsy on Mr Harrington's body."

"And what did you discover to be the cause of death when you carried out the autopsy?"

"We discovered a small puncture mark on the victim's left arm just above the elbow, which indicated that he'd been injected with a hypodermic needle. I sent a blood sample off for a toxicology report, which showed he'd been poisoned with tetrodotoxin."

"Can you explain to the jury what tetrodotoxin is, please?"

"Tetrodotoxin is a poison found in the organs of pufferfish. It's one of the deadliest poisons known to man."

"Is it widely available in the UK?"

"It is not the easiest poison to get your hands on," he replied. "You can buy pufferfish from companies that supply tropical fish for aquariums. But then you would have to know how to extract the poison. Alternatively, you could buy the poison from the dark web."

"But don't people die from ingesting minute traces of tetrodotoxin present in badly prepared pufferfish? It can't be that difficult to obtain."

"I would agree with you that it would not be difficult to buy a pufferfish, cook it and disguise a small amount of it in another fish dish, such as a fish pie. Only, Mr Harrington didn't die that way. He was injected with neat tetrodotoxin, which had been extracted from the fish in a laboratory. As a result, I think that purchasing it from the dark web is the most likely way it came into the hands of whoever did this."

"Let's turn to Mr Harrington's clothing. Can you tell the court what he was wearing on the upper part of his body?"

"He was wearing a shirt and tie."

"A long-sleeved shirt?"

"That's correct."

"Was Mr Harrington injected through his shirt or was the sleeve rolled up?"

"When we examined the shirt under a microscope, we discovered a small puncture mark indicating that he'd been injected through the shirt."

"Is it normal for someone to inject themself through their clothing?"

"No, it's highly unusual. If someone was injecting themself, you'd expect them to do it directly into the skin rather than through a shirt."

"Thank you, Dr Fletcher," said Miss Cartwright. "I have no more questions for you."

Steve stood up.

"Dr Fletcher, would you say that poisoning by tetrodotoxin is uncommon in this country?"

"It's the first time I've ever come across a case of tetrodotoxin poisoning, and I've been in this job for 25 years."

"I'd like to ask you a bit more about the way the poison was injected into Mr Harrington. You said he was injected through his shirt."

"That's correct."

"And you also said that it's highly unusual for someone to inject themself through an item of clothing."

"That's because it is."

"But if someone wanted to disguise suicide as murder, and in the process frame my client, wouldn't that be precisely what they'd do?"

"I suppose so."

"Can you tell the court whether Mr Harrington was right or left-handed?"

"I'm sorry, I don't know."

"Well, let me tell you. He was right-handed. Isn't it true that a right-handed person would inject themself in their left arm?"

"Usually, yes."

"And, of course, it was in Mr Harrington's left arm where you discovered the puncture mark."

"It was, but that doesn't mean he injected himself."

"Now, when you carried out the autopsy on Mr Harrington, did you discover anything else of note? For example, was there any evidence that he'd been in a fight?"

It was clear to me that Steve had thrown in that question in order to disprove that there had been a violent argument between myself and Barnaby Harrington. This particular piece of information hadn't been divulged yet. But Steve knew it would form part of Mrs Booth's evidence later.

"There was no evidence of that. The only other thing I discovered was that there was some deterioration of his brain."

"Really?" said Steve. "What do you think caused that?"

"In my opinion, Mr Harrington was suffering from the early symptoms of Creutzfeldt–Jakob disease, more commonly known as CJD. It's the human form of so-called mad cow disease, which is usually caught from eating infected meat products. However, I must stress that the disease was in its early stages. He might not even have realised he had it."

"Would you mind telling the court what the symptoms of CJD are?"

"The disease is caused by prions that can remain dormant in the system for many years after someone becomes infected. The average age when someone starts showing symptoms is around sixty and Mr Harrington was 58. The first symptoms include memory loss, deteriorating eyesight and personality changes. Later symptoms include total blindness, involuntary movements and dementia. About ninety percent of sufferers die within three years of being diagnosed. There is no treatment for CJD and it is not a pleasant death."

"Thank you very much, Dr Fletcher," said Steve. "That's most interesting."

He turned to me and put his thumb up. Dr Fletcher's evidence had added weight to our argument that Barnaby Harrington had committed suicide. After all, he was far more likely to want to kill himself if he knew he had CJD than if he was just going blind. We still had to prove that he did know about his condition, of course. But if he did, then we'd hopefully be able to convince the jury that he'd decided to take me down with him in the mistaken belief that I was responsible for his brother's death.

The next witness called by the prosecution was Dr Jason Richards who had treated me at the hospital.

"Dr Richards," said Miss Cartwright. "You were the consultant who treated Mr Hillman after he was admitted to A & E on the 17th of December last year."

"That's correct."

"Can you tell the court what state he was in when he was admitted?"

"He was in a coma and it looked as if he'd been poisoned."

"And did you later discover that this was indeed the case."

"Yes, we ran blood tests that showed he'd been given flunitrazepam, which is more widely known as Rohypnol."

"The date rape drug."

"That's correct."

"And was the drug administered orally or through an injection?"

"He had a puncture mark on his left arm, so he was injected."

"Thank you, Dr Richards."

It was now Steve's turn to cross-examine him.

"Dr Richards, you stated that Mr Hillman's coma was caused by being injected with flunitrazepam and we don't dispute that. However, my client will state that he was first given the drug orally, causing him to pass out, before being injected. Is that possible?"

"It is possible. Mr Hillman was not vomiting when he was admitted to A & E, so we never examined his stomach contents. We knew he'd been injected with flunitrazepam and that in itself is extremely serious. He could have died. Our main priority was to try and remove as much of the drug from his system as possible. To do this we had to put him on an intravenous drip containing flumazenil."

"Flumazenil being the antidote to flunitrazepam."

"That's correct. It was immaterial whether the flunitrazepam was in his system through injection or through a combination of oral ingestion and injection. We just needed to treat him immediately."

"Was it possible to say if Mr Hillman injected himself or if someone else had done it?"

"That's impossible to say, I'm afraid."

"Which arm was he injected in?"

"His left arm."

"And would someone who injected themselves in their left arm normally be right-handed?"

"Usually, yes."

"For the court, Mr Hillman is left-handed," added Steve.

"One final question, Dr Richards. Was there evidence that Mr Hillman had been in a fight before he was admitted to A & E?"

"No, there wasn't," he replied.

The judge told Dr Richards he could stand down. Nothing he'd said was very controversial. However, I didn't think the same could be said of the final two witnesses for the prosecution. DI Cowling was next up.

"DI Cowling," said Miss Cartwright. "When did you first meet the accused?"

"DC Gethin and I interviewed him in the hospital following the death of Barnaby Harrington."

"Would you mind telling the court how Mr Hillman ended up in hospital?"

"A patrol car was sent to Mr Harrington's house following a 999 call from his next-door neighbour. When they arrived, they discovered Mr Harrington's body in the kitchen and Mr Hillman lying unconscious next to him. Mr Hillman was taken to the hospital, and we closed off Mr Harrington's house as a crime scene and called in scene of crime officers."

"Did they find any sign of anyone else being present at the time of Mr Harrington's death?"

"DNA from several other people was discovered, as you would expect. But there was nothing to suggest that anybody else was in the house at the time Mr Harrington was murdered. We also discovered two Wayne Rooney mugs with the remnants of coffee in them. These were the only mugs that had been used recently. This suggested to us that the only two people who were present were Mr Harrington and Mr Hillman."

"We've heard that Mr Harrington was killed with tetrodotoxin. Can you tell me if any tetrodotoxin was found at the scene?"

"Yes, a syringe full of tetrodotoxin was found on the floor in Mr Harrington's kitchen. Another empty syringe containing traces of tetrodotoxin was found on the kitchen table."

"We've also heard that Mr Hillman was admitted to hospital following an injection with flunitrazepam. Can you tell me if any flunitrazepam was found at the scene?"

"Yes, a syringe containing traces of flunitrazepam was also found on Mr Harrington's kitchen table. In addition, we found a plastic bag in the bin at Mr Harrington's house. This bag had minute traces of both tetrodotoxin and flunitrazepam on the inside. It also had Mr Hillman's fingerprints on the outside"

"And from that you deduced what precisely?"

"I believe that Mr Hillman brought the three syringes to Mr Harrington's house in the plastic bag. Once there, Mr Hillman accused Mr Harrington of murdering his friends and an argument ensued, following which Mr Hillman injected Mr Harrington with tetrodotoxin. After that, Mr Hillman must have disposed of the plastic bag before he injected himself with flunitrazepam. The reason he did this was so he could claim that Mr Harrington had intended killing him with the tetrodotoxin before committing suicide but that Mr Harrington messed up and injected him with the wrong drug instead."

"Did Mr Hillman say that was what he thought had happened?"

"He did. He claimed that Mr Harrington must have prepared all three syringes. One syringe containing tetrodotoxin was intended for him, the other was going to be used to commit suicide. The syringe with the flunitrazepam was there for putting a small amount of the drug into his coffee."

"What did Mr Hillman claim had gone wrong with this plan?"

"He said Mr Harrington only needed to put a small amount of flunitrazepam into his coffee, which would have left most of the drug still in the syringe. When Mr Harrington attempted to kill him, he thought Mr Harrington must have mistakenly picked up the syringe containing the rest of the flunitrazepam and injected him with it instead of with the tetrodotoxin."

"And you didn't believe his story?"

"No. I think Mr Hillman deliberately placed the syringe with the tetrodotoxin under the table to make us believe it had rolled there accidentally, thereby explaining Mr Harrington's so-called mistake. Mr Hillman said Mr Harrington couldn't have realised he'd injected him with the wrong drug, and thought he'd killed him. He also wanted us to believe that Mr Harrington got rid of all the evidence like the email he claims Mr Harrington printed off and the plastic bag."

"When did Mr Hillman claim Mr Harrington did this?"

"He said it must have been after he had injected him and before committing suicide using the other syringe of tetrodotoxin. He also said he was very fortunate that Mr Harrington had injected him with flunitrazepam by mistake, otherwise he would have been killed."

"Well, that sounds like a perfectly reasonable explanation to me. Why don't you believe that was what happened?"

"Firstly, no trace of flunitrazepam was found in either of the coffee mugs. Also, flunitrazepam is a clear liquid, which is why it often goes unnoticed when it's slipped into a drink. Flunitrazepam is the generic name for Rohypnol, which is also known as the date rape drug. The fact that it's a clear liquid is one of the reasons it's so effective. Tetrodotoxin, in comparison, is a yellow liquid. There's no way anyone could confuse the two."

"Why do you think Mr Hillman wanted to kill Mr Harrington?"

"Mr Hillman believed Mr Harrington was going to kill him after killing all his friends."

"What proof do you have that this was what he believed?"

"He came into the police station along with Mr Bowler and told DC Gethin that was what he believed. Later, under caution, he repeated this accusation to DC Gethin and me."

"And did Mr Hillman provide any evidence to back up his theory?"

"Yes, he said a lady called Olga Alferov was friends with both Mr Harrington and the person who set up the Facebook account in the name of his brother. He claimed that this was proof they were the same person. He believed that the person who had set up the account in the name of Mr Harrington's brother was the same person who had murdered his friends."

"And yet we know that it was Mr Hillman himself who set up the Facebook account in the name of Mr Harrington's brother," Miss Cartwright stated.

"Objection, my Lord," said Steve. "We know no such thing. Mr Hillman strongly denies that he set up the account. He believes someone took over his computer remotely and set up the account."

The judge summoned Steve and Miss Cartwright.

"I thought Mr Bracher had shown that it couldn't be possible because of the timeline," the judge said.

"We intend bringing in our own expert witness who will show that it could be done," replied Steve.

"Very well, I'll accept that," he added before sending Steve and a mightily pissed off Miss Cartwright back to their seats in the court.

"Strike Miss Cartwright's last statement from the record," the judge ordered.

Miss Cartwright continued.

"Did Mr Hillman produce any other evidence to back up his claim that Mr Harrington was murdering his friends?"

"Yes, he produced the list of names of all the intended victims."

"And was this the list in exhibit number one, already shown to the court by my learned colleague?"

"That is correct."

"And if it is proven to be Mr Hillman who established the Facebook account," she added, choosing her words very carefully, "would it be reasonable to assume that he also posted the list?"

"In my opinion, yes, it would."

"Do you know why Mr Hillman believed that Mr Harrington was killing his friends and intended to kill him as well?"

"It was because he realised Mr Harrington had discovered that he and his friends were responsible for the death of his brother and three other people in August 1981."

"The jury will ignore that last statement," interrupted the judge. "DI Cowling, you cannot say that the defendant was responsible for the death of Mr Harrington's brother when the inquest into his death said he wasn't."

"Sorry, my Lord."

The judge summoned Miss Cartwright to speak to him.

"Miss Cartwright, I will not tolerate either you or any of your witnesses stating as fact that the defendant was responsible for the death of Giles Harrington in 1981. Can I remind you that Mr Hillman is not on trial for killing Mr Harrington's brother?

The result of the inquest into his death was unequivocal. It blamed Giles Harrington's brother for his own death and that of three other people."

"However, new evidence about what happened in 1981 has now come to light and it has a bearing on this case," Miss Cartwright retorted.

"I will accept references to what happened back in 1981 and you can say that new evidence has come to light that might suggest Mr Hillman was involved. But you and your witnesses must not state as fact that he was involved. Do I make myself clear?"

"Yes, my Lord."

Miss Cartwright returned to questioning DI Cowling.

"Wasn't Mr Hillman cleared of any involvement at the subsequent inquest into the death of Giles Harrington?"

"He was. However, it now turns out that not all the evidence was presented to the inquest. For a start, the only other witnesses to the crash were the parents of Mr Hillman's girlfriend. It was also never disclosed that Mr Hillman's car had to go into the garage for bodywork repairs after hitting something that was painted red. Giles Harrington's car was red. These two things only came to light in comments on a Facebook post by the person pretending to be Giles Harrington. Barnaby Harrington was a member of the closed group and therefore he would have seen it. Then there was the letter we discovered whilst carrying out a search of Mr Harrington's house."

"For the record, I am showing the court exhibit number two," said Miss Cartwright. "It's a letter purportedly from a Mrs Martha Cook to a girl called Danica. Mrs Cook has subsequently died, and we have been unable to trace Danica."

DI Cowling put his reading glasses on and read out the letter to the court. Miss Cartwright continued to question him once he'd finished.

"DI Cowling, if this letter is genuine, do you believe Mrs Cook saw something that night that made her think Mr Hillman and his friends were complicit in the deaths of Giles Harrington, his girlfriend and two people in the car that Giles Harrington hit?"

"I think it's perfectly clear that this is what Mrs Cook meant. Also, it would appear that Mrs Cook was writing to the daughter of the people killed in the other car."

"And do we know who they were?"

"Yes, the people in the other car were a Mr and Mrs Fields and their baby daughter. Mr and Mrs Fields were pronounced dead at the scene. Their baby daughter was in the back of the car and was injured. She was taken to hospital where she later recovered. Doctors at the time praised the child seat she'd been in for saving her life."

"And this daughter was called Danica, was she?"

"The little girl was only two weeks old at the time and her birth hadn't yet been registered. It must have been registered later, but we don't know what her surname is, or where she is. She was adopted, you see."

"But surely her name is Danica Fields, isn't it?"

"No, she would have been registered under the surname of the people who adopted her after her parents were killed. All we know is her Christian name."

"So Mr Harrington was confronted by three pieces of information showing that Mr Hillman and his friends may have had a hand in the death of his brother. Therefore, are you completely sure that Mr Harrington wasn't carrying out these murders as acts of revenge?"

"Absolutely certain. For a start, all three police forces involved in the murders believe that none of these deaths are linked. In addition, Mr Harrington couldn't have left the country because he doesn't have a passport. "

"Did you put this to Mr Hillman?"

"I did and he changed his story."

"Really. What does he say now?"

"He said that a lady called Georgia Pearce had killed his friends and had probably killed Barnaby Harrington as well."

"And what made him say this?"

"He told me that Barnaby Harrington had suggested that she was carrying out the murders. Georgia Pearce was supposedly the sister of Sue Pearce, Giles Harrington's girlfriend."

"And is this true?"

"No, it isn't. Sue Pearce didn't have a sister. She was an only child."

"Did you tell Mr Hillman?"

"I did."

"And what was his response?"

"He changed his story again."

"Really. It seems to me that Mr Hillman changes his story about as often as most people change their socks. What did he say this time?"

"He said Mr Harrington confessed to killing his friends just before he died."

"What, even though we know that he couldn't have done it because he didn't have a passport?"

"That's correct. But I think by this point he was clutching at straws. He probably realised that we knew he had killed Barnaby Harrington."

"But couldn't it have been someone else who was in the house who killed Barnaby Harrington and at the same time drugged Mr Hillman?"

"We could find no evidence that anyone else was in the house. Indeed, Mrs Abigail Booth, Mr Harrington's next-door neighbour, heard raised voices and can confirm that the only people she could hear were two men arguing. It was Mrs Booth who raised the alarm by calling 999."

"I believe that Mr Harrington had previously shown concern about the way that Mr Hillman was behaving."

"That's correct. He said as much to Mrs Booth. In addition, he emailed us to express his concern."

"I'm showing DI Cowling exhibit number three. Can you confirm that this is the email you received?"

"It is."

"Can you read it out for the court, please?"

DI Cowling put his reading glasses on again and read out the email. When he'd finished, Miss Cartwright continued.

"Can you tell the court when you received this email?"

"It was on the morning of Sunday the 17th of December."

"Which was the same day Mr Harrington was killed."

"That's correct. The time on the email was 13.46, which was an hour and eight minutes before we received the 999 call."

"Why didn't you action it immediately? You might have saved Mr Harrington's life."

"We always tell the public to call 999 in an emergency. Email communication is considered non-urgent. Nobody read it until the next day."

"By which time he was dead."

"Precisely."

Chapter 28

Steve rose to his feet to cross-examine the witness.

"DI Cowling, you mentioned that no flunitrazepam was discovered in either of the coffee mugs that were found in the kitchen."

"That's correct. Forensic tests were carried out on both mugs, the only ones that had been used, and those tests revealed no traces of flunitrazepam."

"And the coffee mugs were presumably both brushed for fingerprints?"

"That's correct. One of the mugs had Mr Harrington's fingerprints on it and the other had Mr Hillman's."

"But how can that be? Surely, if Mr Harrington made the coffee, the mug he gave to Mr Hillman should have had his fingerprints on it as well as Mr Hillman's."

DI Cowling hesitated.

"DI Cowling," said the judge. "Please answer the question."

"I would have thought so, yes."

"Thank you. My client tells me that he never drank out of a mug with a picture of Wayne Rooney on it, which you discovered at Mr Harrington's house. Instead, he told you that the mug he drank out of had a picture of his old PE teacher from school on it, which would tie in with what it says in exhibit one."

"No other mugs with pictures of people on them were found in Mr Harrington's house. In addition, Mr Hillman's fingerprints were found on the mug with Wayne Rooney on it."

"Well, my client has an explanation for that, and it's one that fits all the facts, unlike your explanation. He believes that Mr Harrington had an accomplice who took away the mugs after he'd been drugged and replaced them with the Wayne Rooney mugs. Of course, this was only once they'd placed my client's fingerprints on one of them whilst he was unconscious. The person responsible would have had to wear gloves or used some kind of cloth because you'd have become suspicious if you'd discovered an unidentified set of prints on the mug. But at the same time as doing this, they forgot that Mr Harrington's fingerprints should be on both mugs."

"But your client could be lying, and he really did drink from the Wayne Rooney mug and there was no flunitrazepam in it."

"That's true, but it doesn't explain why the mug doesn't have Mr Harrington's fingerprints on it, does it?"

"Perhaps Mr Hillman removed Mr Harrington's fingerprints to add credence to his story."

"If that were the case, he would have been better off just squirting a small amount of flunitrazepam from the syringe into the bottom of the mug instead. That would have added weight to his argument that Mr Harrington drugged him first before injecting him. I mean, if you were correct, he would have had the syringe full of flunitrazepam with him."

"Perhaps it slipped his mind."

"But learned council has described my client as cool and calculating. However, now you are asking us to believe that he wouldn't do the obvious thing to cover his tracks. I mean, why would he bother to lie about the mugs? Why wouldn't he just place a small amount of flunitrazepam in the bottom of one of them and be done with it?"

"I think it's because he'd become so convinced by the conspiracy theory that he wanted the mug to have a picture of his old gym teacher on it. It was the same reason why he placed the Facebook post that we saw in exhibit one."

"Except he didn't post it, as we will demonstrate tomorrow. DI Cowling, you are not only asking us to believe that my client, my ruthless, cold, calculating client wouldn't do the obvious thing to conceal what he'd done. You are also asking us to believe that he made the basic mistake of carrying out his plan even though flunitrazepam and tetrodotoxin are different colours. I mean, if your theory is correct then my client would be relying on you believing his story about Mr Harrington mixing up the two syringes. But surely the fact that one of the drugs is clear and the other was yellow would have scuppered his plan, so why did he still carry it out?"

"Well, perhaps he's not as clever as he thinks he is."

"Perhaps indeed. But I've got a far simpler explanation. My client didn't know they were different colours because he's never seen either of them. If he's never seen them, then he couldn't have murdered Barnaby Harrington with one of them."

"That's one explanation. However, the same argument goes for Mr Harrington. If we are to believe Mr Hillman's version of events, it means that it was Mr Harrington who didn't notice the difference in colour between the two drugs which is highly unlikely.

"I think you are forgetting that the court has already heard from Dr Fletcher that Mr Harrington had Creutzfeldt–Jakob disease and would have had problems with his eyesight. In fact, he was going completely blind. It's no surprise that he didn't notice the difference in colour."

DI Cowling sighed and folded his arms.

"Turning now to the plastic bag with my client's fingerprints on it. I believe that forensic analysis of the inside of the bag showed minute traces of tetrodotoxin and flunitrazepam, which led you to deduce that this was the bag used to transport the three syringes to Mr Harrington's house."

"That's correct."

"And were the three syringes dusted for fingerprints?"

"They were, but none were found."

"That's a bit odd, isn't it? Why do you think that was?"

"I presume your client wiped his prints from them after he'd used them."

"You are asking us to believe that my client would meticulously clean the three syringes but would carelessly toss the bag he'd brought them in into the bin without a care in the world."

"He must have forgotten that his fingerprints were on it."

"Which is most unlikely. If we now focus on the syringe containing the flunitrazepam. Are you seriously suggesting that my client would be capable of wiping the fingerprints from this syringe after he had injected himself with its contents?"

"Flunitrazepam isn't like tetrodotoxin. Its effects aren't instantaneous. He would have still been conscious immediately after injecting himself. He would have had plenty of time to clean the syringe before he passed out."

"However, an alternative is that it was Mr Harrington's accomplice who wiped the fingerprints from the syringes and put my client's fingerprints on the plastic bag. She had to clean them because they had Mr Harrington and her fingerprints on them rather than my client's."

"So why didn't this person transfer your client's fingerprints onto the syringes?" asked DI Cowling.

"My job is to ask the questions, DI Cowling. Your job is to answer them. However, I will make an exception in this case. The reason why she didn't try to place my client's fingerprints on the syringes is because it is relatively easy to place the fingerprints of an unconscious man onto a coffee mug or a plastic bag. It is far harder to do that with a syringe where the thumb must be on the plunger and the rest of the fingers around the barrel."

From the expression on DI Cowling's face, I could tell he felt uncomfortable with the way the cross-examination was going.

"Let's move on to the so-called conspiracy theory you say my client believed," Steve continued. "I'd like to ask you the same question I asked your colleague. Do you know what the odds are of three school friends being randomly selected by different murderers and killed within three months of each other?"

"I do now."

"Yes, it's one in fifteen million, isn't it? In all probability, it wasn't a conspiracy theory at all, was it? It was a very real threat to my client."

"Just because something has long odds of occurring doesn't mean it didn't happen. After all, someone has to win the lottery."

"But then again, millions of people don't win it. Not only that but the letter you discovered in Mr Harrington's house proves that someone must have suggested to him that my client and his friends were somehow involved in the death of his brother."

"Mr Hillman was probably involved in Giles Harrington's death. But that doesn't mean Barnaby Harrington embarked on a killing spree."

"My client has not been charged with killing Giles Harrington as you well know, DI Cowling," said Steve. "Therefore, I would stick to the facts of this case if I were you."

"I said he was probably involved. The reason I think that is because of the new evidence."

"If that were true, a new inquest would have been called, but it hasn't. The letter known as exhibit number two was addressed to a lady called Danica. I think she has been carrying out these murders. She is also the person who, in all likelihood, assisted Mr Harrington in committing suicide after he discovered he had CJD. It is apparent from the letter that this lady is the daughter of the couple Giles Harrington crashed into in August 1981. She would probably have a motive based on the letter sent to her by Martha Cook. That letter erroneously pointed the finger at my client and his friends. So I ask you, DI Cowling, what have you done to find this woman?"

"We didn't have much to go on. Only the name Danica and the fact that she appeared to be in Mrs Cook's class when she died of cancer. We contacted the school but there was nobody by that name in her class that year."

"You also know that she was the daughter of Mr and Mrs Fields who were killed in the crash."

"Yes, but she was only two weeks old at the time and her parents hadn't registered her birth yet."

"What happened to her?"

"We don't know. I can only assume she was adopted."

"Well, it seems to me that you haven't tried hard to find her. You could have interviewed all the people who knew Mrs Cook back in 1995 and asked them if they knew who Danica was."

"We could have done that but it would have cost a lot of time and money."

"So you don't mind sending an innocent man to jail, just to save a bit of money?"

"That's not true."

"You took the easy way out, DI Cowling, didn't you?"

"No, I did not."

"You decided my client was guilty from day one and you didn't look for anyone else. It's sloppy police work, isn't it?"

"I don't accept that. Don't forget that Mr Hillman first thought Mr Harrington had carried out the murders, which we know wasn't true. Then he pointed the finger at Georgia Pearce, which we also know wasn't true. Next he claimed Mr Harrington admitted to him that he'd killed them all and once again we know that couldn't be true. Mr Hillman is a liar and a fantasist. There is overwhelming evidence that he murdered Barnaby Harrington and probably his brother as well."

"DI Cowling, I suggest to you that the overwhelming evidence in this case points to an elaborate plot to frame my client. In no way did he murder either Barnaby or Giles Harrington."

"Well, I don't believe it."

"In which case, it's fortunate that the decision in this case is down to the jury and not to you. Earlier today my learned friend asked you a question about exhibit number one. She asked if it were to be proven that Mr Hillman established the Facebook account, would it be reasonable to assume he also posted the list? You answered yes to that question. I am going to turn that question on its head. If it is proven that it wasn't Mr Hillman who established the Facebook account, would it be reasonable to assume that he did not post the list?"

"I believe that it was him though."

"The question is a very simple one, DI Cowling. The answer is either yes or no."

"Yes."

"And if my client didn't put the post on Facebook, someone else clearly did, someone who murdered Mr Hillman's three friends and has tried to frame him for murder. I suggest to you that that person is Barnaby Harrington, the computer expert, who was facing an agonising death from Creutzfeldt–Jakob disease. He did it along with Danica, who you have failed to identify."

"Except that the statement we took from Mr Harrington's neighbour makes no mention of a woman being in the house. She states that Mr Harrington and Mr Hillman were in there by themselves, and she heard them arguing."

"If we now turn to the email that Mr Harrington supposedly sent to the police."

"He did send it. Our experts have confirmed that it was sent from Mr Harrington's laptop."

"I'm sure I don't have to tell you again, DI Cowling, that Mr Harrington was a computer expert and that what might seem obvious to you is often not the case. However, there is no need for us to be in dispute about this. We also believe it was sent from his computer. However, don't you think that it's a little convenient that he sent it a little more than an hour before he was killed?"

"He was obviously concerned that Mr Hillman would attack him."

"But he was not concerned enough to dial 999 and raise his concerns with you over the phone."

"He must have underestimated the threat posed to him by Mr Hillman."

"Yes, but I have another explanation. I believe that Mr Harrington deliberately contacted you by email because he knew full well that you treated emails as non-urgent, and he'd be dead by the time you read it. Mr Harrington was a dying man. He had Creutzfeldt–Jakob disease, the human equivalent of mad cow disease. He had no desire to go mad and blind when he knew he was going to die anyway. That was why he lured Mr Hillman to his house so he could frame him. He'd probably already typed that email. All he had to do was press send once he knew Mr Hillman was on his way. It was Mr Harrington who believed the conspiracy theory, not my client. He believed that my client had a hand in the death of his brother. That was why his last act was to frame my client before he took his own life. Do you not agree that this is what happened?"

"That's your theory. Mine is that it was Mr Hillman who believed the conspiracy theory that Mr Harrington was murdering his friends. That was why he went to his house and killed him."

Chapter 29

"How do think it's going so far?" I asked Steve in the break between witnesses.

"Not bad but you can never tell with a jury," he replied. "However, we are at least clarifying our position. As I said in there, I believe this is a conspiracy between Barnaby, who lost his brother in the crash, and Danica, who lost her parents. The only issue is that we don't know who Danica is. DI Cowling says there was no one by that name in Martha's final class at Tupton Hall School. I've got the headmaster checking for me and I hope he's wrong. It would help our case tremendously if we could identify her."

A few minutes later, we were back in the courtroom just before Abigail Booth, the final witness for the day, took to the stand. Mrs Booth was the last witness called by the prosecution.

"Mrs Booth, can you tell the court how long you've known Mr Harrington?" asked Miss Cartwright.

"For three years," she replied. "I moved in next door to him in 2021."

"And how would you describe your relationship?"

"Cordial. I mean, I never went around to his house for drinks or anything like that. But we'd chat sometimes over the garden fence or if we bumped into each other in the street."

"And did he say anything to you recently that might be relevant to this case?"

"He told me that a man had been around to his house and had threatened to kill him. He seemed afraid. He said he was convinced this man had killed his brother and now he wanted to kill him as well."

"What did you say to him when he told you this?"

"I told him to go to the police."

"And how did Mr Harrington respond to your advice?"

"He told me he was going to get in touch with them."

"Can you describe the events of Sunday the 17th of December last year?"

"At about half past ten in the morning, I was looking out of my window when I saw a man pull up outside my house. I wondered who he was but pretty soon realised that he was calling on Barnaby rather than me. Then I remembered what Barnaby had told me about the man who'd threatened to kill him. So I continued to look at him as he approached Barnaby's front door. I could see him quite clearly as I've got a bay window in my living room."

"And is the man you saw present in court today?"

"He is."

"Can you point him out to us, please?"

"Yes, he's the accused."

"Thank you, Mrs Booth. What happened next?"

"Barnaby let him in. I presumed he wasn't the man he was referring to. Otherwise, why would he do that? However, after about forty minutes, I heard an almighty calamity coming from next door. There were screams and banging noises, as if furniture was being thrown around. Then it all went quiet and I dialled 999."

"Mrs Booth, did you see a woman either entering or leaving Mr Harrington's house on the day of his murder?"

"No, I did not, and I was looking out of my front window all the time between hearing the argument and the time the police arrived. I might have missed someone going in before I went to the window. But I am absolutely certain nobody left."

"Thank you, Mrs Booth, I've no further questions."

It was Steve's turn to cross-examine the witness.

"Mrs Booth, didn't you think it was odd that Mr Harrington should let my client into his house if he had previously threatened to kill him?"

"That was why I didn't phone the police immediately. When Barnaby let him in, I presumed he wasn't the man he'd told me about. It was only later when all hell broke loose that I realised it had to be him."

"So Mr Harrington lets the man into his house, who had previously threatened to kill him, and promptly makes him a coffee. It doesn't add up, does it?"

"No, it doesn't."

"Also, you say you heard no shouting for the first forty minutes after my client had gone into Mr Harrington's house. Why do you think that was?"

"I presumed it was because they had a discussion that later got out of control."

"However, my client tells me he was only in the house for about twenty minutes before he passed out. Are you absolutely sure it was forty minutes later when the arguing started?"

"It was definitely forty minutes. I'm absolutely certain."

"You see, my client thinks there might have been a third person in the house and that person was a woman. Could it have been a man and a woman you heard arguing?"

"The walls are very thin between our two houses. I could hear quite clearly that it was two men."

"Could you make out what was said then?"

"Not all of it because I was listening to the radio at first. But as the voices got louder, I switched it off and that was when I heard Barnaby say, 'I've told you before that I had nothing to do with the death of your friends'. Then the man shouted, 'Well, I don't believe you. You're a lying bastard.' Barnaby told him to get out of his house and I heard a series of loud bangs. It was as if two people were fighting and furniture was being knocked over. Then it all went quiet, which is when I phoned the police."

"It sounded as if they were having a fight?"

"That's correct."

"However, we've heard from Doctor Fletcher that there was no evidence from the autopsy that Mr Harrington had been in a fight. There was also no evidence at the crime scene that any struggle had taken place in Mr Harrington's kitchen."

"As I said, it sounded like a fight. But it might just have been something else."

"Like what?"

"I don't know. My initial impression was that there was a fight going on next door. I know what I heard."

"You know what you heard, even though you heard it through the wall?"

"As I said, the walls are very thin between our two houses."

"Why do you think nothing was discovered by the police when they examined the crime scene?"

"I presume it was because whoever had killed Barnaby tidied up after the argument."

"Are you seriously suggesting that whoever killed Mr Harrington did some cleaning immediately after murdering him?"

"I'm not suggesting anything. I'm just telling you what I heard."

"Mrs Booth, one final question. You say you were looking out of the front window of your house whilst this was unfolding. However, if there was somebody else in Mr Harrington's house that day, could they not have climbed over the fence at the back?"

"I doubt it. Mr Harrington has a six-foot-high hedge all around his garden."

"But surely there must be a garden gate?"

"There is, but it would lead him back to the front of the house and, as I've already said, I saw nobody leave the house."

Chapter 30

Steve and I were discussing the case on the way home after the trial had been suspended for the day.

"I could see the jury nodding as Mrs Booth was giving her evidence," I told him.

"Unfortunately, she's probably done more harm to our case than any other witness," added Steve.

"Do you think she could be Danica?" I asked.

"We know she was adopted as a baby, so she could be Danica," Steve replied. "I'll see if I can find out if she was out of the country when Martin, Alex and Dan were killed."

Before we arrived back in Chesterfield, Steve phoned the headmaster of Tupton Hall School. He wanted to discover if he had found out if there was a girl called Danica in Martha's last class before she died.

Unfortunately, it was not good news. The headmaster backed up what DI Cowling had said in court. There was no one by that name in her class.

"Not only that but I've looked at her previous classes," he told us. "Martha was with us for four years between 1991 and 1995 and none of the students who were in her class during any of those years were called Danica. In fact, I don't think we've ever had a pupil with that name."

Steve thanked him for his help.

"Shit," I said. "That's no use to us at all. Perhaps Danica was in one of Martha's classes when she taught at St Helena's."

"Not if she was born in 1981, she wasn't," Steve replied. "She'd only have been ten years old when the school closed."

He was right, of course. I'd been clutching at straws and I knew it.

"Still, not to worry," said Steve. "Tomorrow, we'll be presenting the witnesses for the defence, and we'll put this matter to bed once and for all."

Steve seemed confident. But I didn't share his optimism, which was probably because I was facing a life sentence, not him.

"How many witnesses have we got?" I asked him.

"Four," he replied. "I thought I'd start off with Dr Miller, Barnaby Harrington's GP. Then Andy Geek, followed by Mrs Parker, Barnaby's other neighbour, and then you."

I had to admit that I was not looking forward to giving evidence tomorrow and even less so to being cross-examined. I thought about Bert, my last boss at Newlands Brewery. He would be calm and collected at times like these. I realised just how much I missed my former colleagues in South Africa. My happy carefree days in Cape Town seemed like a lifetime ago. Why had I ever decided to return to Chesterfield? I could have bought a villa in Hout Bay instead. I looked over at Monica who sat with her head in her hands. It was obvious that we were having similar thoughts.

Chapter 31

Court started at ten o'clock the following morning. The first witness to give evidence was Dr Miller, Barnaby Harrington's GP. Because he was a witness for the defence, Steve questioned him first.

"Dr Miller, we have already heard from Dr Fletcher, the pathologist who carried out the autopsy on Barnaby Harrington that Mr Harrington's brain was showing the early signs of Creutzfeldt–Jakob disease. Can you tell me if Mr Harrington was aware of his condition?"

"Yes, he came to see me in June last year complaining of memory loss. He was also having problems with his eyesight."

"Both of which are classic symptoms of CJD. So what did you do?"

"You say these are classic symptoms of CJD and that's true. However, there are many other conditions with similar symptoms. I sent him for a series of tests at the Hallamshire Hospital in Sheffield. These eventually showed that Mr Harrington was suffering from CJD."

"And when was he finally diagnosed?"

"In July last year."

"For the court, that was the month before the post saying YOU KILLED ME appeared on Facebook. What was Mr Harrington's reaction to his diagnosis?"

"He was shocked, upset and angry, the normal reactions when someone has been given devastating news like that."

"And did he say what he intended to do?"

"At first, he said he wanted a second opinion. But I told him that the doctors at the hospital were world experts in the diagnosis of CJD. They wouldn't have made a mistake."

"And what did he say to that?"

"He went quiet and then asked me if I knew how he could get in touch with Dignitas."

"And as we all know, Dignitas is a clinic for assisted suicide in Switzerland. You are saying that Mr Harrington was contemplating suicide."

"He must have been, yes."

"Thank you very much, Dr Miller."

Next it was Miss Cartwright's turn to cross-examine the witness.

"I presume you didn't provide Mr Harrington with the information he required?"

"No, I'm Catholic. I believe it is a mortal sin for someone to take their own life."

"So what did you do?"

"I tried to persuade him not to take his own life."

"And were you successful in doing that?"

"I thought so at the time."

"You say that one of Mr Harrington's reactions on being given the news that he was suffering from CJD was anger. Can you tell me how this manifested itself?"

"He presumed he'd caught CJD by eating contaminated meat products, in particular the spinal cord of an animal with mad cow disease. He was angry that such a contaminant had been allowed to get into the food chain."

"No plots to murder anyone then, either with or without an accomplice?"

"Well, you must understand that people suffering from CJD often undergo personality changes. I wouldn't rule it out."

"But if that was to happen, would it not be later on in his illness?"

"Not necessarily. It could occur at any stage."

"Thank you, Dr Miller. I've no further questions"

The next witness was Andy Geek. He'd put a suit on especially for the occasion and looked very uncomfortable.

"Mr Geek," said Steve, "can you start by telling the court when you first met Barnaby Harrington?"

"It was in September 1997."

"And how did you meet him?"

"I'd enrolled on an evening class in computing. I was only fifteen at the time and Barnaby was the course tutor."

"I understand you and he became quite friendly."

"Yes, that's correct. He was quite a bit older than me but we both shared a passion for computers."

"How would you describe him?"

"He was intense and had a few weird ideas, for example, his belief that the USA and USSR were covering up alien sightings. He also used to tell lots of lies."

"But you remained friends despite the lies."

"Yes. You've got to understand that this was 1997 and there weren't many people in Chesterfield who knew anything about computers."

"Can you give me an example of the type of lies Mr Harrington told?"

"He once told me that his father had been awarded the VC during the war. However, I had to remind him that he'd told me on a previous occasion that his father was 58. That meant he'd only have been sixteen when the war ended."

"And what did he say to that?"

"He said that he'd meant the Korean War. However, it was easy to look this up. I discovered that only four people had been awarded the VC during the Korean War and none of them were his father."

"And did you confront him with this?"

"I did. He said his father was in the SAS, and they had to keep his name out of the papers, which blatantly wasn't true."

"Why wasn't it true?"

"Because one of the men who had really been awarded the VC was in the SAS and there was no attempt to cover up his name."

"Now, my client says that Mr Harrington told him he'd taken his computer into your shop for you to unlock it after it had been hacked. Did he do this?"

"No, he didn't."

"Why do you think he'd say that if it wasn't true?"

"Because he was a compulsive liar."

"We've heard from the prosecution expert that Mr Harrington was a convicted computer hacker, but when asked if he was the best in the world, he declined to rank him. You knew him. Would you like to rank him for us instead?"

"Barnaby Harrington was definitely one of the best. I would say he was one of the top three computer hackers in the world."

"Yes, we've already heard how he hacked into the computer at the Kremlin and the Northern Rock Building Society. Then whilst he was in prison, he completed a PhD in Computer Science. Now, one of the things the prosecution expert said was that if Mr Harrington had hacked into my client's computer, he couldn't have set up the Facebook account with his computer the previous month. Is that true?"

"Yes and no."

"Can you please explain to the court what you mean by that?"

"Whilst it is true that he couldn't have set up the account on the 3rd of August using Mr Hillman's computer if he hadn't taken it over by then, he could have set up the account on another computer. Then, after hacking into Mr Hillman's computer, he could have substituted its IP address for the IP address of the computer that was originally used to set up the account."

"And how would he do that?"

"He would have to hack into Facebook."

"And how easy would that be?"

"Very difficult indeed. Their firewalls are state-of-the-art."

"So you'd probably have to be one of the top three computer hackers in the world then?"

"Leading the witness, my Lord," shouted Miss Cartwright.

"I'm going to allow it," replied the judge. "It's all gobbledegook to me anyway."

"You would have to be a very accomplished hacker," replied Andy.

"If he was able to change the IP address at a later stage, wouldn't it show the date of the substitution rather than the date the original account was set up?"

"Under normal circumstances, yes. However, once he was in the Facebook server, he could turn the clock back, make the substitution, then put the clock back to the correct time."

"But wouldn't that show up? I mean, if anybody put a post on Facebook whilst the clock was turned back, it would have the wrong date on it, wouldn't it?"

"It would. However, I've checked this. At 3am on the 2nd of September last year, the Facebook server went down for 27 minutes. During the time it was down, no posts could be put on Facebook anywhere in the world."

"For the court, the 2nd of September is the day after Martin Howarth was murdered in Macau and his phone was stolen. It is also the day after my client received an email that we believe was the route Barnaby Harrington used to take over my client's computer. Was any reason given for the Facebook server going down on this date?"

"I believe they said it was caused by a power surge."

"But it could have been caused by someone deliberately shutting it down to hide what he was doing?"

"That's correct."

"Thank you, Mr Geek."

Miss Cartwright's stepped forward to cross-examine the witness.

"Mr Geek, when did you last have any contact with Mr Harrington?"

"June 1999."

"So 25 years ago? This hardly qualifies you as an expert on what he was like just before he died, does it? I mean, one white lie a quarter of a century ago, in which he exaggerates his father's achievements, doesn't really make him a compulsive liar, does it?"

"That was only one example, though. There were plenty of others I could have used instead."

"All of which occurred more than 25 years ago."

"A leopard cannot change its spots."

"Which, if I may say, is a very pessimistic view of man's ability to change. Would you remind the court when Mr Harrington hacked into the computer at the Kremlin, please?"

"That was in 1999 as well."

"And when did he hack into Northern Rock?"

"I believe that was in 2001."

"And has he hacked into any other computers since then, as far as you are aware?"

"As far as I'm aware, he hasn't. But that doesn't mean he hasn't."

"I would argue that it indicates that he gave up hacking computers 23 years ago. Can you tell me how sophisticated computer firewalls were back in 1999 compared with the present day?"

"Obviously, they weren't as sophisticated as they are now."

"And presumably the technology hadn't moved on much by 2001?"

"It had moved on a bit."

"But not as much as it has moved on in the 23 years since then?"

"No."

"You see, I'm just trying to work out why you regard Mr Harrington so highly as a modern-day computer hacker. His last hack was 23 years ago after which firewalls got far more sophisticated. Why do you still rate him as one of the top three hackers in the world?"

"He's a legend in the world of computers. He's still the only person to get past the Russian firewalls and break into the computer at the Kremlin."

"Something he did 25 years ago. Mr Harrington was 58 when he died. He would have been 33 when he completed his last known hack. Tell me, what's the average age of a computer hacker in this country?"

"I really wouldn't know."

"Well, I'll enlighten you, shall I? It's nineteen and getting younger every day. Computer hacking is a young man's game, is it not, Mr Geek?"

"Yes, on the whole it is."

"In fact, I'm told that most hackers consider themselves too old by their mid-thirties. So I'll ask you again. Was Mr Harrington really one of the top three hackers in the world?"

"Perhaps I didn't make myself clear. I meant one of the top three of all time."

"A bit like Pele being one of the top three footballers of all time. However, he would struggle to get into a pub team nowadays let alone the Brazil national side."

"I suppose so, especially since he's dead."

There was laughter from the jury and from the public gallery.

"I'm glad we cleared that up," Miss Cartwright continued. "We know that Mr Harrington served twelve years in prison for hacking and as far as we know has never committed an offence since. On the face of it, he appears to be a reformed character. Why do you think he would hack into the Facebook server?"

"I didn't say he had. I only said he could have done."

"And there is not a scrap of evidence to suggest that he did in fact carry out a hack of Facebook's computer systems. Thank you very much, Mr Geek. You may leave the witness box."

Chapter 32

Next in the witness box was Carol Parker, Mr Harrington's other neighbour. Mrs Parker was a divorcee in her mid-forties. She'd made an effort and looked very smart.

"Mrs Parker," said Steve. "Can you tell me how long you have known Barnaby Harrington?"

"I moved into my current house in 2019, so five years."

"Which means you've known him for two years longer than Mrs Booth, his other neighbour."

"I believe so, yes."

"And how did you get on with him?"

"Okay, I suppose. We weren't what you would call friends. I knew he'd been in prison, so we were never going to become bosom buddies. But we would chat occasionally."

"If I can take you back to the morning of the 17th of December last year. Can you talk me through what you were doing that day?"

"I got up around half past seven, made myself some breakfast and did a bit of housework. Then, because it was quite a nice day, I decided to clean the car. It had been raining a lot and I hadn't had the opportunity to do it before then. I cleaned it both inside and out. When I finished, I went back into my house and had a shower. After I got dressed, I noticed there were two police cars and an ambulance parked outside. I'm not

261

normally a nosey person but I thought something terrible must have happened. I went and asked one of the officers what was happening and he told me they were investigating a possible crime scene. It was only later that I realised Mr Harrington was dead."

"Can you remember what the time was when you went outside to clean the car?"

"Not precisely. But it must have been around ten o'clock."

"And did you hear any noises coming from next door, any shouting or raised voices either when you were in the house or outside cleaning the car?"

"No, I did not."

"Could you be mistaken?"

"Definitely not. It's a very quiet street. I would have noticed if there had been an argument going on next door."

"Thank you, Mrs Parker."

Miss Cartwright rose to her feet.

"Mrs Parker, whilst you were outside your house, did you notice anyone call on Mr Harrington?"

"Yes, I did."

"And is that person in court today?"

"Yes, he is."

"Would you mind pointing him out to us?"

Carol Parker raised her hand and pointed at me.

"For the record, Mrs Parker is pointing at the accused. Can you tell me if you saw anyone else either entering or leaving Mr Harrington's house, a woman for example?"

"I don't think I've ever seen any women call on Mr Harrington. He wasn't the type of man to have lady friends. He was a typical bachelor."

"Mrs Parker, how long does it take you to clean your car?"

"Not long. Usually about twenty minutes, half an hour if it's really dirty."

"Well, let's say half an hour then. We've already heard from Mrs Booth that the argument she heard didn't start until forty minutes after Mr Hillman entered the house. Therefore, if you saw Mr Hillman, it must mean you were back inside your house by the time any argument started. Would you not agree?"

"Well, now that you've said that, I guess you must be right."

"And in all probability, you were in the shower."

"Probably, yes."

"Your house isn't attached to Mr Harrington's, is it?"

"No, it's attached to Mr and Mrs O'Gara's house. They're my other neighbours."

"And would you mind telling us where in the house your shower is located?"

"It's in the bathroom."

"Which is where?"

"At the top of the stairs."

"What I actually meant was, is it on Mr Harrington's side of the house or Mr O'Gara's side?"

"It's on Mr O'Gara's side."

"Good," said Miss Cartwright. "So to clarify, there were three walls, a bedroom and a driveway between you and the kitchen where Mr Harrington was at the time of his death."

"That's correct."

"Whereas Mrs Booth only had a partition wall between her and Mr Harrington."

"I suppose so, yes."

"Mrs Parker, you said that the first time you noticed the police vehicles and the ambulance was when you looked out of the window. Are you sure that's correct?"

"Yes."

"You didn't hear them when they arrived?"

"No, I must have been in the shower."

"The reason I ask is that the ambulance and the first police car on the scene both had their sirens on as they entered your street."

"Did they?"

"Yes, they did," replied Miss Cartwright looking very pleased with herself. "No, further questions, my Lord."

Chapter 33

After Carol Parker had finished giving evidence, the judge called a one-hour lunch break. I could tell that Steve didn't like the way the morning session had gone and neither did I.

"The prosecution barrister ripped our last two witnesses apart," he said as he tucked into his chicken salad. "I think we just about came out level with Andy's evidence. As for Carol, well, I wish I'd never put her on the stand. I don't want to put you under any pressure, Nigel, but you need to put in a really good performance or we might lose this case."

I was up next and I had already been feeling extremely nervous before Steve's comments about the previous witnesses. I was acutely aware that the next hour would probably determine what type of bars I'd be looking at for the next twenty years, metal ones or the ones in our local pub.

I didn't know how I was going to stand up to cross-examination by Miss Cartwright. But I was about to find out, as we were due back in court. If anything, Monica looked more worried than I did and I was absolutely terrified.

Once inside, I took to the stand and swore to tell the truth, the whole truth and nothing but the truth. Steve stood up.

"Mr Hillman, there's something I want to clear up right from the start. Did you have anything to do with the death of Mr Giles Harrington in 1981?"

"No, I did not."

"And whilst you could be lying, I think we can safely rely on the decision of the police, the forensic scientists, the other witnesses and the coroner, all of whom came to the same conclusion. Of course, my honourable colleague would suggest that new evidence has come to light since then, the first of which is that you took your car to Walton Motors at the end of August 1981 for some bodywork repairs. Is that true?"

"Yes, it is."

"Why wasn't this fact released to the inquest into the five deaths that occurred that night?"

"Because it had nothing to do with the crash. I clipped a gatepost in my parents' driveway five days later, which was why I damaged the wing of my car."

"And that gatepost was painted red, the same colour as Giles Harrington's car?"

"Yes, it was."

"I'd like to show the jury exhibit four, a photograph that was taken in 1980 of the outside of Mr Hillman's parents' house, which clearly shows the red gatepost."

The clerk of the court handed the photo to the foreman of the jury who passed it around.

"The second piece of 'new' evidence was that the two witnesses in one of the other cars were friends of yours. Is that true?"

"No, but they were known to me. They were the parents of one of my ex-girlfriends. They were hardly friends of mine as I'd recently broken up with their daughter."

"Precisely, and we can't ask them why they didn't mention that they knew you as they are both dead. Perhaps they just weren't ever asked that question."

"I wouldn't know. I haven't spoken to them since 1981."

"The third piece of evidence is a letter written by Martha Cook on the 3rd of June 1995. This letter was discovered in Barnaby Harrington's house and suggests that you and your friends somehow interfered with Giles Harrington's car in the car park of the Kelstedge Inn. Is that true?"

"That's not true. We were just admiring its interior."

"And once again, whilst you could be lying, the fact is that the wreck of Giles Harrington's car was thoroughly examined after the crash and was found to have no mechanical defects. If we could now move on to the Facebook post that was placed on the Chesterfield School former pupils' site by someone pretending to be Giles Harrington. I believe this said YOU KILLED ME. Is this correct?"

"Yes, it is."

"And it didn't say who the post was directed at."

"No, but there were several replies, some suggesting that I was the target."

"And was it these replies that mentioned the red paint and the fact that two of the witnesses were known to you?"

"That's correct."

"I believe Martin Howarth was one of the people who replied."

"That's correct. He said he was in the car with me, and he backed up everything I said."

"Although this post has subsequently been taken down, we have several witnesses who can confirm that everything you've just said is correct. Can I ask when you first began to suspect that Barnaby Harrington was responsible for the post?"

"It was first suggested by a friend of mine called Richard Hobart."

"Mr Hobart is currently on holiday in the Caribbean," said Steve, whilst looking at the jury. "But we have a sworn affidavit from him confirming this."

He then turned back to face me.

"However, I believe you didn't confront Mr Harrington about your friend's suspicions at this stage."

"No, I didn't go and see him until after my friends, Martin Howarth and Alex Singleton, were murdered."

"If we turn now to the murders of you friends. Can you tell me how long after the post on Facebook appeared was Martin Howarth murdered in Macau?"

"It was just over three weeks later."

"Mr Howarth was killed in an Airbnb let he owned, which had been rented by someone calling themself John Smith. However, nobody ever saw this person. Is that correct?"

"That was what Dan Podgorski found out and told me."

"And as we have already demonstrated, Mr Podgorski got this information through his diplomatic contacts. Furthermore, since nobody saw the person calling themself John Smith, there is every possibility that it was a woman who killed him. The police report into Mr Howarth's death states that an injection with flunitrazepam immobilised him before being tied to a chair and suffocated with a plastic bag. Why do you think he or she did that?"

"My Lord, my learned colleague is asking the witness to speculate again," said Miss Cartwright.

"Mr Bowler," said the judge giving him a stern look. "I'll not tell you again."

"Sorry, my Lord," replied Steve.

"At this stage, did you link the death of your friend to the post on Facebook?"

"Not at this stage, no."

"How long after the death of Mr Howarth was your second friend, Alex Singleton, murdered in Long Island?"

"Martin was killed on the 1st of September. Alex was killed twelve weeks later on the 29th of November."

"And did you connect the death of Mr Singleton with Mr Howarth's?"

"Yes. When Alex was killed, someone left a message in his house indicating that it was a present from Luigi."

"For the court, John Smith was the name of the deputy headmaster of Chesterfield School in the late 1970s and early 1980s. Luigi was the headmaster's nickname. When did you link these two deaths with the Facebook post?"

"When I looked on the Facebook page of the person pretending to be Giles Harrington, I saw he'd only posted once more."

"For the court, this was the post already shown to the court as exhibit one," explained Steve. "And was it at this stage that you first went to see Barnaby Harrington?"

"Yes."

"Why did you do that?"

"Because I suspected he was involved but I had no proof."

"And did you confront him about your suspicions?"

"I did and he flatly denied any involvement."

"How would you describe the atmosphere during that meeting?"

"I told him that I thought he was involved. So it was never going to be very friendly. But he made me a coffee and when I left, he promised to try and help me."

"What made you suspect that Barnaby Harrington hadn't been telling you the whole truth?"

"The person who'd pretended to be Giles Harrington had very few friends. But one of them was also friends with Barnaby Harrington, which I considered too much of a coincidence."

"And this person who was friends with both men was called Olga Alferov?"

"She was."

"Was this when you went to see Barnaby Harrington for the second time?"

"It was. Mr Harrington denied knowing anyone called Olga Alferov."

"How did he explain that she was his friend on Facebook then?"

"He said his computer had been hacked and that must have been when she was added to his list of friends."

"But we've already heard that it was Barnaby Harrington himself who was a computer hacker. In fact, he'd served twelve years in prison for hacking."

"I didn't know that at the time though, so I believed him."

"And we have already heard what an expert liar Barnaby Harrington was. Did he tell you who he thought had hacked his computer?"

"Yes, he said it was Georgia Pearce, Sue Pearce's sister."

"We now know this was a lie, because Sue Pearce was an only child."

"That's correct. I presume he only said that to deflect attention from himself."

"If we can move to the murder of Dan Podgorski, the British High Commissioner to the Seychelles. Mr Podgorski's name was on the list you had seen on Facebook. Did you not warn him that his life might be in danger?"

"I did. I warned him on two separate occasions."

"And yet he still ended up dead."

"Dan was always far too laid-back for his own good. I believe the killer was able to get to him because he gave his bodyguard the day off."

"For the court, there was a witness to this murder who said the killer was a woman. We believe this is true and that Martin Howarth and Alex Singleton were also killed by a woman. The police report into the death of Dan Podgorski shows that he was killed with tetrodotoxin, the same poison used to kill Alex Singleton and the same poison that was found in Barnaby Harrington's body. Yet no link was made between Mr Singleton's death and that of Mr Podgorski by the two police departments involved. After Dan Podgorski's death you went to see Barnaby Harrington for a third time on the day he died. Why did you go?"

"Because he phoned and said he had an email from Georgia Pearce, which made accusations about me. He told me he had printed it off."

"And yet no such email was recovered from his house, no email was found on his laptop, and we know he must have been lying because Georgia Pearce doesn't exist."

"That's correct. But he did show me an email."

"Which, being as though he was a computer expert, he must have faked."

"Objection, my Lord," shouted Miss Cartwright. "We know no such thing."

"Keep to the facts please, Mr Bowler," said the judge.

"Sorry, my Lord," replied Steve. "So what did this email say?"

"I was only able to read half of it. But it mentioned the two things that never came out at the inquest into the crash in 1981, the fact that I had known two of the witnesses to the crash and had damaged a wing on my car."

"Neither of which were damming evidence against you and both of which were in the public domain through the comments on Facebook."

"That's correct."

"You said in your interview with the police that Mr Harrington drugged you by putting flunitrazepam in your coffee. Yet, the only flunitrazepam discovered at the scene was in a syringe. How do you account for that?"

"I believe there was a third person in the house that day who removed the coffee cups and replaced them with the ones with a picture of Wayne Rooney on them. I believe that person was the same woman who killed my three friends. I also believe that she is the woman called Danica referred to in Martha Cook's letter and that she was the daughter of the two other people killed in the crash in 1981. She wrongly believed that my friends and I had something to do with her parents' deaths, which is why she and Barnaby Harrington concocted this whole thing between them."

"You also said that Mr Harrington confessed to you that he'd killed your friends."

"That's correct. I believed him because he'd drugged me and knew all the same details about their deaths that I knew, some of which had not been released to the public."

"And yet we now know that he couldn't have killed them."

"His female accomplice must have killed them and then told him how she'd murdered all of them."

"But why should he lie?"

"Because he wasn't going to kill me. Instead, he was going to frame me for murdering him, when he was actually intending to commit suicide assisted by his accomplice. He lied because he wanted my story to sound ridiculous in court."

"The prosecution says you killed Barnaby Harrington because you believed in a conspiracy theory that Mr Harrington was killing all your friends and was due to kill you next."

"It wasn't a theory. Their deaths are linked. But I didn't want to kill Mr Harrington. I wanted to bring him to justice."

"Part of the prosecution evidence against you is the email sent to the police by Mr Harrington. How do you explain this?"

"He sent it because he knew it wouldn't be read until after his death. It was part of his plot to frame me. He must have sent it after he'd phoned me, and I was on my way to see him."

"What about Mrs Booth's evidence, that she heard the two of you arguing?"

"We didn't argue. I had passed out after being in the house for only twenty minutes. I couldn't have had an argument with him twenty minutes later. I don't know what she heard. But she is mistaken if she thinks she heard an argument between us."

"Another key part of the prosecution's evidence is that you ordered tetrodotoxin and flunitrazepam from the dark web. Did you?"

"I wouldn't have a clue how to get onto the dark web, let alone order anything on it."

"Have you ever seen tetrodotoxin or flunitrazepam?"

"No, I have not."

"In which case you wouldn't know that one of them is a clear liquid and the other is yellow."

"That's correct."

"Mr Hillman, did you kill Barnaby Harrington?"

"No, I did not."

"Thank you, Mr Hillman."

"I think we'll take a ten-minute break before we continue," said the judge.

Chapter 34

Steve used the break to urge me to keep calm during cross-examination by Miss Cartwright.

"It's important that the jury feels sympathetic towards you," he said. "Consequently, it's vital that you don't lose your temper. I doubt whether Miss Cartwright will ask you any questions about the death of Giles Harrington. That's because you are on trial for the murder of Barnaby Harrington and not his brother. I will jump in and challenge her if she does ask you about it."

A short time later, I was back in the dock. I wasn't aware of the jury looking at me while Steve was questioning me. But under cross-examination I was acutely aware that twelve pairs of eyes were scrutinising my face intently.

"Mr Hillman," said Miss Cartwright, "why did you move away from Chesterfield as soon as you left university?"

"Because I was offered a job in a brewery in Nottingham. I couldn't get a similar job in Chesterfield because there weren't any breweries in the town at that time."

"And seven years after that you moved to South Africa."

"That's correct."

"And then your parents moved to Cornwall."

"Yes."

"And your sister moved to Cambridgeshire."

"Yes."

"It seems to me that you and your family couldn't get away from the town quickly enough. Did you ever return to Chesterfield after you emigrated?"

"No."

"That means that you never set foot in the town for 31 years. So why now?"

"Because I'm retired and I always wanted to move back here."

"It's not because you thought there was a big enough gap between now and what happened back in 1981 then?"

"My Lord," said Steve, "learned counsel is implying that my client felt guilty over the death of Giles Harrington when he had no reason to because he wasn't involved."

"I was only seeking to discover if Mr Hillman had been affected by the traumatic events he witnessed that evening," said Miss Cartwright.

"I fail to see where this line of questioning is going, Miss Cartwright," the judge replied. "Move on, please."

The judge might not have been able to see it, but I could. She couldn't accuse me of killing Giles because the judge had warned her against that. But she was attempting to persuade the jury that the reason I had moved away was because I was feeling guilty after killing him.

"Mr Hillman," said Miss Cartwright, "you have been charged that you murdered Barnaby Harrington in his own house on the 17th of December last year. You're an intelligent man, so why do you think you are facing this charge?"

"Because someone is trying to frame me."

"Really? That sounds like a conspiracy theory to me. You like conspiracy theories, don't you?"

"No."

"Well, you believed that Barnaby Harrington was murdering your friends, didn't you?"

"That wasn't a theory. He was really killing them."

"But we've already heard that he couldn't have killed them because he didn't have a passport."

"No, but he had a partner who committed the murders."

"Really? Why has this so-called partner of his never been identified?"

"She has been identified. She's called Danica."

"Ah, the mysterious Danica. She's a bit like the scarlet pimpernel, isn't she? They seek her here, they seek her there, they seek her everywhere, but nobody can discover who she is."

"That's because the police didn't look very hard. They believed I was guilty and never looked for anyone else."

"But they did look for her and they couldn't find her, which is probably because she doesn't exist."

"She does exist. The police discovered a letter to her in Barnaby Harrington's house."

"And do you think that this Danica woman used to be a pupil in Martha Cook's class at Tupton Hall School?"

"I do, yes."

"In which case, why does the headmaster say that there was never a girl with that name in any of Martha Cook's classes? In fact, a girl with that name has never attended Tupton Hall School."

"I don't know why."

"Well, I know why. It's because she doesn't exist. You wrote the letter that was discovered in Barnaby Harrington's house, and you hid it there. You did it to prove that there was a plot to murder you and all of your friends. You also did it to throw suspicion on her rather than yourself, didn't you?"

"No, I did not. The post on Facebook linked all the deaths."

"A post which you put there. That post and the entire Facebook account have been traced back to your computer."

"But that post was set up by Barnaby Harrington after he hacked my computer."

"There is no evidence to support that he hacked your computer. Barnaby Harrington was a reformed character. He hadn't done any hacking since 2001 and computers have moved on in the meantime. He probably wouldn't have had the ability to hack your computer."

"But he must have done. He had a PhD in Computer Science, and he ordered flunitrazepam and tetrodotoxin from the dark web on my computer."

"No, Mr Hillman, you ordered them to murder Barnaby Harrington and to render yourself unconscious."

"I did no such thing."

"Mr Hillman, why did you visit Mr Harrington's house twice before making the visit on the day you killed him?"

"My Lord, I must object," said Steve.

"Rephrase the question please, Miss Cartwright," said the judge.

"Sorry, my Lord," she replied. "Mr Hillman, why did you visit Mr Harrington's house twice before the visit you made on the 17th of December?"

"The first time was because I wanted to find out if Barnaby Harrington had any involvement in the deaths of my friends and the post on Facebook by the person pretending to be his brother. The second time was because I wanted to confront him about Olga Alferov who, as I discovered, was friends on Facebook with both him and the person pretending to be his brother."

"Ah, Miss Alferov. You like Eastern European names, don't you, Mr Hillman? What with Olga and Danica. When I think about it, even Georgia is an Eastern European name. Tell me, do you always go to Eastern Europe when you make up a name?"

"I don't make up names."

"But we know that Georgia Pearce was made up."

"That was made up by Barnaby, not me."

"But we only have your word for that, don't we? Then there's Olga who appears on a Facebook page that you set up."

"Objection, my Lord," said Steve. "My client did not set up the Facebook page and Olga Alferov also appeared on Barnaby Harrington's Facebook page."

"Objection sustained," said the judge, and instructed the jury to ignore Miss Cartwright's last statement.

"Finally, there's Danica," continued Miss Cartwright, "whom nobody can find and where the only clue to her existence is that she is mentioned on a piece of paper, which just happens to be found in a house that you visited three times. Tell me, did you go there twice before the 17th of December to check the lie of the land so you could plot the murder of Barnaby Harrington? Was this when you planted the letter? Or did you do it on the day you murdered him?"

"I didn't murder him and I never saw the letter until after it was discovered by the police."

"Mr Hillman, did you threaten Barnaby Harrington?"

"No, never."

"Why did he email the police telling them that you had?"

"Because he wanted to frame me."

"Really? So why did Mrs Booth confirm that she heard you having a fight with him?"

"I don't know why. She must be mistaken."

"She's not mistaken, Mr Hillman. She said she heard you arguing with him because that's precisely what happened. However, let's go along with your explanation for a moment. If you didn't kill him, who did?"

"He must have committed suicide, because he knew he had CJD."

"In which case, who cleared away the coffee mugs that you claim you drank from and replaced them with the ones with Wayne Rooney on them?"

"It must have been his accomplice."

"You mean the elusive Danica who we wouldn't even know existed if it were not for the fact that she is mentioned in a letter discovered in Mr Harrington's house?"

"But she does exist."

"She must be a bit like the tooth fairy then. Because nobody has ever seen her and, most importantly, nobody saw her on the 17th of December. Mrs Booth didn't see her and she was looking out of the front of the house all the time. Mrs Parker didn't see her either. Nor did any of the other neighbours. How do you explain that?"

"I can't."

"The reason you can't is because she doesn't exist. You killed Barnaby Harrington because you believed he was going to kill you. Mr Harrington was a frail man with a terminal illness but you believed he was a serial killer. So you injected him with poison and then tried to cover it up by knocking yourself out and inventing this Danica woman. You're a fantasist who believes in conspiracy theories. But worse than that, you're a calculating cold-blooded killer, aren't you?"

"No, I'm not," I replied.

Chapter 35

After being cross-examined by Miss Cartwright, the judge called a halt to the day's proceedings. I was eternally grateful as I didn't think I could take much more. Steve explained that tomorrow would be the summing up.

"First the prosecution will provide a summary of their case," he told me. "Then it will be my turn for the defence. Finally, the judge will give instructions to the jury before they retire to consider their verdict."

I wasn't at all sure how well the trial had gone. I'd never been in a court before and the only ones I'd seen were in TV dramas. Steve, on the other hand, had seen the whole thing many times. I asked him how he felt about the possible outcome.

"I won't lie to you, Nigel," he said, "it's 50:50 at best. I've been in this job too long to be able to predict the verdict a jury will come up with. Sometimes, I'm astounded by what they decide. Take the trial of OJ Simpson, for example. He was as guilty as sin but the jury still found in his favour."

"You're not exactly putting my mind at ease," I replied.

"Well, if there's one thing that hopefully will, it's the fact that the vast majority of bizarre decisions I've come across have gone in favour of the defendant. What I'm trying to say is that, if the jury are uncertain, they are more likely to find you not guilty than they are to convict you."

Steve was trying to keep my spirits up about the possible outcome. However, that didn't stop me from being unable to sleep that night. I couldn't get the thought out of my head that this could be the last night I might be spending in my own bed with Monica. Tomorrow night, I could be sharing a cell with a tattooed safe cracker from Doncaster instead. Monica didn't get any sleep either. She spent the entire night sobbing.

The following morning when Steve picked me up, he had some news. It seemed that Abigail Booth had not been out of the country since May 2022. She was not Danica.

"It was a long shot," I replied after Steve had told me.

"It would have made our case that much stronger though, if we could find out who Danica is," replied Steve.

Court started at ten o'clock again and Steve gave me a thumbs-up sign as I was led to the dock. A few minutes later, Miss Cartwright started her summing up.

"During this trial, there has been two versions of what happened on the 17th of December last year. One thing that everybody can agree on, however, is that this was the day when Barnaby Harrington met his death after being injected with tetrodotoxin in the kitchen of his house. The defence would have you believe that Mr Harrington decided to commit suicide and, at the same time, embarked on some bizarre plot to frame Mr Hillman for murder. But let's look at the facts. The two drugs that were used that day were ordered from the internet by someone using Mr Hillman's laptop. His laptop has face recognition software on it, which means that he is the only person who can use it. Furthermore, there is no evidence that Mr Harrington has ever ordered either of these substances."

I looked up at the public gallery and smiled at Monica. She tried to smile back but I could see the concern on her face.

"So why did Mr Hillman choose tetrodotoxin and flunitrazepam? Well, he's given you the answer to that. He chose them because he had discovered through his contacts that tetrodotoxin was the drug used to kill his friend, Alex Singleton. Flunitrazepam was used to render his other friend, Martin Howarth, unconscious before he was suffocated. That was why he chose them so we would believe his story that Barnaby Harrington killed his friends and attempted to murder him. Mr Hillman had visited Mr Harrington on two previous occasions prior to that fateful day. His visits caused Mr Harrington to worry so much that he not only told Mrs Booth, his neighbour, but he also sent an email to the police outlining his concerns. Then there is the fact that Mrs Booth heard an argument between two men in Mr Harrington's house. She became so concerned that she phoned the police. We know what they discovered a few minutes later when they arrived at the house."

Miss Cartwright paused to catch her breath.

"The defence argues that there was a third person in Mr Harrington's house that day," she continued. "It was a woman who helped Mr Harrington to commit suicide and who also helped frame Mr Hillman. But there is no evidence that this woman existed. In fact, Mr Hillman originally said that this woman was Georgia Pearce, the sister of Sue Pearce. But we now know that Georgia Pearce didn't exist. Then he changed his story and said that this woman was a lady called Danica who was in his friend Martha Cook's class at Tupton Hall School. But we know that nobody by that name was ever taught by Mrs Cook. So who is this mysterious woman? The police haven't been able to trace her. Do you know why that is? It's because she doesn't exist either. The only evidence we have of her existence is the letter Martha Cook wrote to her just before she died. I suggest to you that Mr Hillman wrote this letter himself and planted it in Mr Harrington's house. It was his insurance in case his first plan failed, the one blaming Georgia Pearce. The truth is that there wasn't anyone else in the house that day. No woman was seen either entering or leaving Mr Harrington's house and the police found no evidence that anyone else had been there."

"Surely that's enough," I thought to myself. "I don't know how much more I can take."

But Miss Cartwright was nowhere near finished yet.

"Let me tell you what really happened," she continued. "Mr Hillman became obsessed with the idea that Mr Harrington was murdering his friends and that he was next. Yet, we know this wasn't true. Mr Hillman's friends were all killed abroad and Mr Harrington didn't have a passport. Not only that but all three police forces involved didn't believe that the murders were linked and even if they were, they disagree about the sex of the murderer. Despite this, Mr Hillman became so obsessed with this conspiracy theory that he decided to kill Mr Harrington, a man who was terminally ill with CJD and who probably couldn't defend himself. He looked up tetrodotoxin and flunitrazepam on the internet and embarked on a plan to murder him. At the same time, he made it look as if he was the victim and that Mr Harrington had committed suicide. Mr Hillman had been plotting against Mr Harrington for months. This was probably because he feared Mr Harrington was compiling evidence that could result in the inquest into the death of his brother being overturned. This was why Mr Hillman set up the bogus Facebook page. It was all part of his plot to show that he was the victim. But when three of his friends were killed within three months of each other, he became really paranoid despite the fact that the deaths of his friends weren't linked. It was just pure coincidence that they died so close together."

I wanted to shout out no, it wasn't, but feared I'd be charged with contempt of court if I did.

"Fuelled by his paranoia and his belief in this conspiracy theory, he bought the drugs he needed to carry out his plot from the dark web. Then on the 17th of December he went to Mr Harrington's house and confronted him. The two of them argued. We know this because Mrs Booth heard them. Shortly afterwards, he injected Mr Harrington with tetrodotoxin, killing him instantly. Then he went upstairs where he hid a letter pretending to be from Martha Cook in one of Mr Harrington's drawers. This was quite a clever move as he knew it would be found by the police. Also, whilst it appears to accuse him of being complicit in the death of Mr Harrington's brother, he knew that he would never be charged with this. No, the real purpose of this letter was to back up his story that Mr Harrington had a female accomplice, the mysterious Danica."

I'd stopped listening by this stage. I knew the jury were going to find me guilty.

"The person Mr Hillman originally wanted to blame was Georgia Pearce, the supposed sister of crash victim Sue Pearce. But that was never going to work. He realised that the police would discover that Sue Pearce didn't have a sister. So he decided to blame the woman he called Danica instead. She was, in fact, his plan B. After planting the letter, Mr Hillman went back to the kitchen again where he injected himself with flunitrazepam. This was his final ploy to prove that he was the victim. It was supposed to make it look as if Mr Harrington had mixed up the two drugs and had injected him with the wrong one. But that was when Mr Hillman made his final mistake. In his arrogance, he ignored the fact that flunitrazepam is clear and tetrodotoxin is yellow. He probably thought that the police were too stupid to realise this. It is this mistake coupled with all the lies and the changes to his story that prove his guilt."

Miss Cartwright had finished and the judge called a ten-minute break.

Chapter 36

I couldn't stop shaking during the break. Miss Cartwright was very good, so good, in fact, that she'd even convinced me I was guilty. So what chance did I have with the jury? Steve told me not to worry, however, as he hadn't started his summing up yet. He reminded me that since he was going last it was his words the jury were more likely to remember. Five minutes later, I had the opportunity to find out whether that was going to be true or not. We were back in court and Steve was about to speak.

"My learned colleague has told you that there are two versions of events that took place on the 17th of December, and I agree with her. There is the version according to the prosecution and then there's the truth. Let's clear one thing up from the very start, shall we? My client had absolutely no involvement in the death of Giles Harrington back in 1981. He was just driving the car that Giles was overtaking when he crashed. I was there that night and, whilst I didn't see what happened, I know that he wouldn't do anything that would endanger life. But you don't have to take my word for it. Take the words of the witnesses, of the police, of the scene of crime officers and the forensic scientists, and finally, take the word of the coroner. If any substantial new evidence had come to light, a new inquest would have been ordered. But there are simple explanations for this so-called new evidence, which is why a new inquest hasn't been called."

Miss Cartwright might have been good but fortunately I had Steve in my camp. He was equally as good, if not better than she was.

"Once you accept that, the whole of the prosecution's case against my client starts to fall apart," he continued. "The prosecution argues that my client started plotting against Mr Harrington before any of my client's friends were murdered and that he did this because he feared what Mr Harrington might discover about the crash in 1981. But my client wasn't afraid of this because he'd done nothing wrong back then. Why should he set up a bogus Facebook page and post something on it? The prosecution say it was to make himself look like a victim, all part of an elaborate plot to get away with murdering Mr Harrington. But it was not my client who was plotting anything, it was Mr Harrington. He believed the rumours that my client was somehow involved in the death of his brother, and this was fuelled by the letter he received from the woman calling herself Danica. Danica does exist and the reason why we haven't been able to find her is purely down to tardy police work. Not only does she exist but she is almost certainly Mr Harrington's co-conspirator. Mr Harrington was the person doing the framing. We've heard that he was a computer expert who served twelve years of a sixteen-year sentence for hacking. My client, in comparison, has never been in trouble with the police. He's never even received so much as a fine for speeding before. Now, whilst Barnaby Harrington may have been a convicted criminal, he wasn't a murderer. That was Danica, his co-conspirator. It was she who travelled to Macau, Long Island and the Seychelles to murder my client's friends. And why did she do it? It was because the letter from Martha Cook led her to believe that the three of them plus my client were responsible for the death of her parents."

I looked at Monica again to see if her mood had improved. But she still looked worried.

"Barnaby Harrington was due to die a horrible death caused by CJD. That is why he committed suicide. After he had taken his own life, Danica switched the coffee cups and removed the printed copy of the email that was purportedly from Georgia Pearce. Then she left. We know she didn't leave through the front door of the house because Mrs Booth would have seen her. We know she couldn't have climbed over the back hedge, because it was too tall. But there was nothing to stop her escaping via Mrs Parker's garden next door. Mrs Parker wouldn't have seen her as we know she was in the shower at the time. All this started with a misinterpretation of what Martha Cook saw when four lads looked at Giles Harrington's car and she thought they were doing something to it. But they weren't, they were just admiring the upholstery. We know that must be true because the GT6 was examined after the crash and was found to be mechanically sound. Several years later as she was dying, Mrs Cook wrote to Danica, who was the daughter of two of the victims of the crash and expressed her concerns. This letter led to the chain of events that resulted in three people being murdered. In fact, it's four if you include Barnaby Harrington. Please don't let there be another victim. You need to find my client not guilty. You need to do this because he is innocent."

Steve sat down and gave a smile in my direction.

Chapter 37

I was happy with Steve's summing up and I told him so over lunch. Monica thanked him as well.

"I just needed to sow a seed of doubt in their minds whether you are guilty," he said. "If I've managed this they can't find you guilty beyond reasonable doubt."

However, both Monica and I were extremely nervous about the verdict. We didn't know which way the decision was going to go. I could only hope Steve was correct about sowing a seed of doubt in the jurors' minds. Anyway, I didn't have long to discover whether this was true or not. There was only the summing up by the judge to go before the jury would retire to consider their verdict.

"Ladies and gentlemen of the jury," the judge began. "I want to remind you that Mr Hillman is not charged with killing Giles Harrington. The inquest held at the time was quite unequivocal in its findings that Giles Harrington alone was responsible for his own death and those of three other people. The defence barrister was correct when he said that if substantial new evidence had come to light, the inquest would have been reopened. The fact is that it hasn't. Let's now turn to the crime that Mr Hillman has been charged with, that on the 17th of December last year he did murder Mr Barnaby Harrington. The prosecution and the defence have painted two completely different pictures of what happened on that day. The prosecution would have you believe that Mr Hillman went to Mr Harrington's house because he wrongly believed Mr Harrington had murdered his three friends and was intent on murdering him as well. They would also have you believe that this was why Mr Hillman injected him with tetrodotoxin. It was because he wanted to kill Mr Harrington out of fear that Mr Harrington was going to kill him."

The judge stopped briefly and took a sip of water.

"The defence would have you believe, however, that Mr Harrington along with an accomplice really did murder Mr Hillman's friends and they lured Mr Hillman to Mr Harrington's house in order to frame him for murder. The defence would also have you believe that Mr Harrington was not murdered. Instead, he committed suicide after being diagnosed with CJD. Your task is not to decide which one of these two versions of events is correct. The only thing that you must decide is whether Mr Hillman is guilty beyond reasonable doubt. In other words, the defence do not have to prove that Mr Hillman is innocent. It is down to the prosecution to prove guilt. If you feel they have done this, you must bring in a verdict of guilty. But if you have even the slightest of doubts, you must find the defendant not guilty. Now, please rise and go and consider your verdict."

As the jury left the courtroom, I felt sick to the base of my stomach. It was a feeling that didn't go away for the next three hours as they hadn't returned by then.

"Why are they taking so long?" I asked Steve.

"There's only one reason," he replied, "and that's because they can't make a decision."

Finally, at half past five, the jury returned to the courtroom.

I returned to the dock in order to hear their verdict.

"Will the foreman of the jury please stand," said the clerk of the court.

"Have you come to a verdict on which you are all agreed?" asked the judge.

"No, my Lord, we have not," replied the foreman.

"Please God, no," I thought to myself.

"In which case, you are going to retire to a hotel for the night. You will continue to discuss the case and when you return in the morning I will accept a verdict on which at least ten of you agree. All rise."

That was it for the day. At the very least, it meant one more night in my own bed, one more night of agony and worry. I sat in Steve's car in total silence as he drove us home that evening. Then I suddenly blurted it out, "They're going to find me guilty, aren't they?"

"You don't know that," he replied. "Just remember what I said about undecided juries eventually coming down on the side of the defendant."

I didn't believe him in the slightest. Instead, I couldn't help but think I was going to spend the rest of my life in prison.

Steve eventually dropped us off and suggested we get a good night's sleep. However, I knew that wasn't going to happen. Monica made supper, but I couldn't eat. Instead, I just sat down and watched *BBC News 24*.

It wasn't a major news day and every half hour you'd get the same piece of news repeated. Not that I cared. I was well past the point of caring about the news.

At half past ten, it was time for the papers where a group of journalists review the headlines for the following day. Most of the papers had a headline about a minor cabinet reshuffle. This had been caused by the resignation of the Justice Secretary who wanted to spend more time with his family. *The Sun* featured the same story on its front page but with a twist. They'd been able to discover the real reason why he'd resigned from the cabinet. They'd obtained CCTV footage of the cabinet minister being tied to his desk and whipped by a dominatrix brandishing a cat-o-nine-tails. It took up most of the front page, but not all of it. There was still room for one other story, and it was this that caught my eye. The headline said, "I caught British diplomat's murderer on film."

My transformation was immediate. Until that point I had been lethargic and uninterested in what was happening in the world. Now I sat bolt upright and turned the sound up as the journalists reviewed the story.

It appeared that someone had been filming a selfie in Victoria market on the day Dan had been killed. They hadn't noticed what was going on in the background at the time but they'd since realised that they'd also caught Dan's murderer injecting him with tetrodotoxin.

They were back in the UK before they discovered this and hadn't gone to the police. They'd gone to *The Sun* instead and had posted the video on YouTube.

"Why would they do that?" I asked Monica. "Surely, it's their duty to go to the police."

"That's the world we live in nowadays, I'm afraid," she replied. "It's all about self-publicity. Also, if they're able to get more than 100,000 views on YouTube, they'll start making money out of their video."

I reached for my iPad but Monica was one step ahead of me. She was already typing Murder of British High Commissioner to the Seychelles into the search engine on YouTube. A few seconds later she found it. My heart was beating wildly, and I had my fingers crossed. Would we be able to make out who the killer was?

The cameras in modern smartphones produce a far clearer image than anything that has gone before. Consequently, I needn't have worried that the image would be blurred. The picture was as clear as daylight and the murderer's face was right in the middle of it.

"Good God," I said. "She was the last person I thought would be Danica."

Chapter 38

"Well, that explains why she was such a crap witness for the defence," said Steve after I'd phoned to tell him that Carol Parker had killed Dan.

"What do we do next?" I asked him.

"We go and see the judge first thing tomorrow," he replied. "We'll present him with this new evidence and get him to call a halt to the trial."

"And do you think he will?"

"You can never be certain," Steve replied. "But I strongly believe that he will. Let's see if we can gather some supporting evidence before we see him."

I was more relaxed that evening than I'd been in a long time, and I even allowed myself a glass of wine before I went to bed. That said, I still found it difficult to get to sleep. There were too many thoughts going through my mind. I was thinking about my friends and the final moments before they had died. I was also wondering what had been going through Carol Parker's mind when she'd killed them all. I had no doubt that she was responsible for killing all three of my friends.

Steve picked me up at half past eight the following morning. This time, he asked Monica to drive as he had a few phone calls to make. He'd already bought a copy of *The Sun* from a local newsagent, plus he'd been able to find out the previous evening that Carol Parker's maiden name was Higson. Armed with that information, the first person he phoned was the headmaster of Tupton Hall School. He was able to confirm that Carol Higson had been in Martha Cook's class the year she'd been diagnosed with cancer.

"Why was the person Martha sent the letter to called Danica rather than Carol?" asked Steve.

"Well, it was a personal letter rather than a school letter," replied the headmaster. "Perhaps Danica was a nickname. I can always ask Miss Davidson. She took over Mrs Cook's class when she went into hospital. She still teaches here."

Steve thanked him and asked if he could do it as a matter of urgency. Next, Steve phoned the UK Border Force and was able to establish that Carol Parker had been out of the country when Martin, Alex and Dan were killed.

"It's getting better and better," he said to me.

Five minutes later, it was looking better still when the headmaster from Tupton Hall School phoned back.

"I've spoken to Miss Davidson," he said, "And she did know why the letter that Mrs Cook sent was addressed to someone called Danica. She told me that Carol bumped into one of her mother's former friends when she was thirteen. She told her that her mother was going to call her Danica. She was of Belarusian descent, you see. Her father, Carol's grandfather, had been taken prisoner whilst fighting for the Nazis during the war. It was quite common for people from countries like Belarus to fight for the Germans as they thought that Stalin was a bigger threat than Hitler. Their country had been swallowed up by the Soviet Union and they saw Hitler as the person who could drive the Soviets out. Anyway, after the war he couldn't go back to Belarus as he'd have been shot as a traitor. So he stayed in the UK where he eventually got married and had a daughter. That daughter was Carol's mother who was killed when Giles Harrington had a head-on collision with the car she was in. Carol insisted on being called Danica after she discovered that was what she would have been called if her parents had survived the crash. However, I believe she'd reverted back to Carol by the time she was in the sixth form."

Steve thanked him for that piece of information. It added weight to the rest of the evidence we had at our disposal.

As soon as we arrived at the courthouse, Steve went to see the judge in his chambers along with Miss Cartwright. Half an hour later, he reappeared with a beaming smile on his face.

"He's going to instruct the jury to find you not guilty," he told me.

I let out a huge sigh of relief. Monica kissed me and Steve hugged me. An hour later, it was all over. The jury had been dismissed, I'd had my electronic tag removed and I was a free man again. My sister and mother came down from the public gallery and they kissed me as well.

"Thank God for that," said my mother. "I never doubted your innocence. There was one thing that came out that I didn't understand, though. I don't ever remember you hitting the gatepost."

"I did, Mum. But I'm not surprised you don't remember. It only took Dad a few minutes to touch up the paint. Unfortunately, it took far longer to repair the damage to my front wing."

I had lots of questions that needed answering. One of them, of course, could never be answered. Would the jury have found me guilty if someone hadn't been filming a selfie in Victoria market on the day Dan was murdered? Monica told me to stop worrying about it. However, I never could, and it was destined to give me nightmares for years to come. These would usually end with me waking up in the middle of the night, my pyjamas soaked in sweat, shouting I'm not guilty as I'm led away in handcuffs.

The person who could answer the rest of my questions was Carol Parker but she was nowhere to be found. She had disappeared and nobody knew where she was.

Still, I was able to get answers to some of my questions a week after my trial collapsed. DI Cowling had called me to the police station to update me on what they had discovered after searching for evidence in Carol Parker's house.

"We believe it was pure coincidence that Carol Parker moved in next door to Barnaby Harrington," he told me. "They probably didn't know they both had relatives who were killed in the same car crash until it came out during one of their conversations. Until then we think Barnaby had probably believed the official version of what happened. But when Carol Parker gave him the letter she'd received from Martha Cook, he changed his mind and thought you and your friends were responsible."

"But we weren't," I added.

"We know that now," continued DI Cowling. "But unfortunately for you, they fed off one another and this fuelled their belief that you had done something to Giles Harrington's car. Then Barnaby was diagnosed with CJD and that was when they started hatching their plot."

"So was Abigail Booth involved as well?" I asked.

"No, Mrs Booth is completely innocent. The reason why she didn't see anyone emerging from the front of the house was because Mrs Parker went straight from the backdoor of Mr

Harrington's house to her own backdoor. Mrs Booth was also duped into believing there was an argument in Mr Harrington's house. We've discovered a recording of an argument between Mrs Parker and Barnaby Harrington on an iPad in Mrs Parker's house. They must have played it over a Bluetooth speaker after you passed out."

"But Mrs Booth was adamant that the argument was between two men."

"Yes. But you are forgetting that Barnaby Harrington was a computer expert. He used an app which altered the pitch of Mrs Parker's voice on the recording. It made it sound as if he was arguing with a man, when he was really arguing with a woman. Our experts have been able to restore the original recording."

"You know, I was convinced that Abigail Booth was Danica at one stage. She was about the right age and was adopted as a baby."

"Except that Mrs Booth wasn't born until six months after the car crash. She was also born in Luton. Who told you she was adopted?"

"Steve told me, and I think he got it from Carol Parker."

"That's no surprise. It was really Carol Parker who was adopted, not Abigail Booth. Abigail was brought up by her natural parents and only moved to Chesterfield in 1985 after her father got a job with Royal Mail."

"What I don't understand is why link the murders to masters from my old school?"

"Well, that was so you would see they were linked but we wouldn't. Something like that is straight out of an Agatha Christie novel, so they knew we'd think that it was a conspiracy theory you'd dreamt up instead. In fact, we believe Harrington and Parker didn't consider that the police would withhold the information about the message from Luigi left in Alex Singleton's house. They got lucky that you were still able to find out about it through Dan Podgorski."

"But there was no link to Cec Thompson when Dan was killed, was there?"

"Actually, there was. The day after Mr Podgorski was killed, the High Commission received this addressed to him in the post."

DI Cowling showed me a photo of a book. Its title was *Born on the wrong side*, Cec Thompson's autobiography.

"The book also had a bookmark made out of a Rohypnol box in it and was wrapped in a plastic bag."

"That means all three murders and the suicide of Barnaby Harrington were linked by four things, tetrodotoxin, flunitrazepam, a plastic bag and the name of a teacher from our old school."

"I don't think there was any connection between tetrodotoxin and Martin Howarth's murder," said DI Cowling.

"Yes, there was," I replied. "After Carol Parker had murdered Martin, she took his phone. As soon as she did that Barnaby must have been able to take control of it remotely and he sent me a photo of Martin and his wife. The caption underneath it said they were enjoying a meal of pufferfish. It was this email that allowed him to take over my laptop."

"And that was something that different police forces all over the world would never have been able to link."

"But I could."

"Which was precisely why they did it."

"Have you been able to discover anything else?" I asked

"We have," replied DI Cowling. "Remember Olga Alferov from Minsk? Well, her Facebook page was set up by Barnaby

Harrington. Olga Alferov is actually the name of Carol Parker's mother."

"But I thought her mother was a Mrs Fields."

"Fields was her married name. Her maiden name was Alferov."

"Have you made any progress towards finding Carol Parker?"

"Not yet. Given her history of foreign travel, we've issued an international arrest warrant and an all-ports warning. She'll turn up eventually. I've no doubt about that."

Chapter 39

Three months later, Carol Parker still hadn't turned up. It was as if she'd disappeared into thin air. My life had pretty much returned to normal. There was shopping on Saturdays, walks in the Peak District on Mondays, drinks with my former classmates once a month on a Friday, and the occasional dinner with Steve and Jessica. Monica and I even got to go up into the tower of the Crooked Spire at long last. If it wasn't for the nightmares, the court case could just as well have never happened. Then one day in September, I received a phone call out of the blue. I recognised the caller's voice immediately. It was not surprising really as she'd tried to frame me for murder.

"Hello Nigel," she said.

I went quiet.

"Do you know who I am? Are you going to speak to me?"

"Why don't you give yourself up?" I said. "You can't keep running forever."

"What you really mean is that I can't get away with murder forever, which is pretty rich coming from you. After all, you've been getting away with killing my parents for the past 43 years."

"I didn't kill your parents. What Martha saw that night was just the four of us looking through the window of Giles's car."

"You don't really expect me to believe that, do you? After all, Martin told me exactly what happened before I killed him. I must say you are an extremely lucky man, Nigel. You are lucky because Barnaby kept the letter from Martha that I'd given him. I told him to destroy it but he never did, the idiot. Then there was the person filming a selfie in Victoria market. If it hadn't been for their narcissism, you would have been found guilty and would have spent the next 25 years in prison. That was our plan A anyway. So now it's time to switch to plan B. Who was it that said that? Ah yes, it was Bruce wasn't it, shortly before you killed my parents? At least, that was what Martin told me before I killed him."

"I told you, I didn't kill your parents. Neither did any of my friends. You're mad if you think otherwise."

But she wasn't listening to me.

"Instead of sending you to prison, I'm going to kill you," she continued. "You'll never know when I'm going to do it. But one day when you're least expecting it, I'll strike."

"You're psychotic," I replied.

"Or maybe I'll kill one of your sons," she continued. "After all, you killed my relatives. Perhaps I'll fly out to Vancouver and kill Ben. Or maybe I'll go to Osaka and kill Johannes. I really haven't made up my mind yet."

"Why are you doing this?" I pleaded.

"Because you denied me the chance of being brought up by a loving family. My adoptive parents were abusive towards me both physically and mentally. Not only that but the injuries I sustained in that crash prevented me from having any children of my own, which ultimately led to my marriage breaking down. In fact, everything that's gone wrong in my life can be traced back to you and your three friends. That's why I'm doing it, Nigel."

"But it's all based on a lie," I shouted. "I had nothing to do with the death of your parents."

"No, you're the one who's lying, Nigel, and worse than that, you are lying to yourself. You may have convinced yourself that you are innocent but you will never convince me. I don't live in a world of self-delusion like you do. Goodbye, Nigel, and don't forget to check that you've closed all the windows and locked the front door when you go to bed tonight. In fact, you'd better not forget to do that for the rest of your life. Because if you do, I may just enter your bedroom and inject you with tetrodotoxin."

"No, don't go," I shouted. "We need to discuss this rationally.

Only it was too late, she'd already hung up. She'd done it, of course, to put the fear of God in me. For the rest of my life, I would never know whether she would come up behind me and inject me with tetrodotoxin. Worse than that, I'd never know whether she would carry out her threat to kill Ben or Johannes. Should I phone and warn them? Or should I let them continue in blissful ignorance? In the end, I decided that I would contact them. Both of my sons told me not to worry as she was probably playing mind games with me.

That was almost certainly correct but for the rest of my life, there would always be this nagging doubt.

Chapter 40

In the middle of the Bristol Channel, Carol Parker dropped her mobile phone over the side of the inflatable dingy she was sitting in. She had been living in a caravan in Brean for the past three months and had used the time to decide what to do next. Deep down, she knew it was inevitable that the police would eventually catch up with her. She had no desire to spend the rest of her life in prison. She also wanted to punish me, which is why she decided on the perfect plan. She would kill herself and ensure that her body was never found. I would always wonder if she was coming after me, not knowing that she was dead.

After disposing of the phone, she ripped a large gash in the side of the inflatable, before injecting herself with tetrodotoxin. She'd already tied a weight to her ankle and a few seconds later both the inflatable and her body disappeared beneath the sea.

13th of August 1981

"Come on everybody," I shouted as soon as Giles had disappeared into the gents. "Let's leg it."

We all dashed out again leaving a bemused looking Sue wondering what the hell was going on. We were laughing as we emerged into the car park.

"Bloody hell," said Alex. "I could have done with a waz myself."

"You'll have to cross your legs until we get to the Red Lion," said Martin.

However, if truth be told, I should also have gone to the toilet, which was when the idea entered my head. It came to me as we were walking past Giles's car. The GT6 had a chrome filler cap operated by a push button. It was just the right height. I went over to it and started to relieve myself into the car's petrol tank. The others all gathered around laughing. Steve, meanwhile, was pulling out of the car park in the other car.

"Hurry up, I'm bursting," said Alex.

I soon finished and Alex took over.

"Be quick," said Martin. "Otherwise, he'll catch us."

"He won't get very far if he decides to chase after us," said Dan taking over as soon as Alex had finished.

"In which case, it's all for one and one for all then," said Martin as he unzipped his fly.

By the time Martin had finished, Giles still hadn't appeared.

"He must be having a dump," said Alex.

We were all giggling as we got into my car. Just as we were about to set off, Giles appeared at the door of the pub looking perplexed. Sue was just behind him.

"Quick, let's go," said Dan.

I started my car and reversed out. In my haste to get away I misjudged the distance between my Avenger and Giles's GT6 and clipped his rear wing with the front wing of my car as I turned the wheel.

"Shit," I shouted out.

"You didn't hit him very hard," said Martin. "He'll probably be able to rub out any scratches with some T-cut."

Mind you, Giles had noticed what had happened and was racing towards my car screaming blue murder.

"Go," shouted Alex.

I didn't really need him to tell me that. I put my foot down and shot out of the pub car park. Realising that we were getting away, Giles and Sue got into the GT6 and set off in pursuit of us.

A few seconds later, I was held up at the road junction. There was quite a lot of traffic heading towards Matlock on the main road and I had to wait for a gap. After waiting for what seemed like an eternity, I eventually pulled out. However, this delay meant that Giles wasn't very far behind me.

His car was a lot faster than mine, of course, and he was catching up at a rate of knots. Fortunately, there was another car between the two of us.

"There's no need to panic," said Dan. "As soon as the piss gets as far as the carburettor, his engine will cut out."

"How far do you think he'll be able to go?" I shouted.

"Only about half a mile," he replied.

Giles, of course, was totally oblivious to the fact that we had urinated in his fuel tank. He tried to overtake both me and the car behind me. It was a dangerous manoeuvre, especially since there was a car coming in the opposite direction. As he pulled alongside me, the other car sounded its horn. Giles probably would have made it if his engine hadn't cut out. But at that precise moment, it died on him and despite the driver of the other car breaking hard, he ploughed straight into the GT6.

There was a horrible bang and the sound of breaking glass. Then there was silence. I pulled over to the side of the road.

"Jesus, what have we done?" said Dan. "We'll all go to prison. I'm due to go to Loughborough University next month. My parents will kill me."

Similar thoughts were going through my mind and the minds of my other friends. We could see all our hopes and dreams going up in smoke before our eyes. My parents had been so proud when I got the grades I needed to go to Heriot Watt University. I was the first person in my family to get into university and nothing was going to take that away from me.

"Look," I said. "Nobody can link this to us. They will think Giles crashed because he was over the limit. No one will ever be able to discover that we pissed in his fuel tank. All we have to do is keep quiet and we'll be alright."

"We must never speak about what really happened tonight ever again," added Martin. "Are we agreed?"

"Yes," we all replied.

"Right, let's go and see if there's anything we can do to help."

We got out of the car and wandered back towards the scene of the crash. I noticed that Giles's fuel tank had ruptured in the collision spilling petrol all over the road. I secretly breathed a sigh of relief. There was no way anyone would be able to prove that the petrol had been contaminated with urine and that was especially true after the fire brigade arrived and sprayed foam all over the road and the remains of the GT6.

Of course, there was nothing any of us could do. The scene was one of total devastation and the people in both cars were dead, all of them apart from a baby who was in the back of the Austin Maestro that had hit Giles's GT6.

The end

Author's notes

I was the first amongst my group of friends to pass my driving test two months after my seventeenth birthday. Soon most of the people in my year were driving. My friends and I used to meet at the Portland Hotel on Fridays and Saturdays and travel out to various pubs in the Peak District. We'd always visit a chip shop as well.

When I look back at it now, I'm amazed that nobody was killed, given some of the things we used to get up to. One of my friends regularly climbed out of the back window whilst I was driving and clung to the side of my car. I'd also try and get my mother's Hillman Avenger to go at a hundred miles per hour on the downhill bit of road between Wadshelf and Chesterfield. However, one of the most dangerous things one of my friends ever did was to go around the Baslow roundabout the wrong way to get past another car. The camber of the road was against him, and he went backwards into a drystone wall. Fortunately for him, the only damage to his car was a broken brake light.

By the time I was in my second year at university, I was already on my third car, a red Triumph GT6. It was my pride and joy and I could only afford to buy it because my dad got me a summer job as a tank cleaner for Whitbread's in Sheffield. Imagine my horror when the engine cut out one day after I'd only travelled half a mile from my hall of residence. The mechanic I took it to said that someone had put water in my petrol tank. But my dad had another idea. He said someone must have pissed in it, which was probably true.

About the Author

Ian Walker was born in Chesterfield in 1956. His father was the chief clerk for Scarsdale Brewery and his mother was a ballet teacher.

He went to Chesterfield School before gaining a place at Leicester University where he studied Chemistry and Maths.

After graduating, he got a job working in the laboratory at Truman's Brewery in Brick Lane, London. The following year, he transferred to Watney's Brewery in Mortlake where he moved into the sales department eighteen months later.

A variety of sales roles followed until he became Regional Sales Director for Scottish and Newcastle in the West Country.

All this came to an end in 2006 when, aged just 50, he suffered a stroke and had to give up work. After 12 months of physiotherapy, he felt sufficiently recovered to buy a pub in the North York Moors National Park with his wife Eunice.

In the eight years that they owned the pub, they achieved listings in both *The Good Beer Guide* and *The Good Pub Guide*. They were also included in *The Times* list of the top 50 places to eat in the British Countryside.

In 2016, he decided to retire and move back to Chesterfield after forty years of living elsewhere. He and his wife live just around the corner from the house where he grew up. He has two grown-up sons from a previous marriage.

You Killed Me is his eighth novel.

Printed in Great Britain
by Amazon